You Be The Judge

Kathie Keppler

CENTRAL PARK SOUTH PUBLISHING

Copyright © 2020 by Kathie Keppler

All rights reserved. No part of this publication may be reproduced, distributed or transmitted in any form or by any means, without prior written permission.

Publisher: Central Park South Publishing

Website: www.centralparksouthpublishing.com

Publisher's Note: This is a work of fiction. Names, characters, places, and incidents are a product of the author's imagination. Locales and public names are sometimes used for atmospheric purposes. Any resemblance to actual people, living or dead, or to businesses, companies, events, institutions, or locales is completely coincidental.

You Be The Judge by Kathie Keppler -- 1st ed. © 2020

ISBN-978-1-7352964-5-6

Dedicated to Big Bill

Prologue

Her movie star face adorned the covers of all the top magazines, *Vogue, Mademoiselle, People, Better Homes And Garden, Vanity Fair,* and many others. Time had her listed as one of the top ten richest women in America. But this weeks' *Time* and *New York Post*'s page six do not have this world-famous best-selling mystery writer radiating her perfect smile, in her signature Chanel suit. Instead, the magazine covers show her being hidden behind two policemen escorting her to a jail holding cell in Rockland County for allegedly killing her boy toy second husband.

Could a woman this brilliant and renowned for her writing about crime be capable of committing the most heinous one herself...?

CHAPTER

One

When Burke entered the jurors' room, a woman a bit older than herself, in the second row, smiled at her with just a touch of intelligent mischievousness playing across her face. It was as if she was beckoning Nora Burke to sit next to her.

When Burke sat down beside her, her neighbor looked upward and said, "Open a bloody window, please dear Lord, do you hear me?" She then turned to Burke and said, "It's a cauldron in here, don't you think?"

Burke nodded. "You're British."

Jackie nodded. "I am and I don't see why they're punishing US with no air conditioning. We're not guilty!"

Burke laughed. "You're right."

"I'm Elizabeth," the English woman added, smiling, and put her hand out to shake. "Half of my class in school were named Elizabeth, after the Queen. But I prefer Jackie. Nice to meet you, dearie."

"My name's Nora but I prefer Burke." Nora didn't feel the need to explain that she preferred her last name because she never identified with that legendary renegade Ibsen's wife nor some Irish girl crooning to her baby.

"Burke suits you," said Jackie.

"Think so?"

Jackie nodded. "It's strong." She continued, "I like Jackie – it's good as a stage name since I am a singer. I am soon auditioning for Mary Poppins."

"On Broadway?" Burke's eyes widened. So, it *is* true when they say you never know who you'll meet on jury duty.

"No, a community theatre not too far from here."

"Oh, well, wonderful. What's the difference," Burke said. "Don't forget to invite me."

"Also, I plan to audition, with my British accent, for that lizard that advertises insurance."

"Geiko?"

"Yes."

"But he's male," Burke replied.

"Oh, don't be so particular, Burke. With the Me Too movement and how everything has to be equal nowadays, that cockney lizard is going to have to have a charming female sister or counterpart or something."

Burke studied her and hoped Jackie would be selected for the same jury as her because clearly she is fun but, she thought, Jackie's best chance to be selected would be to keep her mouth shut. The lawyers don't like feisty types.

"What do you do?" Jackie asked.

Burke said, "I'm a teacher. An exhausted burnt out teacher. Special ed. That's why I want to get picked. I still get paid by the schools if I'm on jury duty, while actually getting a rest, just listening."

They both turned at that moment to a disheveled man in his forties who suddenly sat down on their bench. It was a bit late to have just arrived, thought Burke. Why did he come in now?

"Oh, I know," Burke explained to Jackie, who had not asked. "He must have just been dismissed right before a jury selection. People often settle at the last minute to avoid going to court."

Jackie whispered, "Odd bloke, isn't he? Must shop in the Salvation Army."

"The clearance rack even there," Burke added.

Jackie laughed. "You've got that Galway humor, Burke. With your red hair and blue eyes, you've got to be Irish." Before Burke could affirm that she is indeed Irish, her new friend turned to the man and said, "I'm Jackie. We're waiting too."

He said, "Peter." Luckily, he didn't offer to shake hands.

Jackie leaned into Burke, "His shirt is 50 shades of blue. Must have washed it that many times."

Burke said, "The real question is how does he keep it buttoned with that stomach? I hope he filled out his form as Poor Potbelly Pete."

Jackie smiled.

"By the way, besides being a theatrical, I'm a nurse," Jackie said, to pass the time.

"Oh, what kind?" Burke asked. It was nice to have someone to be friends with during what could turn out be interminable hours here, Burke thought.

"Well in England I nursed the old vets from WW2 who loved my singing, I might add, I know all the old war time songs because I was a Wren"

"A what?"

"In the Royal Navy."

"But you don't look that old..."

"After the war, of course. It was fabulous. But, when I left, I came to the land of the free to make my way and did a few stints and am now a nurse in the ICU in Hackensack in New Jersey."

"Why are you at a jury selection in Rockland County?"

"I rent a room in the Tuxedo Park mansion area. I bike to the station and then take a train to my job."

"Impressive. Will you get paid if you're picked?"

"Yes."

"Good."

They had each already noticed that the other was not married. Although, Burke had been married at one time, like everyone else. Hers had been to her college sweetheart and it lasted only six months. He turned out not to like women that much. Burke was actually on the hunt for a new husband and men did notice her with her almost natural red hair and her being tall, usually referred to as "statuesque." Being younger than Jackie, she still longed for the house, a city pied-a-terre, twins and a red convertible paid for by her brilliant, well-groomed and taller-than- herself husband.

This was proving difficult to find.

Jackie, however, seemed like she had lost interest in the whole thing.

Maybe she had seen too many men in the altogether at her nursing jobs.

"I wonder what the lawyer is like on this case," Burke said.

"What do you mean?"

"I wonder if he is single."

"Who knows?" Jackie replied. "Married men pretend they're single. Single men are metrosexuals nowadays. What does that mean? They have sex with the subway? Who knows what's going on anymore?"

The man who was the emcee of potential jurors called out, "Okay, these names go to Room 3C where you will meet your lawyer and go through jury selection for your case. Once you have completed, come back here and drop off your number. If you are selected, you will go to the court you are told to be in on Monday, this being Friday. If you are not selected, come back here to see if you are called to another case."

Burke looked to see if he was wearing a wedding ring, even though he wasn't her type. It was a habit at this point. Of course, he's wearing a ring. Men must get married five seconds after they divorce. God forbid, they should miss a meal.

She and Jackie began their walk to Room 3C in a crowd of what seemed like lost souls, judging by the lackluster way everyone walked. Jackie made a joke as they headed downstairs, "Who will be chosen? Who will be left abandoned on the shore?" as if she was a movie narrator or a religious preacher.

Burke smiled.

"Stand by me, lovey," Jackie said. "It's the only way we'll get through this."

* * * * *

Room 3 C turned out to be a courtroom and they all filed into jury seats. Burke was overjoyed at the sight of a very tall, very handsome attorney sitting at one of the lawyer's desks facing the judge's bench. Next to him at the other desk was the DA, shockingly another handsome man right out of the centerfold of GQ. He wore a pinstriped three-piece suit, white shirt and a red power tie. She noticed a gold pocket watch with a Harvard Law bob (Burke stayed abreast of these insignia) dangling on a gold chain. He had blonde hair and a smile like Brad Pitt, which really should be illegal itself, she thought. He was not wearing a ring. She didn't think she'd seen one on the very tall lawyer, either.

It is a pleasure, she thought, to serve one's country.

As she looked more attentively, she noticed that the DA looked to be in his thirties. Burke was 36, and wanted a man of proven gravitas. The other very tall lawyer seemed more her type.

She and Jackie exchanged a quick look at they sat down, approving the excellent scenery.

The tall one, 6'5' to be exact, with thick brown hair and a pleasant face, stood and began to walk toward the potential jurors.

"I am Attorney McGuinness," he said.

Burke thought, big guy, notice me. I will say or do whatever it takes to get on *this* jury.

He then placed his manicured hands on the mahogany rail. She immediately took in the gold cufflinks and the large class ring with a garnet stone on his left hand. It also had a large ram on one side.

"Oh my God," Burke whispered to Jackie.

"What?"

"He's wearing a Fordham ring. I went to Fordham."

"Really?"

"And I wear the ring, too." She held her hand up for Jackie. Had that lawyer quickly looked at her hand when she walked in, she wondered, or was that her imagination. He was now looking at the list of jurors.

Why didn't she meet him in college instead of Mister Wrong? This lawyer seemed like the poster boy for an Irish gentleman. All he needed was a white horse.

Then the handsome DA stood up with his list of jurors, strode over to the jury box, and said, "I am the prosecutor on this case, Attorney Christopher Lloyd."

Jackie thought, and now, for the first act.

Attorney McGuinness began, "This is going to be a high-profile case and I will have to ask you all some questions. You of course will not be able to talk to each other outside of the jury deliberation room during your time of jury duty, if you are selected."

Burke and Jackie gave each other a look as if to say—Fat chance, Counselor!

On the other hand, both Burke and Jackie were happy to never ever have to talk to the woman next to them who had been knitting in the jury hall and was still unbelievably doing so in the jury selection room. How could they possibly pick her? Anyway, she seemed to be knitting a coverlet for a Volkswagen. That sound of click-click of her needles. I hope they stop her immediately, Burke thought. And Shalimar? Who still wears Shalimar?

Attorney McGuinness and Attorney Lloyd took turns asking the potential jurors different questions. Both attorneys had the filled-out forms, so they had the requisite information on whomever they addressed. That meant that any writers, lawyers, union members who were here would, most likely, be thrown off. Burke was not sure where teachers stood. On the other hand, she had seen Attorney McGuinness' head move imperceptibly when he saw herself, a tall redhead, walk in.

They'd now learned this case was called The People vs Maura Howard Craig St. Claire.

Attorney Lloyd asked Burke if she had read of any of Maura Howard Craig's books?

"No," Burke said, "I haven't." And in fact, this was true. They seemed too boring, aren't all those crime books formulaic?

Burke answered her questions elegantly and wonderfully and before McGuinness turned to question the next juror, the skies opened: he smiled at her.

This is my kind of case, she thought.

Once everyone had been asked different questions and Jackie had not said too much, thankfully, the lawyers conferred at the front tables and seemed to check off some names and cross out others. Christopher Lloyd stood up and said," I will read out the names of who is to be on the jury. If you are not called, please leave."

A well-dressed man of 60ish was selected juror number one. He was losing a battle to grow a goatee and he had a distant circle of plastered hair combed forward over his forehead. This was an instant where Burke was delighted to see a wedding ring.

Jackie whispered, "Why doesn't Combover Ken just go bald?"

A very pretty platinum blonde girl of 30 was chosen juror number two. She said her name was Belinda—

"Did she say Blender?" Jackie asked.

Burke shook her head.

And Belinda had never read Maura Howard Craig since she had no time to read fiction. She was becoming a nurse practitioner and had to study all the time. She seemed innocent and sweet. Both Burke and Jackie wished they could be more like this young ingénue, she seemed destined for a good life. They called her "Marilyn," for her blondness and delicate featured good looks.

The attorneys next chose Too Tall Paul, who was so pretty he could have been a girl himself, or a model. He'd said he was studying for a degree in Pharmacology and he seemed to be armed with books and an iPad.

Burke whispered, "You know they said Peter O'Toole was so pretty he could have been a girl. So too with Too Tall Paul."

"They'll be married before the case is settled," Jackie said.

"Quiet, please," said Attorney Lloyd, and Burke sat up straight. That comment was for her and Jackie.

Burke looked over at Too Tall Paul and Marilyn, and they did seem to be a match.

The next juror was Dangerous Dan. Why they chose a man who looks like a gigolo, or worse a ballroom dancer, and has an Elvis duck-tail on his head, and resembles a thief himself, Burke did not know. He winked at Jackie, then Marilyn, and then Burke.

Oh, great, a buffoon lothario, Burke thought.

Burke whispered, "This is more a freak show than a jury, so far. Doesn't seem like a jury of peers of a famous writer."

Then they chose Fatty Arbuckle, at least this man had the same shape as the silent film actor. He had a box of fish shaped crackers coming out of his pockets. He also had never heard of Maura Howard Craig. Had there been a casting call for an illiterate jury?

The clinker with her knitting needles, Lilian Edwards, also turned out to be selected for the jury. Burke was sure they would never allow the knitting. Ms. Edwards didn't even stop when they called her name.

Others were chosen, and then Elizabeth's name which for a moment confused Burke, but when she saw the smile on Jackie's face, Burke remembered. And then she heard her own name.

Good. Great. But even better, when her name was called, Attorney McGuinness turned around and winked at her.

The Judge now came in and sat down. She was of a certain age, perhaps not the age to still be working, but she was chic and you could see, sharp.

"My name is Judge Egan, and I will be hearing this case. I am glad to meet you all. You may of course go to lunch now," she announced. "Be back at 2 pm to be told some details of the case and where to be on Monday and some house rules. Thank you so much for serving."

And out she went.

* * * * *

On this very first day, Burke and Jackie followed the instructions not to interact with each other to the letter. Anyway, Burke had plans so she officiously left the jury room.

"See you later, Jackie."

"Yeah, sure." Maybe Jackie needs to study her lines for Mary Poppins, Burke thought.

Burke, on the other hand, wanted a smoothie and then to get herself to a newsstand. Perhaps she wasn't allowed to do that but how would they ever know?

The New York Post would have the dirt.

She paid the Pakistani man for the newspaper and found a remote bench in the shady part of the park near the courthouse.

"Did Maura Howard Craig St. Claire murder husband #2?" Burke's pretty blue eyes focused intently as she read that this was not the first time Mrs. Craig had been up for murder. That was unbelievable! As Burke read, she saw that Mrs. Craig had been found innocent of the first murder. Mr. Craig had died on a boating accident and there was not enough proof to convict Mrs. Maura Howard Craig.

Burke sat back, what are the chances of being up for murder of two husbands? "Open mind." Who are they kidding? She *must* be guilty.

She continued studying the paper. Besides being rich, Burke also could see that Mrs. Craig was gorgeous. She looked like Elizabeth Taylor. Burke put the paper down, she had always thought writers were supposed to be nerdy looking. Not this one. She looked at the pictures again and this writer positively looked like a film actress. She reread the caption to make sure it wasn't a film actress portraying Mrs. Craig. No, this is her.

Well, we'll see if she stands up to her photo at the trial or is this one of those book jacket things where the photo is 40 years out of date.

She took a draw of her smoothie to reflect. Well, she thought, a murderer or potential murderer shouldn't be competition for the affection of that attorney. Who wants to marry a possible murderer? Of husbands, no less. Much better to marry a juror. After the case is completed, of course. But he IS defending her. Hopefully, the money is good.

The Post had another article on the first husband. Craig, it seems, had four wives who remarkably all looked alike. Well, they say men like the same type, but this is ridiculous, she thought. It must have been plastic surgery. She studied the photos, and then continued reading. They testified at the trial that Thomas Craig insisted his wives dress and wear their hair identically to his dead first wife. He called them all "Baby." That didn't seem very personal to Burke. Each wife only lasted a few years, she read on, and they all received a generous cash settlement along with having to sign a clause never to reveal secrets of their marriage during his lifetime. Bizarre. She continued reading and apparently, he'd left his entire publishing empire to his wife, Maura. That was nice of him. Also convenient for a writer to have her own publishing house.

Oh, she's written twenty books. Where did she find the time to murder husbands?

Burke finished her skinny smoothie only to see on her phone, when she looked it up, that the skinny smoothie was anything but skinny with its 400 calories and headed back to the courtroom. She is going to have to talk to Jackie about all this. It's too interesting.

* * * * *

All the jury members re-entered, looking each other up and down, and waited.

The two lawyers came in and stood up for Judge Egan. Judge Egan now returned and, again, Burke had to admit she felt partial to her. Her hair was an attractive auburn that waved around her face, which flattered her dark piercing eyes. She wore a pinkish lipstick and a blue suit, which you could hardly see under her robes. She wore heels, which made Jackie and Burke both respect her. She had an air of firmness, independent competence, and tremendous sanity about her.

This was now her moment. She turned to the jurors.

"Ladies and Gentlemen of the Jury, thank you again. You will see quite a bit about this case in the news since the defendant is very well known but I ask you to not let the news have any effect on you. Do not read it. Take a break from papers and television news. You have no idea how good it will be for your health. The allegation of murdering a husband is always good for hard copy so it will be everywhere. Let us hope it will not result in a rampage of dead husbands."

The jurors laughed. The DA looked appalled.

She continued, "You know your job is to listen for testimony that proves guilt and not go by any of your own biases. You have two very capable lawyers here making their arguments. We will meet in the main courthouse in Rockland County on Monday at 9 am sharp. Please do not speak of or about this case to anyone at all, including each other. The main request I have is that you keep an open and receptive mind to all you are about to hear. Have a good weekend and I look forward to seeing you all on Monday morning. Court adjourned."

Out she went, the lawyers began packing up their briefcases, the other jurors began walking out, and Jackie and Burke were both quietly deciding whether they should have a drink right now or wait for another day.

CHAPTER

Two

They were not to watch the news or follow the case anywhere else.

However, both women got home and respectively went onto google. They would bet many other jurors were doing the same, well not Marilyn who clearly was a good girl, a person who followed the rules, as probably was her as-yet-unknown-to-her fiancé, Too Tall Paul.

Maybe Jackie and she were the only outliers but, Burke rationalized, as she fired up her computer, as Malcolm Gladwell said, Outliers are the inventors and the ones who accomplish things. As she thought that, it occurred to her that information may not be empiric. If only one of her students would understand the word empiric.

First, let us look up our darling attorney. She can even go into the Fordham annals. She was sure he noticed her ring, because aren't attorneys supposed to notice everything?

Since this was going to be a long night, she got up and got herself a white wine. Walking back to her computer, she noticed that she herself owned four Maura Howard Craig novels. Probably people gave them to her. She picked one out of the bookcase and yes, there she was in all her glamorous glory. No wonder all these rich men were marrying her all over the place. She's got talent and good looks. It seemed a bit unfair. God should have more compassion and pass out these assets more equitably.

She went onto the Fordham site and looked up Attorney Eugene

McGuinness. He had gone to Fordham on the GI bill, having been in the air force. There was a picture of him walking in the St. Patrick's Day Parade, representing Fordham. Wait, there's Maura Howard Craig, herself.

She went to Fordham, too?

Burke then began looking up Maura and the Fordham alumni newsletter had done several profiles of her as their most famous English Literature graduate. Burke read that Maura's first book, "Little Bo Peep," had been published during her senior year, and from then on, her books paid for her tuition.

Hmmm... so he went on the GI bill and she went on her books, so there was no family money in either case. Plus, they know each other! But then, Burke herself had gone to Fordham to get her Ph.D. in Psychology and she didn't know either of them. But the lawyer and the possible murderer were there in the same years.

She then googled the Attorney again and got his business website and saw he had graduated top of his class, flew his own plane, and was not married. He also had won over 120 trials. He seemed to be a star lawyer with his firm.

There were loads of articles on Maura Howard Craig, but they interested Burke less. She'd look at the photos, instead. That way she'd be almost following the request of Judge Egan not to read up on the case.

Burke was most impressed at the wedding photos with the now deceased Mr. Craig, who turned out to be 20 years Maura Howard Craig's senior, handsome in an expensive dark suit, perfectly cut silver hair, powerful looking, which apparently, he was. Maura looked lovely in an antique ivory gown and matching crown, with mountains of black curls, blue eyes and a porcelain skin.

She then saw pictures of the second wedding with Guy St. Claire, the man she is being prosecuted for murdering. In the pictures, he is quite the knockout, tall, elegant, and this time 20 years younger than Mrs. Maura Howard Craig. She must be 40 in this picture, although she doesn't look it, and he must be in his twenties. He seemed to have worked at Craig Publishing, also. Mrs. Craig is beaming next to him in a lace off-white dress and he stands gentlemanly and proud, full blonde hair, dapper blue suit. There's a picture of a yellow Cadillac and him giving her the keys. And a picture of a black Ferrari and she giving him keys. They were married at the Craig mansion in Tuxedo Park, the caption read. Most of the other pictures were book readings or book jacket photos. Some charity events.

Interesting.

That was enough. Burke shouldn't do this. She got off the sites and emailed Jackie about drinks tomorrow night. She knew Jackie was renting a place nearby and her work friends probably were in Jersey so she must be a bit lonely. They'll need to go somewhere where they won't be seen. Maybe New York?

Tomorrow Burke wanted to buy something extremely tasteful, flattering, and very noticeable to wear to the first day of the trial.

* * * * *

Jackie and Burke went back and forth on where they should meet so they would not be sighted. Should it be upscale or downscale? Well, the lawyers were successful so better to go downscale. They were pretty sure the other jurors were not the drinking type and were further downscale than they would even think of going.

They settled on a Karaoke bar in Hoboken so Burke could hear Jackie's voice.

Burke had never been to a Karaoke bar before and, oddly, expected to see lots of Japanese people for some reason. Instead, there were mostly couples of every race, quietly drinking away, waiting for the music to start. Jackie sipped her cosmopolitan and Burke her martini, when Jackie asked, “Does your psychology doctorate make you able to read people’s faces and body language?”

“Yes, I think so,” Burke said. “It certainly helps. We were told some peculiar things, though.”

“Like what?”

“Like people who smoke pipes aren’t aggressive. Crossed legs are defensive, things like that.”

“Do you think you’ll be able to tell if she’s guilty?” Jackie asked.

“Well how many people are up for murdering two husbands? It does seem a bit of a coincidence.”

Jackie nodded.

Jackie said, “Anyway she should be convicted for just being so good looking and talented in one lifetime. It’s not considerate of other people.”

Burke smiled. “I am not one to be upstaged so I bought myself a beige silk blouse, and a blue skirt. Very shapely and perfect for listening to the arguments.”

Jackie laughed, “And for capturing an attorney’s eye.”

“I hope so.”

“Jolly good,” Jackie said.

Now it was Burke's turn to ask, "Do you think she did it?"

Jackie said, "I think so although I read up about him. No idea why she would. He's quite cute."

Burke said, "Oh I didn't read about him, just looked at the pictures. What did you find out?"

"He's of French extraction. Very good breeding. Upper class. A doting husband. Hard working at Craig Publishing. That's how he met her. One of those men who are so handsome that you sort of melt around them."

"Why would she kill him?" Burke said. "A younger, doting husband."

"Who knows? We'll find out. The DA – that Lloyd guy – will have some assumptions. Maybe St. Claire was fooling around with her money, or women."

"She has enough money for him to fool around with. If he was, it wouldn't make much difference to their lifestyle," Burke said. "She wouldn't kill him over that."

"Rich people never feel they have enough money," Jackie said. "Neither do poor people, for that matter."

"The papers are not saying why they think it is her," Burke said. "Except she was seen leaving the scene of the crime, of course. That could do it."

Jackie wagged her finger, "You're not supposed to be reading the papers."

Burke said, "You're not supposed to be sitting here with me, either."

Jackie said proudly, "We Brits are eccentrics. We don't do what other people tell us to do."

"But I wonder why the papers are not saying exactly what happened," Burke said.

Jackie posited, "Maybe they don't know. Maybe people aren't talking. If so, it's unbelievable. Mind if I sing now?"

Burke said, "Go ahead."

Jackie got up onto the stage without any hesitation and grabbed a mic very professionally and confidently. She whispered a song to the DJ. People were talking but once she started, she had such a clear and melodic voice, a professional's indeed, that people stopped their conversations and watched her. Burke laughed at her choice of music. Jackie winked at her as she sang, Johnny Cash's FOLSOM PRISON BLUES.

The eight people in the bar loved it.

When it was over, everyone applauded loudly and Jackie broke into a sudden little girl smile and said, "Thank you, all of you. You're all loves," and then made her way back, shaking people's hands as she went through the bar to where she had been sitting. "It's such fun to sing, I must say," she said.

"You're wonderful at it. Excellent choice of song," she laughed. "Maybe you can sing that in the jury room!"

They ordered two more drinks and then Jackie said, "You know, I keep wondering how they actually got her."

CHAPTER

Three

A month before Jackie and Burke had been out drinking that night, the quietude in the surrounding town to one of the most upscale boroughs in the state of New York was interrupted by the noise of a singular siren. It was 5 pm and the residents of the town were beginning to arrive home from New York and White Plains, cities where most of them went to work. Usually, a siren at this time was a local police officer putting the chase on a neighbor's car for exceeding the 25 mph limit on the roads. The state coffers always needed to be replenished and speeding tickets was one of the most reliable ways.

There'd been a heavy snow so perhaps the police were right to be vigilant in their speed watch. And it was definitely a police siren, an ambulance siren being more repetitive and insistent, trained to communicate Get Out of Our Way Now, and a fire department siren sounded more like what one remembered from childhood when little brothers got a firetruck at Christmas.

After the initial siren that evening, there was a silence of about ten minutes. They must have got the transgressive driver. Until that silence was once again broken by the screaming sound of a mournful, piercing ambulance, followed by the cacophony of a series of police sirens, all of it as if a cavalcade was coming down the road.

Those people sitting in their homes and hearing those sirens had visions of their offspring being involved in some terrible accident. A number of inquisitive neighbors, or rather those who were looking for some reason to get out of the house, immediately got in their cars to drive to the scene. Most of them knew how to access the police news to locate the exact address where all the sirens were converging.

Once they arrived at Montebello's snowy Main Street, the inquisitive stayed put in their cars and found themselves gaping at a tarpaulin covered body awaiting a lift into an ambulance. The police, on the other hand, were out of their cars and asking any and every one, who were not in cars, what they had seen. Those who had been there from the beginning, who had been on errands stocking up on groceries for the snowstorm, were stunned and overcome as they reported that the shooter had been a woman driving a yellow Caddy convertible.

The snow was still coming down. By now, the victim had been identified and the ever vigilant Rockland County press had managed to ferret out of one of the policemen that the owner of the bereft Ferrari covered in snow and blood from which the victim had tried to emerge, perhaps stopping for some groceries himself, was that of Guy St. Claire of Tuxedo Park.

Another witness, who chose to remain anonymous, also informed the journalist that she'd heard that Guy St. Claire and his rich wife were divorcing. She'd seen it, she thought, in *Vanity Fair*. He was a man, the witness said, whose looks you did not forget.

The yellow Caddy was cited more than once, as bystanders gave their impressions of what they saw.

Patrolman Haber said to his partner, Patrolman Williams," I hate to tell you this, but St. Claire's wife drives a yellow Caddy. I remember my own wife commenting on it. She reads all about society people. It usually drives me crazy."

Patrolman Harry William's said, "Your wife is right. I just called in.

Guy St. Claire is married to that famous writer in Tuxedo Park. Maura Howard Craig and, what's more, she does drive a yellow Caddy."

Patrolman Haber looked on silently. "Well was she the one driving it? Someone else could have taken her car."

Patrolman Harry Williams was grabbing his CB to call the precinct detective. 'Someone reported the dark hair, the scarf, the whole look. She's kind of good looking I hear and the alleged killer seemed to match her looks."

Patrolman Haber said, "Well she didn't cover her tracks very well, driving her own car and all. Doesn't she write mysteries? She probably would be more careful in a book."

"Look, Haber, this is not a book club meeting. It's murder." Then Patrolman Williams got the Chief. "Me? Yes, I can go out there. Don't I need a warrant or something? Oh, just to let her know about his death. I see. Yes, I've got the address."

* * * * *

As Patrolman Williams drove to Tuxedo Park, with Haber at his side, he remembered she had been up for the first husband's death.

He mentioned this to Haber who said, "She certainly leads an unusual life. It seems to be hazardous to be married to her."

Both men laughed, each one secretly believing that one of the traits necessary for police work is a gallows humor.

When the policemen arrived at the mansion, Maura answered the door. Patrolman William's first impression was that her response was a little quick for someone who normally would not have expected company, especially on an inclement night like tonight. When he walked into her opulent house, with its huge marble foyer with a staircase waiting for Vivian Leigh to come down in a long white dress, he had a second impression. Mrs. St. Claire's hair seemed to be slightly damp, as if she'd just taken a shower, and her manner not that of a woman who might have just shot her husband.

She was incredibly chatty. How long had they been on the force? What part of the county do you two gentlemen live in?

While his partner, Haber, answered, he looked out the window and noticed that the tire tracks that led into her four-car garage were only slightly covered.

That's interesting, he thought.

"I have some bad news, Mrs. St. Claire," Patrolman Williams said.

"Oh really? What? Not about Patricia, I hope?"

"Who?"

"She's my maid. I am very fond of her. We're friends really. Nothing happened to her, did it?"

"No, this is about your husband, Mr. St. Claire."

"What about Mr. St. Claire, whom, by the way, no longer lives here," she said.

"Yes, well he won't be living anywhere now. I am afraid to report he has been shot dead."

"What?" she looked genuinely shocked and sickened.

"He's been murdered."

"By whom?"

"We don't know, Mrs. St Claire."

"Maura, please," she corrected him, graciously.

She sat down then and motioned that they should sit down. "If Patricia was here, she could get us all a drink."

"We're on duty, ma'am," said Haber.

"Oh of course."

Patrolman Williams was withholding the yellow caddy part being at the scene just to see how she reacted. I really should be in the detective department, he thought.

"Tell me more," she said, "about what happened."

* * * * *

Patrolman William's phone rang at that moment. "Excuse me a moment," and he went into the next room, a well-appointed second drawing room with red walls and furniture covered in greens and blue velvet.

"Desk Sargent here."

"Go ahead," said Williams.

"We've got other witnesses saying they saw a yellow Cadillac near the scene of the crime."

My God, he thought, looking out the window again and tilting his head, that's a yellow Caddy in the four-car garage with the fresh tire tracks.

The desk Sargent continued. "Another witness said a woman was seen at the scene of the murder and one witness claimed the deadly shot came from that car."

"Thanks," said Williams, and hung up. As he got up from his blue velvet chair, he thought, *this* seems like a shoo in to me. Then he sat back down.

He dialed the station. "Get me the Captain please."

The Captain came on and Patrolman Williams expressed his impressions to him.

The Captain then said, "We'll grab another policeman and a female cop, Evelyn Alford, and get out there. We've got grounds for an arrest. You keep talking to her until they get there. When they arrive, tell her she is going to have to come down to the station and wait in a holding cell. We'll get an attorney to sign the card which sets forth her rights and make sure you read all of them to her."

The Captain put the phone down and gleamed with delight. He always thought that Maura Howard Craig woman got away with the murder of her first husband. There was just something about it. They were fighting on the boat. Of course, they were. He looked down at the witness reports on this murder and thought, we have a perfect case against her and I do not want her fleet of expensive attorneys to buy her out of her crime this time. Under no circumstance do I want any of this station talking to her when she gets here, complimenting her on her books or whatever they would say, or making any reference to the evidence at hand. With the millions she's made writing books on murder, she probably knows a lot of tricks. I want this to be the last one she writes, and I do not want any probable buyers of her books who might be potential jurors to start thinking they can get clues from her books. These mystery writers make their readers think they are amateur detectives or police captains. The readers actually mistake the books as crime solving training manuals. Her no-sex, no-violence stories are for housewives, plain and simple, who are best at solving where to buy chocolate donuts but, let's face it, he thought, as he went in search of some of his staff, they would consider themselves heroines if they found a way to save the famous author from being fingered.

He went back into his office.

He dialed Squad 52. "Yes, Cap?"

"I want you to go round to the local bookstores and local library in Rockland County to collect names of purchasers of Maura Craig Howard novels."

"I beg your pardon, Cap?"

The two Squad 52 policemen looked at each other like the Captain might have been having a few.

"You are not joking, are you?"

"No, I am not. Just get those names. Make them give you lists."

"Okay Cap."

They began to look at their phones. "Why would he want those?" one asked the other. "God, there are 10 bookstores in the Rockland County area."

"Well look at the bright side," said Patrolman Kennedy.

"What?"

"Hard to get shot at in a bookstore and you can meet some interesting people there."

"How would you know?" laughed Patrolman Duckworth.

They drove off to the first Barnes and Noble in their area, each commenting that it was going to be a long, boring night.

* * * * *

Maura sat in the small cage of a jail cell that she shared with a very drunk young lady who looked no older than seventeen. The steel commode in the corner of the cell was a far cry from her home custom-made bidet in sapphire blue, her favorite color. The police kept walking by her, either because they found Maura and her cellmate attractive or were confused why Maura seemed unaffected by the environment.

Maura knew she was entitled to one phone call. But to whom? she wondered. Her corporate lawyers were money grubbing fools and not that smart, not that she needed someone that smart, but what she really needed was a friend. In truth, she wasn't too worried about this case. She was positive they wouldn't convict her.

She sat down on the worn bench and tried to think whom she should call. What about her old grade school friend, Eugene John McGuinness? As her jail cell mate lay on a bench talking to herself, Maura remembered how Eugene had hated his first name in school and grown to over 6'4" and become known as "Huge." He dropped that name when he passed the bar.

When she and Eugene had been at school together, they had both been poor, bright, and he used to kiss her in the locker room. He was always focused on his schoolwork, never became a player, but then neither had she. She too had been focused on her work. But she never forgot how, when in grade school and her father died, the parents of her classmates felt it would be too traumatic for their young children to see a dead man in a box. Huge was the only one who came to the funeral to say he was sorry for her loss. She had the feeling he would have defied his parents, even if they had given him the same message. To this day, it meant a lot to her. He'd even congratulated on her $25 paycheck from Readers Digest for her first story. Nobody else had done that either.

They used to kiss a lot, now that she thinks about it, out of sight of the nuns. He was diligent in his kissing, as he was about doing his work. She laughed to herself.

They went onto parallel lives, she thinks. He joined the air force and then went to law school on the GI bill. She'd paid her own tuition by writing a book a year. Everyone thought he was gay because there were no girls. But she had a sneaking suspicion he carried a torch for her.

And then they'd both gone to Fordham and had seen each other at various alumni parties in the early years after graduating. He went onto law school at night at St John's and she had already begun her writing career. The only time they ran into each other was when they marched side by side in the St Patrick's Day Parade down Fifth Avenue, stopping at St. Pat's for the Cardinal's blessing.

The parade was a ritual for both of them, a sentimentality, she guessed. One needs rituals in this topsy-turvy world, she thought as she looked round the jail cell. They'd both had hard childhoods. Her mother never made much money after her father's death. Maura had to wear hand me downs to school dances and parties. Huge's father was cruel to his mother, she now remembered, and also to his studious son.

She was enjoying remembering all this as she sat on that scarred bench. It gives one solace, she thought, to remember the past. Even in jail, she rued, smiling a bit to herself.

At one of the St Patrick's Day parades, she'd told him about her marriage to Craig. He'd graciously said how happy he was for her and that he would always be there for her. She'd been moved by that. Maybe that was why he was coming to mind right now. He himself had never married and she remembered during the Craig trial, he was still attending St John's Law at night and managing a yacht club giving sailing lessons during the day. When they had put her on the stand and she testified that she and her very drunk husband had fought on the boat, just as the witnesses had said, over her refusal to wear the green contact lenses he'd bought for her so she would look like all the other Baby's he'd married. She'd forgotten to mention he was also angry that she was wearing the lavender dress he'd asked her to wear and she'd chosen a sweat suit, instead. Perhaps she had done it to spite him.

Maura's reverie was interrupted by her cell mate saying *Ommmmm*. Maura looked over and she could see that the girl was sitting cross legged on her bench trying to meditate away her anxiety. With the way her cell-mate's fingers were tapping, it wasn't working.

She thought back to McGuinness and that trial. Oh yes, the fight with Craig and his absurd obsession with his first wife who died in childbirth having twins. One of the twins, a boy, had died too. Craig refused to get over it. No wonder she wrote *Down Will Come Baby,* as one of her best novels.

Gene would never have put her on the stand like that, he told her years later at one of the parades. Anyway, she had convinced the jury that it was an accident. She was the victim in that case, not that rich bastard Craig. The women jurors teared up as she spoke. She could see them thinking, who could be married to such a strange character making women all look the same? The men in the jury looked like they wanted to take care of her.

But now she was mostly conjuring up the vision of Gene catching her eye when she was on the stand and smiling and then rushing off, presumably, to night school at St John's Law.

Should she call him? She had no family. And she wanted an outsider to defend her. Eugene Huge McGuinness was now a 6'5" (he'd grown another inch after high school) senior partner at O'Connor, McGuinness and Goldberg.

* * * * *

"Who?"

"Maura Howard Craig," said his secretary.

McGuinness excused himself from the client meeting in his all-windowed New York office to take the call. He would have walked on hot coals for a call from her. He'd read of the news of the murder and arrest on the internet. As he picked up the phone, Gene had visions of his beautiful Maura sitting in the over-lit Rockland County jail, her Jimmy Choo's replaced by shoelace-free sneakers provided by the good citizens of Rockland County, New York.

"Hi, Gene. I just have one call, as you know. Have you heard about why I'm in jail?"

"I have, Maura. Don't worry. I'm sure it's some incorrect technicality."

"You know what the allegations are, right?"

"I do. Are you in a holding cell?"

He was surprised at how calm she sounded.

"Yes, but I did nothing but be a trusting wife. I'm not saying I'm not glad he's dead but I had nothing to do with it. I think I was framed for his murder."

Gene listened. Then he said, "I'm on my way. Don't talk to anyone and I mean anyone."

* * * * *

As he drove to the jail, he thought that running to rescue Maura was something he had always been in preparation for. Up to now, he had only given devoted passion to his job, but also perhaps to the memory of her.

Maura had become very successful but then he, too, had met most of his own goals:

Gain or earn a partnership in a successful law firm: Check

Drive an S-class Mercedes-Benz: Check

Buy a summer home on the water complete with a Le Comte 33 Medalist Sailboat: Check

Pilot his own plane: Check

Sing like an Irish tenor and dance like Michael Flatley: Pending

Argue a case in the Supreme Court: Also pending

Marry his childhood sweetheart, Maura, even though she didn't know she was his childhood sweetheart: Seemingly a Mission Impossible.

Over the years, he'd enjoyed seeing the maturing pictures of Maura on her book cover jackets. But he clung to his favorite picture of her, a cherub faced beauty wearing her school uniform which, in those years, she'd told him was her best dress. Her rich husband, Craig, had changed all that, of course. Her short curly bob was now shoulder length with extensions. A team of designers jazzed up her wardrobe transforming her into a fashionista which exchanged her innocent bearing for hard glamour.

When she'd married Craig at 25 years old, Maura seemed to have it all.

Her novel, *Down will Come Baby*, published with Craig, went to number one. She was on her way. There had been pictures of them celebrating on Craig's yacht. The 112-foot boat had a full staff including a Captain aboard, he'd read.

Gene now knew he was formally out of her league and no longer would she ever need his protection.

And then ten years later, Thomas Harrison Craig was lost at sea, his body never recovered.

Gene remembered reading that Craig's staff said the couple quarreled over the dress Maura wore, that it wasn't one Craig picked out for her and her sudden weight gain. Maybe it was over contact lenses, he wasn't sure. Rumor had it that she was pregnant. If she was, the press suspected that it was terminated as Mr. Craig did not want another child, having lost the first Mrs. Mary Craig who accidentally drowned in a pool right after giving birth to his twins. One of the twins died in the hospital, Gene thinks.

He remembered how Maura had been arrested and charged with the murder of her first husband and labeled a gold digger by the media. The tabloids showed her as a fabulous looking, cold-blooded widow. But between her highly priced lawyers, the inept prosecutor, compounded by the poor testimony of the first-year detective, Maura was acquitted. The DA, Thomas Dunn, or, as he was known by everyone in Gene's office, "Undone Dunn," could not prove without a doubt that Maura had anything to do with the accidental death of her husband. It was deemed more likely that Thomas Harrison Craig probably fell overboard after a heavy night of drinking. He was not reported missing until the next morning when he failed to appear for breakfast. It seems the two often slept in separate quarters after an encounter. They never got around to signing a prenup and Maura was now CEO of Craig Publishing.

Since then, Gene had read all her mystery novels and even gone to many of her book signings but strangely she never seemed to recognize him.

* * * * *

He parked at the jail and entered the stone building.

One thing about being this tall is that people tend to give you respect. Never fails.

"Go ahead, Attorney."

He stopped at the Chief Bailiff. "I am representing Ms. Maura Howard Craig St. Claire. I would like some time with my client."

"Understandable, Mr. McGuinness. Wait in that office over there. I'll bring her in."

He was nervous standing there waiting. How would she perceive him after all these years?

"Here she is, Attorney."

And he turned and you would have thought she'd been waiting to meet him at the Ritz tearoom, not a jail cell in Rockland County.

"Hi Gene," she smiled, not a hair out of place, her silk blouse pressed, her pencil skirt smart and expensive.

"Hi Maura. Are they treating you okay?"

"Just great," she said.

Just great? he thought.

The policeman left them alone.

"I didn't do it," she said.

"I'm not worried about that," he said. "I'll get you off."

She smiled and chuckled. "I know that, Gene."

"First I have to set an arraignment and get you out of here on bail. I know the judge and maybe I can do all that with the DA and Judge Evans without stalling for court. We're all friends up here. I'll put up the bail myself till I get you out."

"That's so wonderful, Gene," she said, smiling, as if was telling her where they were going for dinner.

"You are certainly the most relaxed alleged murdered I've ever seen. It must be the Irish in you," he said, laughing.

"No, it's just I have the ultimate confidence in you," she said.

And at that moment his 6'5" frame soared to 7'5" and he knew there was nothing in the world he wouldn't do to get her acquitted.

CHAPTER

Four

Opening day began with Judge Egan facing everyone in their places.

Jackie and Burke were situated next to one another in their juror seats, Burke in a most attractive blue skirt, and silk cream blouse that showed her figure to effect. Her hair was up, accentuating her slender neck and piercing blue eyes. Jackie was wearing a yellow flowered dress, in contrast to how soberly she was taking in the pageant before her.

Judge Egan looked fresh and gracious, her auburn hair gracefully shining under the courtroom's institutional light. Attorney Lloyd's blonde hair also shone as he looked down at his files in front of him, and then nodded to the female assistant attorney next to him, indicating they were good to go. Attorney McGuinness sat tall beside his defendant, Ms. Maura Howard Craig St. Claire, who looked petite, well-coiffed, and surprisingly at peace for someone accused of murder and facing possible life in prison or worse. Maybe there wasn't anything worse than possible life in prison.

Actually, Burke was finding what was worse than prison was witnessing the silent sort of camaraderie between McGuinness and his defendant as they sat so companionably together. As he looked at his notes, he'd break to steal fond looks at her, while she would be glancing curiously over at the jury, always with a gentle and wise demeanor, then back at him with a little smile. They were so easy together, they could have been waiting for *My Fair Lady* to start. Burke told herself, "Well they're old friends but still...he should be stealing looks at *me* more often, not a potential murderer."

Maybe this idolatry on his part is part of his defense strategy.

Judge Egan called for court to begin and this was the time for opening arguments. Attorney Lloyd assured the jurors that he could provide evidence beyond any doubt that Maura Howard Craig, a woman who had the rare resume of being twice accused of murder of a husband, was at the scene of the crime and had been seen with a gun, the very same night and time that the unfortunate, hard- working, devoted husband Guy St Claire had been heinously murdered.

This was followed by Attorney McGuinness getting up to his full height, and somehow managing to smile at all the women jurors without seeming sexist or lecherous, simply by projecting a romantic kindness. He assured the jury that it would be literally impossible for a woman of such stature, beauty, intelligence, refinement to do something as base or stupid as murder Guy St Claire. He stated that the jurors would see conflicts abound in testimony and, rather like *Rashomon*, a film he would highly recommend to the jurors, everyone who will give testimony will have witnessed events differently. He asked that the jurors listen carefully and wisely and, if they do, they will see that this is a case where the police and the DA arrived at the easiest, cheapest solution to a murder that would put them in the greatest spotlight with the least amount of effort.

He sat down. Jackie raised her eyebrows to Burke as if to say—Interesting.

Judge Egan said, "Attorney Lloyd, call your first witness."

Attorney Lloyd said, "I call Sandra Frost."

Ms. Craig turned around to the back of the courtroom to look with interest at this first witness. Up strode a tall blonde about the same age as Ms. Craig. She sat down and swore to tell the whole truth and nothing but. Burke and Jackie were so in synch as to both privately and philosophically think, "Who could ever tell the whole truth and nothing but?"

Attorney Lloyd said, "Ms. Frost, you and Ms. Craig shared an apartment in the West Village, did you not, after completing your studies at Fordham?"

Sandra said, "Yes, we did."

Attorney Lloyd asked, in a slight accusing tone, "Why the West Village?"

Sandra replied, "We were best friends and young—"

McGuinness stood up and called out, "Objection. The defendant is still young."

Judge Egan looked down her glasses and smiled. "Sustained. Not to mention, Gallant."

The women in the jury tittered. Jackie leaned into Burke, "I haven't had this much fun since I was a Wren at the Royal Navy parties."

Sandra continued, "Mrs. Craig, actually Ms. Howard then, had already published books and was writing and it was the right environment for a writer. Plenty of writers lived in the village...Dylan Thomas—"

Attorney Lloyd interrupted her, "Didn't you work on Wall Street?" he asked derisively.

Sandra replied, "Yes, I did, to supplement my painting."

Attorney Lloyd said, "Would you say that already there was a sort of criminal element to your lifestyle?"

Sandra replied, "I beg your pardon."

Attorney McGuinness was listening and watching intently, a bit perplexed.

Attorney Lloyd said, "Half the people currently being found guilty of crimes are or began on Wall Street."

McGuinness rose again, "Objection. Not crimes of murder. Of financial...and, sadly, other..."

Judge Egan said, "Sustained."

Attorney Lloyd, not to be deterred, continued, "It is a Chinese saying that you can know a man or woman by their friends."

Attorney McGuinness rose again. "Objection. We are not looking for Chinese philosophy lessons."

Judge Egan said, "Sustained."

Burke began to wonder if Judge Egan had a crush on McGuinness too.

Attorney Lloyd asked Ms. Frost, "Did Ms. Craig ever speak of murder?"

Ms. Frost actually looked as if she was ruminating on this and said, "She did all the time. After all, it was her subject matter for her books."

"I mean," Attorney Lloyd went on, "of real people."

"Only when discussing how long it took for her royalties to get paid," Ms. Frost laughed.

Attorney Lloyd said, "No further questions," in a voice as if he had scored a point.

Fatty Arbuckle looked like he was having trouble following this and, indeed, it was a rather indirect line of questioning.

As Ms. Frost left the witness box, she smiled at Maura and Maura smiled back.

Jackie leaned into Burke, "Now that was a waste of time but I agree with the DA about Wall Street."

Burke smirked and kept her more Republican attitudes to herself. She saw Dangerous Dan blowing a kiss to Sandra as she went to sit down in the back of the court room. Unbelievable. Combover Ken was also staring at the last witness. Well, those two certainly would vote Ms. Frost innocent even if they watched her murdering someone right in front of them.

Judge Egan instructed the DA to call his next witness.

* * * * *

Patrolman Williams took the stand and also swore to tell the truth. Jackie and Burke were assessing his looks, nice body, clean cut face. I wonder what his life is like, Jackie thought.

Williams went onto to tell the court that the victim had been shot once in the heart as he was getting out of his car and had died quickly of a bleed out. Five witnesses saw the shooter sitting in a yellow Cadillac. Three of those witnesses saw the dark hair under a scarf, the sunglasses. Yes, some claimed to see her writing while she was using the gun. No, Patrolman Williams did not take that seriously.

His precinct had told him go tell Mrs. Craig that her husband had just been shot and was now dead. He drove to Tuxedo Park and, yes, she was there, she seemed to have just taken a shower. She was calm, cool and collected and more worried that their visit entailed something to do with her maid, Patricia. Mrs. Craig was gracious and seemed saddened by the news of her husband although she revealed they were no longer living together.

Attorney Lloyd asked, "Did you see anything suspicious on your call?"

Patrolman Williams sat up in the box, "Yes. I noticed that the snow tracks looked fresh and light to one of the garage stalls, unlike the others that had a good 1 or 2 inches outside the garage door. When I looked inside that garage, where obviously a car had gone out, it was a yellow Cadillac."

Attorney Lloyd said, "Have you reports of all the witness statements that evening of the murder that we can pass on to the jury to read?"

Patrolman Williams said, "I do."

Oh, how Burke wanted to hear those words.

Attorney Lloyd said, "I have had them copied," and then he walked over to the jury and distributed a packet of reports and suggested the jury take a minute to read through them.

Burke quickly went through them, after all she is a teacher and knows how to speed read, only to see Fatty Arbuckle struggling with focusing on the reports. Maybe if they had put some ketchup on them, she thought. Then she softened and thought, I must be nicer to him in the jury room. Help him. There's always a Special Ed person everywhere.

Attorney Lloyd faced the jury, "You have heard that there are more than 5 witnesses reporting they saw Ms. Craig in her Cadillac at the scene of the crime. In actuality, you have read twelve reports. In my opinion, this almost closes the case."

He sat down.

Judge Egan said, "Attorney McGuinness?"

He stood up. "They don't know if it was Mrs. Craig the witnesses saw."

"Sustained. Anything else?"

He surprised the courtroom and the jury by saying, "No questions."

And he himself was surprised, as well as the jurors themselves were surprised, when Mrs. Craig gave her attorney her most captivating smile that had a glint of a lost soul conveying—Help me as you did so many years ago when Tommy Madden taunted me on the school grounds. Then Mrs. Craig bizarrely looked down at her legal-size pad and began taking notes.

Jackie whispered, "Is she writing a book on the state's time?"

Burke said, "Probably. It could be called *You be the Judge*."

Jackie quietly chuckled and then whispered, "What's the plot line, do you think?"

"It's about a rich woman," Burke whispered back, "who is convicted of killing her husband and you be the judge if she gets away with it."

Jackie said, "You're a clever one, lovie, and why the hell does she look so relaxed?"

"He does too," Burke said.

Jackie said, "Maybe they're both taking Prozac or Valium or something."

Attorney Lloyd called one more witness.

* * * * *

She turned out to be a woman who worked at Craig Publishing and the whole point of this testimony was to let the jurors know what a kind, good person Guy St. Claire was. Nobody would want to kill him. At least from work. He was the soul of gentility and generosity. Ms. Maura Howard Craig could be a bit difficult on personnel issues but Mr. St. Claire always had an ear for everyone and really tried to help on their behalf.

Attorney Lloyd thanked the witness who, it seemed, had delivered her paid advertisement to the jury. Or maybe it was true and he was a decent guy. She did marry him, after all.

Jackie leaned in, "We didn't need to hear all that nonsense. Lloyd should have just shown us a photo of Guy St. Clair and we all would have convicted her for not letting him stay single."

Judge Egan said, "Let us all adjourn for lunch. Court, be back in session at 1.15 pm."

* * * * *

This is going to be tricky. "We're not allowed to be with anyone," Burke said. In truth, she didn't really mind that since she liked to be alone.

However, most of the jurors ended up walking together down the court's halls to the exit door. Burke smiled as she saw Blender, with a powder blue pleated skirt and jacket, walk not *with* Too Tall Paul but in lockstep tandem with Too Tall Paul. They were very attractive together, clean cut. And she's becoming a nurse and he's in pharmacology. They could really go into business together. She wondered if she could go into business with the tall lawyer who just gets better the more you watch him. She loves watching him think.

There were six men she noticed and six women on the jury. Like it was an arranged dance or something. Well, those two are paired off. I don't see myself with Combover Ken who just then strode by her on his way to god knows where.

Oh, here's Ms. Edwards and her large bag on the way no doubt to some knitting studio where she can continue working with what looks like steel wool, which is why we think she is knitting for a Volkswagen cover. Maybe it is some kinky outfit. Burke smiled at her and Ms. Edwards looked shocked and then gave a faint return smile. Oh no, Dangerous Dan just swerved by her, as if they were at a dance marathon, en route maybe to the local betting agency. She looked around for Jackie and saw her sitting on a bench with a sandwich and her script, studying her lines.

I really like her, she thought. Jackie sensed Burke looking at her and looked up and gave a thumbs up. Burke wasn't sure for what but it didn't matter.

Ronald McDonald now was walking past Burke, that silly looking man with the red afro. He must not have got the memo that they're not supposed to talk, because he offered, "Nobody who looks as sweet as her is a murderer."

Burke replied, "Murderers don't have a 'look." There isn't a fashion magazine called *Vogue for Murderers*."

"Okay, don't get all upset," he said and gave her a strange look and walked off.

Instead of studying Ms. Craig's looks, thought Burke, he should be wondering if his 1970s polyester athletic suit is something a juror should wear to court.

* * * * *

At 1.15 pm, all were ensconced back in their juror chairs. Dangerous Dan gave her a leering look and she thought, "Jury duty must be the first honest $15 dollars a day he's earned in his life."

The handsome lawyers rose for Judge Egan's entrance. Jackie leaned over, "I really hope this doesn't end soon. It's quite fun."

Attorney Christopher Lloyd gave Jackie a quick reprimanding look.

"Oh," she pretended swooning, "he looked at me."

Burke laughed and said, "Be careful. They'll separate us, like in school."

Judge Egan sat down. Attorney McGuinness also sat, while Attorney Lloyd stood up and called in, "Sister Maureen."

Burke could see the so-called vulnerable defendant turn to her heart-throb, as if she was confused and mouth, "Who is she?

McGuinness smiled. That's what he always does. Smile at her, Burke thought.

That's when a nun walked in. Jackie said, "There's the real murderer."

Attorney Lloyd gave Jackie another swift reprimanding look.

Then after Sister Maureen, "Call me Sister Maureen," swore to tell the whole truth and nothing but the truth, Attorney Lloyd said, "Can you tell us a bit about your relationship withMr. St. Claire.

Jackie whispered, "Why is she wearing a wedding ring?"

"She's married to Christ."

Jackie raised her eyebrows, "I wonder what kind of proposal he made."

* * * * *

This older, motherly type woman began in a soft slight French accent, "He was a beautiful boy. His original name was Gerald McGinty because he was found as a newborn on St. Claire's doorstep by Tom McGinty, the maintenance man."

"What is St. Claire's?"

"It is an orphanage in Newark run by our sisterhood."

"What happened to this baby?"

"We took him in and I was given charge of him and sang to him in French, my first language. You know, I was born in Haiti."

"Did you notify the authorities about this baby?"

"It would not be my job to do that. I don't know."

"Then what happened?"

"He was adopted by many foster homes because he was such a sweet boy but sadly, he was abused, even sexually, and so the only place he felt secure was at St. Claire's. He would return to me over and over and I would care for him. He stayed with us really till he was almost 21 and was, of course, too old for an orphanage."

"Did you stay in touch?"

"Always. He was a sincere person."

"Thank you," and then Attorney Lloyd returned to his table.

* * * * *

Attorney McGuinness stood up to his full height.

Jackie whispered, "Must be like looking up at a crucifix."

He surprised the court by asking Sister Maureen, "Weren't you in a prostitution ring?"

The jury began to pay more focused attention. "Yes, I was sold into one when I was 3 years old."

"Weren't you the favorite wife of the wealthy governor of Port-au-Prince?"

Ms. Craig, seated at her table, kept playing with her pen, thoroughly fascinated by this testimony. Perhaps she was seeing the possibilities of a new book.

"I was," Sister Maureen said, "but since the Governor preferred sex with children, I knew, at thirteen, I was getting a bit old for him and his evil cohorts. This could result in an even worse fate for me, so I took some of his cash and ran away and began my journey crossing to the DR."

"Then what happened, Sister Maureen?"

Burke admired that this Sister was very direct, not hamming it up for the courtroom with false emotionalism. She had obviously come to peace about all this. "In the DR, I found a Christian group from a parish in Upper Saddle River, New Jersey, who were on spring break from high school building homes."

"Did you go back into your old life?"

Jackie raised her eyes to Burke.

“No,” Sister Maureen answered, “I stole a passport and the identity of a look-alike teenager and came to Newark as fast as I could. These Haitian evil men would have been after me with only one goal, to kill me. My name is Sister Maureen because that was her name. I pray for her every day and ask for her understanding and forgiveness.”

“But even so, Sister Maureen, you are well versed with dishonesty and even crime?” Attorney McGuinness asked.

Attorney Lloyd rose, “Objection. Does counsel prefer she stay a sex slave at thirteen or be killed for aging out?”

Judge Egan said, “Sustained.”

Attorney McGuinness changed tack, “Please tell the court what happened when you got to Newark?”

“I took a job at St. Claire’s orphanage and decided to become a nun. This was my first experience of a normal life.”

Jackie mouthed to Burke, “Normal?”

“I was taking my final vows,” Sister Maureen said, holding onto her large cross over her modest beige suit, “when the baby boy was left and, as you know, I was assigned to care for him. At eighteen, he changed his name to Guy St. Claire in honor of how he had been treated with us.”

“How did he get to Craig Publishing?”

“He got his job by translating children’s books from English to French. I had taught him the language well. He made good money there, I think even 6 figures.”

“How was he able to create a good enough resume to get employed?

I don't hear that he went to university, and going back and forth to foster homes, I would imagine his formal education was very sketchy."

Attorney Lloyd said, "Objection."

Judge Egan said, "Not sustained."

Sister Maureen continued, "I helped him write his resume. We did not mention that he was a foster child and had no education. He would not have got a job. We said he was French from a good family and gave some places of education."

"So, his resume was a total fiction?"

"Unfortunately, many people have to do this to find work, Monsieur Attorney. Extreme circumstances sometimes require extreme actions."

"Still, Mrs. Craig would not have had the benefit of the truth of her husband's beginnings."

"I do not know what they discussed, but I am sure she knew he was a fine and loving person," the Sister said.

"Did he ever speak of the defendant, Mrs. Craig St. Claire?"

"Yes, he spoke of Maura Howard Craig with great love and admiration. Theirs was a happy marriage without problems, to my knowledge."

"No further questions. You can cross examine," he said to Attorney Lloyd.

Many of the jurors shifted their legs here and scratched their necks. It was a bit complicated, for a so-called open and shut case,

Attorney Lloyd said, "Did you know that their prenup stated that, if they divorced, Guy would only take away whatever he brought into the marriage, which was, as to be expected, nothing."

"Yes, I knew."

"So, he knew he would virtually be destitute again when Ms. Craig asked for a separation."

She nodded.

"Pardon me?" Attorney Lloyd asked.

"Well, he could work," she said.

"He had been living pretty high."

Attorney McGuinness rose, "Objection—"

"Sustained."

"The couple were not yet divorced, were they?" Attorney Lloyd asked.

"Not that I know of." Sister Maureen looked uncomfortable for the first time, Burke thought. They're giving her a work out.

Attorney Lloyd said, "They were separated, it was thought, because he was spending more and more time and money with a woman in Newark. Depositions have shown that they argued about this. Did he ever tell you about this woman he was spending time and money on, that Mrs. Craig was so irked by?"

"Well sir, this is obvious."

"What is?"

"That woman was me. He sent me money all the time and visited very often. I was all he had. There was no other woman, I am sure."

Burke looked to Maura who could not cover an embarrassed surprise. Ah, she did not know it was a nun in Newark and not some floozy, she thought.

"No further questions," said Attorney Lloyd, looking a bit defeated.

* * * * *

It had been a long session. Judge Egan said, "Court will re-adjourn tomorrow morning. Thank you, again, all for your service and see you tomorrow, and please remember, no talk, no TV, no newspapers, no texts and no contact," and then she left the courtroom.

* * * * *

McGuinness was packing up and Burke decided to be the last out of the juror box. She wanted to hear what Maura Howard Craig would say to him. She lingered in her box as if she was looking for an earring or missing lipstick. Her ruse paid off because she heard Mrs. Craig say to her handsome lawyer, "Well now I know why his French had such a Newark twang. I should have killed him for all his lies."

Her attorney sat down next to her, "I can't understand how this is a surprise to you given how smart you are. What made you marry him?"

Maura laughed, "Good question, counselor. But have you seen his photo?"

At that Burke found her alleged missing earring and left the courtroom. McGuinness looked up as she made her way through the jurors' box and gave her a heart rendering smile. Oh, maybe I should kill the defendant myself, just so I can sit next to him all day, she thought.

She left the courtroom only to see Ms. Edwards and her knitting needles holding back a bit with the express purpose of giving Burke an endearing smile.

Burke returned the smile and kept on walking, thinking, "What did I do to deserve that?"

CHAPTER

Five

It was true that Guy St. Claire was a man who would not go unnoticed. So, when he applied for his job, with his ocean green eyes, tall physique, charming smile, strong jawbone and jaunty mustache, naturally the women in HR thought he should definitely join the firm in *some* position, and began smoothing his way through various senior management in the firm so as to find him a position. His French seemed to be his calling card and HR was recommending him to do translations of English children's books into French.

In truth, his resume was a touch sketchy, a little thin, but when most people, even the men, sat across from him and fell under the spell of his smile and shoulders and long legs, one could forgive a less than stellar resume. No one is perfect, some of the female managers reflected. And the men liked the idea of another man being around, there were way too many women in publishing, there needed to be a balance. And let's face it, they thought, some people are modest about their achievements and maybe he is one of those. Or maybe he just wasn't a star and, if they hadn't exaggerated on their own resumes, they wouldn't have been considered one either.

But no one in Craig Publishing spoke French well enough to test his accuracy. Except for Mrs. Craig herself.

Nicki from HR called up. "I know that you don't usually interview staff but this man – and let me tell you, you won't regret the interview – is fascinating. We are looking at hiring him for translating children's books into French and nobody can test it except you. Do you mind?"

Mrs. Craig liked to not be seen as a snob and as a person who willingly pitched in. She was well liked at the publishing firm. And children's books were her own baby. She had been the one to open the much-needed division incorporating children's literature into the mass market. It was a gamble that paid off.

She gave scholarships to the local schools to promote the division. Her next step was translating classics into various foreign languages. That had also been a success. She was an admired CEO by the press and the staff.

Everyone knew she worked hard, even though she still managed to set aside time to write a book a year. At 35, she'd gained the prestigious honor of Mystery Writer of the Year. The following year she won the Agatha Christie blue ribbon for promoting Women Mystery Writers.

"Of course, Nicki, I would be delighted to help," she said.

* * * * *

When Mr. St. Claire sat in her office and began with, "I appreciate that the head of the company would take the time to interview me. Thank you so much, Mrs. Craig. I realize you must be incredibly busy."

She was and, after she had agreed to it, she was a bit annoyed with herself for wasting her time like this but, she reminded herself, a good CEO stays aware of what goes on in the trenches. "Tough it up," she told herself.

Now she was studying him and distressingly, it was hard to focus on his French. This man was so sure of himself, so attractive, that she found herself unwittingly drifting off into imaginative scenes of him wooing her. What a striking couple they would make, she thought, sitting at a seaside bar. His tall, athletic figure would offset her delicate looks and he seemed just the type to bring something je ne sais quoi to her life. He was shockingly handsome.

He was smart enough not to fawn but he had a ready smile, a kind of insouciance to his smile, and she noticed that he deepened his voice just a bit when speaking, as well as leaned in. She could feel her own pulse accelerate a bit.

She couldn't help but imagine herself being held close to those big shoulders.

So, she made herself focus. "I see that you speak French well enough to translate our children's books?"

"Yes," he said. "Bien sur," he added, smiling.

She wondered if he spoke French in the bedroom. Maybe that would be a bit corny. But nice to find out about.

"Do you speak French?" he asked, conversationally.

"Yes," she said. "That is why they sent you to me. It turns out I am the only one here who *does* speak French. Shall we switch to French?" she asked.

"Est-ce-que vous aimez Paree?" he asked in a quick and confident French.

"Yes," she said, shuffling papers, "I mean, Oui, I do love Paris."

"All beautiful women like you shine in Paris," he said. "Je vous voyez la."

She smiled, suddenly a bit confused. She should be asking him about his French writing abilities but her mind seemed to have a will of its own. "I don't see here if you are married, Mr. St Claire."

"Call me Guy, please.... And no, I am not married."

Excellent, she thought.

"I am surprised a handsome man such as yourself has not been caught. You must be a hunted species," she said with just a touch of a smile.

"I am waiting for the right woman," he replied. "La femme parfait."

He's fast, this one, she thought. "And what would she be like?" she asked, casually.

What kind of interview is this? What am I interviewing him for?

"I like petite women. Often tall men do. Feminine, very smart, flashing blue eyes..."

She was starting to feel herself flush.

"The French, as I am sure you well know, believe the language of love is primary. And you... evoke such a language... I am not being rude, I hope. I am just being honest..." he said.

"Well," she said, with a smile that she was embarrassed to feel had taken over her entire face, "men so rarely compliment me now," she said, "you know, being the boss and all."

"Oh well those men are probably just intimidated. You are a stunning woman, I can't believe it. I am glad I am in the children's book division and not reporting directly to you. Frankly, it would be a bit distracting."

She didn't say so, but she could not agree more.

"My step-daughter, Crystal, is also in the translations division. Did you meet her yet?"

"I did."

"You will interact mostly with her although she personally focuses more on Spanish books. But she is in charge of our foreign rights division."

"I look forward to working with her," he replied.

Maura did not add that, at this particular moment, she was thrilled that Crystal is horsy, big boned and more like a female wrestler in build. This was rather good, if indeed, it is true he likes petite women.

"Do you like children's books?" she asked.

He hesitated, and she said, "I don't either, but they probably are not that difficult to translate. Less words and so on."

He nodded, just taking her in with those green eyes. She actually felt herself wanting to make love.

She stood up and smiled, "Well Mr. St. Guy, I mean Mr. St. Claire, you are hired. And welcome to our company."

"Thank you so much," he said, also standing. "I am very grateful."

"What salary did they offer you?" she asked.

"Sixty thousand a year."

"You must have charmed them." Like you're charming me. "I see, well you will get bonuses and so on with performance, which I am sure they told you."

"They did, thank you so much."

She liked to be careful with her money. Except for her beauty regimen.

She looked down at his resume. He must be about 17 years younger than her. Well, that's never stopped any man before.

She put out her hand and said, "Merci bien and je suis tres heureux que vous allez travailler avec nous."

"Moi aussi et merci bien. I plan to do an excellent job for you and make you very happy."

"Yes," she said laughing, really this interview should go in one of her books, although no one would believe it. "I would love someone to make me very happy."

"Well, I hope I will be able to think up some special ways," he said, taking a bit more control.

And what woman does not swoon to a man taking up a bit more control?

"We'll see you next Monday," she said. "A lundi."

"Yes," he smiled, eyes dancing. "Formidable. Je serai la. A bientot."

* * * * *

The next day when she came into work, a large bouquet of white roses were on her desk. She opened the card but, even before she did, she knew who they were from. "You are more beautiful than your photos. But it is your inner beauty that is most powerful. Merci bien encore."

This is totally inappropriate, she thought.

And totally merveilleux.

* * * * *

After a month of his working there, he sent her an email asking her out for a drink after work. "What French people," he asked, "would pass on un verre ensemble?" She agreed and they met at a local restaurant that was fairly empty, since it was not evening.

They spoke about the office, they spoke about children's books, how they never would go out of fashion for what parent does not want to read to a child eager for a magical mystery tour? They walked to their respective cars and she took such pleasure in his tall easy way that was so gallant.

Then he suggested a drink and dinner in New York at the Pierre. Pourquoi pas? She agreed, for life is to be lived. Plus, no one had asked her to the Pierre since her husband died. Dinner was a bit stuffy and staid but they managed to laugh at tales of people in the company and at some technical mistakes she'd made in her books and she also found she rather liked being photographed with him. This was followed up with gifts from Mr. St. Claire, a perfume, then a framed photo of her he took one day as they took a walk at lunchtime at the office. She placed the photo on her piano.

Patricia, Maura's Polish maid, said, "How old is he anyway?"

Maura said, "Younger. So what? Rich men, even poor men, do it all the time and no one even questions it."

Patricia then said, while bringing them each an old fashioned which she had become very good at making, almost as good as the Plaza Athenee, "I'm not against, but your lawyers look at his resume?"

Maura said, "Why should they?"

Patricia said, "I don't know, feeling."

"You and your feelings," she said, grabbing a handful of nuts. And then thought, Me and my feelings. I can't stop thinking about this "Guy."

But she did have her lawyers look at his resume because Patricia's feelings tended to be rather accurate. Patricia had come up already with 3 plot endings for Maura's books that Maura herself never could have come up with. And this while she was dusting.

* * * * *

"Mrs. Craig, I think his resume is fabricated, I mean some of these jobs translating are at places that don't exist."

Silence from Mrs. Craig. It didn't say much for her HR department.

"Mrs. Craig?"

She was looking round the White Plains office. The hunting pictures. The bust of Thomas Jefferson. The teak credenzas.

"Mrs. Craig? What do you think?"

"Thank you so much," she said to her balding attorney and stood up, gathering her handbag. "What do I think? As Rhett Butler said, I don't really give a damn."

Now Guy asked her out to a play. After dinner their conversation was lively and she had so liked sitting close to him in the theatre. It turned out he liked going to the symphony so that was next, which was ideal for her since she liked to think up plots as the orchestra played. They soon began going to movies on Saturday nights and the best part was that he started holding her hand. Soon they began to kiss at those plays, concerts, movies. And soon they didn't feel the urge for so many plays, concerts, movies and spent their evenings together in her bedroom. Then they went out to those plays, concerts, movies after time spent in her bedroom.

Her friends seemed to like him, the husbands less so. She and Guy St. Claire took to going to the sea together on summer afternoons on the weekend where they would sit on the beach and he would swim and the sight of him wading into the water was worth a thousand ships. They started visiting islands in Maine and then Martha's Vineyard, Nantucket. They stayed in 5-star hotels which she gallantly paid for and had languorous dinners together, which he gallantly paid for. They played tennis. They began to spend their weeknight evenings watching movies or he would translate one of the children's books, while she went over her new novel's pages. They began talking on the phone whenever they were not together, talking about anything. In short, they began to be a couple.

They were driving one early afternoon and going to stop off at a Chinese restaurant they liked to go to, and, as he drove the car, he handed her a box.

"What is it?" she asked, rather thrilled, quite aware what it was.

She opened it and it was a small sapphire and diamond engagement ring. It was pretty in that it had a unique rectangular diamond shape cut.

"I know it's not as big as what Craig could buy you, but it is a special diamond and one day I will get you something bigger."

"No, it's beautiful," and, indeed, the whole idea was beautiful. She would be living with a handsome, gentle, kind man who is an excellent lover and made her feel like she was 25 years old.

"It is very beautiful," she repeated.

* * * * *

They were married at the Tuxedo mansion, with only a few of Maura's friends, her literary agent, her editor and her PR woman. Patricia was maid of honor, dressed in a green knit Chanel suit that actually belonged to Maura since they were both the same size.

She liked to give Patricia her clothes, it made her feel good to help this clever friend who was always available to her. No one knew that Patricia lived rent free on the property which allowed Patricia to send most of her checks back to her family in Poland. In this way, you could say Maura was being philanthropic.

Her lawyers had virtually almost blackmailed her into signing a prenup, where Guy would get nothing if they divorced but Guy was so in love with her, and so sure he could make her happy, and she was the same, that they both signed the document while barely reading it.

As they stood in front of the justice of the peace, Guy turned to her, "You can't believe how young you look," and she did look stunning in her cream lace dress, with a tight waist. Pilates does wonders, she thought.

Her last husband had been almost nothing but critical and saw himself as a Svengali, although he was more like a Rasputin. But this husband, she thought, will be attentive, respectful, he will keep me juicy and happy.

At the party after, her agent said, "You know you can always tell a woman who is loved. It shows on her face and you, Maura, look very loved."

And it was true. She and Guy made love in the night and they made love in the morning and she found she could not keep her hands off him in the middle of the day. She just wanted to keep kissing him.

"Yes," she said, "I am a woman loved."

He swooped by just then, tall and striking in his dark suit, "Hello beautiful. Oh, I mean Mrs. St. Claire. Care for a drive in your new yellow Cadillac?" As if the two of them were alone in the room.

It was the car he had just given her as a present.

"Yes," she said. "But what about the guests?"

"They'll go by 6 pm and then we can just drive to the seaside. I know, I know," he said laughing, "you want to bring your laptop to write."

She nodded, guilty. It was true. She couldn't be without it. She always wanted to be working.

"Don't feel embarrassed," he said. "George Sand also got up to write when she was lovers with Chopin. She'd leave him in bed and go to her desk in the middle of the night. You're in good company."

Really, she knew that fact about George Sand, maybe everybody did, but let's face it, her deceased husband, Craig, would never have bothered to find out.

* * * * *

As they drove to the Massachusetts coast, the warm evening felt sensual and made her feel as if she had all the time in the world. She asked, "Are you going to keep working at the publishing company?"

"Of course," he said.

"You don't have to," she said, "we have plenty of money." She felt so luxuriant and relaxed, she would have agreed to buy them a Greek island. Maybe she should.

"No, I want to earn my own money."

She leaned over and kissed his cheek as he drove. She liked him for that. They held hands as they continued down the highway toward the seashore.

"Do you get on with Crystal?" she asked.

"Yes," he said. "Is that your ex's photo on her desk?"

"Yes. She keeps her father's photo on her desk. But I can't figure out why. He was terrible to her. Besides business, his only interest was in making all the wives look and act alike. I think he blamed Crystal and her dead twin for their mother's death. She died in their swimming pool, she was alone, I don't know what happened but she had just lost one child. A neighbor, Dr. K. K .Rowe, found her. She signed the death certificate as having been accident. Could have been a suicide. Who knows? Craig was with baby Crystal in the hospital when the mother died. I always thought Craig blamed Crystal in some weird way."

"Horrible story," said Guy.

"Yes, it is. Crystal is on anti-depressants since she has tried to commit suicide a few times, herself. She really had no loving parent. I mean he gave her a very fine education and all – but no love."

"Did she want to take over the publishing firm when he died?" he asked.

"I think she thought she would get it but ...she didn't. I did."

* * * * *

After their honeymoon in Gloucester, a small fishing village by the sea, she'd come to think that this second marriage was the second-best thing she'd ever done, besides taking up writing, and he seemed as enthralled as she was, so she didn't once think about the age difference.

When they returned, they both settled back into normal life.

She wrote in the mornings and spent afternoons at the publishing firm.

He spent all day at the office because she needed privacy to write, so he might as well be at his job and leave her alone. He didn't have any vices, at least none she had seen, so he wasn't off shopping or going to the horses or something stupid. He was actually helping them make more money.

* * * * *

His office was situated in the translations section on the 3rd floor. Crystal had the corner office since she managed that department. She was a quiet leader, polite and standoffish; you could tell she came from money.

Her clothes were conservative, perhaps communicating to leave her alone. Maura liked to wear feminine dresses and designer jackets and blouses, as if she was about to be on the cover of some magazine, and in point of fact, she almost always was. Guy felt it was like he had married the Jackie Kennedy of writing.

Crystal, even though she had a famous father, was shyer. No drinking, no smoking, never mentioned a boyfriend. Perhaps she was a bit put off and confused by life, he thought, what with a slew of stepmothers who all purportedly looked like her own mother but weren't. And poor Crystal probably thought all those petite brunettes had little to teach her tall Nordic broad self. And mostly her father kept her away from them anyway, she never even attended any of his weddings.

St. Claire came into her office to show her his latest published French book and to see if she wanted to use the cover in the upcoming Spanish translation.

Besides the photo of her father, she had only one other adornment in her office. A photo on the wall of a small chamber orchestra.

He went up to it to look at it more closely and saw that the woman playing the cello, whose head was down, the hair almost covering her face, looked like her.

"Is that you?" he asked.

"Yes," she said. She looked up briefly at him, it was rare when someone asked her about herself.

"You play the cello?" he asked, surprised.

"Yes," she said, and then she gave a rare smile, "and the violin, guitar and bass fiddle."

"Wow," he said, "you're gifted, like your stepmother."

"Well, not quite as gifted."

"How come you didn't go into music full time?" he asked.

She hesitated, as if deciding whether to be on friendly terms with this man who not only worked with her, but was now married to her stepmother. She always thought keeping a distance was a good idea. The truth was she liked Maura, Maura had been always inclusive and generous with her, which was more than she could say for the other stepmothers, but she never really stopped wondering what exactly went on that fateful night on that boat when she lost her father.

Meanwhile Guy was noticing her long sleeves shirt and felt a bit sad. Maura had told him she'd had a problem with cutting. Maura once posited that Crystal might want to reunite with her dead twin. After she'd said that, Maura had looked off out the hotel window. "Would make for an interesting book," she said.

* * * * *

That night he and Maura had dinner, she read some of her work out loud to him, he listened, they watched *Cat On a Hot Tin Roof*, with an unbelievably good-looking Paul Newman.

"It was one of his first films," Guy, who loved movies, said. Maura listened and noted this passion of Guy's. Maybe that is why he makes our life sometimes feel like we are living in one.

"Do you like Elizabeth Taylor in it?" she asked.

"She's a beauty alright, like you."

Smooth, she thought, but who's complaining? She did get told that quite often but she never got tired of hearing it.

She went over and kissed him, "You do know how to treat a girl."

Yes, she felt like a woman loved.

* * * * *

Attorney McGuinness listened to this tale in his office after their day in court, and then asked, "Did you ever fight with him?"

He and Maura were both sipping some single malt scotch Gene kept for when he won cases. He himself drank hardly anything but his clients usually did.

Her mind flashed to when her accountants called to tell her Guy was sending money to a floozy in Newark.

That he would even have a floozy. That there was another woman. Someone younger than she, most likely. It was a cliché and horribly embarrassing. It infuriated her that he had been a sham. How could he do this to them?

She turned to Gene and, in the evening's quiet light of just a lawyer's lamp and the light coming through the windows from the other office buildings, she replied, "No, we didn't."

CHAPTER
Six

Burke and Jackie sat waiting in their cherry wood juror's chairs. The air conditioning was working and the light came in gently through the courtroom windows. All in all, it seemed like it would be a good day. Burke could just catch a bit of Judge Egan's lovely white and gold flowered blouse under her robes. She was wearing emerald earrings accentuating her bright green Irish eyes enhanced by green contacts.

Nothing had started yet. Burke said, "You know Supreme Court Justice Ginzburg has a different necklace depending on which way she is going to vote."

"Really, love?" Jackie asked. Jackie too looked spiffy in a blue blouse with white trim and blue slacks.

"Very chic," Burke said.

"I am not full of cheek, thank you very much," Jackie laughed.

They stared at the attorneys who were studying their notes in preparation.

Jackie asked, "How is it going with your tall true love over there?"

Burke had also made herself look her best, with her red hair flowing down, wearing a black velvet top and pleated white skirt.

She answered Jackie, "He seems entranced with the murderer."

"Well after all," Jackie said, sanguinely, "that's his job."

"I know. But he should be taking surreptitious glances at me."

"Maybe he's too proper," Jackie said. "That trait will be a bonus when you get married. He won't cheat."

"I like the thought," Burke said. "But they all cheat."

"Maybe why she's a murderer," Jackie added, staring at Mrs. Craig, sitting at the bench in one of her signature Chanel suits, this one pink with gold buttons. For God 's sakes, Jackie wondered, how many does she have?

"Well, they haven't so far brought in a floozy," Burke said. "That nun was too old for the deceased St. Claire."

"Patience, darling," Jackie said. "The curtain hasn't come down yet."

And then the court was called to session.

Attorney Christopher Lloyd, dashing as usual in a dark blue suit, white shirt and red tie, stood up and said he was calling to witness, "Crystal Craig."

"Objection," from the tall one.

Judge Egan looked at him questioningly.

"She is germane to a past case only," Attorney McGuinness said.

The DA was still standing, "Your Honor, Ms. Craig works at Craig Publishing where the defendant works."

Judge Egan said, "Objection denied."

Crystal Craig came striding up to the front of the court. She was a big girl, with ash blonde hair which, in this light, Burke deemed a bit mousy. She should get a colorist, she thought.

Crystal Craig wore a long-sleeved blouse and a bland cream suit.

Jackie whispered, "1977 look. She needs to update."

Burke thought, "We're turning into Joan Rivers and her daughter at the Oscars."

They focused their attention.

Ms. Edwards, sans knitting needles, gave Jackie a reprimanding look.

Jackie, not one to be intimidated, whispered, "Careful. Madame Defarge is on the warpath."

Attorney Lloyd asked, after Crystal was sworn in, "You work at Craig Publishing, your father's old firm that now is owned by your stepmother. This came about rather suddenly as we know, and unexpectedly—"

"Objection," from Attorney McGuinness.

"Sustained."

Attorney Lloyd pivoted a bit and ran his hand through his thick blonde hair and then asked, "Would you say you and Mrs. Craig have an amicable relationship?"

"We don't see each other much," Crystal Craig explained. "We are in different sections of the publishing house. After she married Mr. St. Claire, she was of course busy with that. I saw her more before, never that much. She runs a business as well as writing books—"

Attorney Lloyd tried again, "Are you friendly?"

Crystal looked at Maura as if she was thinking, then turned to Attorney Lloyd. "What does friendly mean?"

Burke and Jackie exchanged glances.

Attorney Lloyd said, "Friendly means you like to go to the movies together, discuss boyfriends, have a drink and talk..."

Jackie whispered, "Thank God. Now I know what friendly means."

Burke's eyes laughed.

Crystal said, "Come again."

Even Attorney McGuinness was enjoying this episode of Lloyd's discomfort. Everyone knew Attorney Lloyd was edging to get Crystal into a diatribe against Mrs. Craig's character, but Lloyd wasn't getting anywhere.

Lloyd smiled at Crystal and any normal woman would have done exactly what he wanted then, or at least had no trouble becoming friendly with him, but Crystal Craig sat stiffly, immune.

Jackie suddenly seemed to be swinging her long arms down under the bench. What was she doing? Burke peripherally noticed it but kept her eyes on the proceedings. Then she felt Jackie punch her leg. She quickly looked down and there was a note. Surreptitiously, she read from Jackie: *Poor love. She doesn't have any friends.*

Lloyd said, "As friends, you would talk on the phone, discuss the latest footwear, rail against the president, talk about Netflix. I guess you two would not want to share books but those kind of things – "

Crystal said, "No we don't do any of that."

Attorney Lloyd looked a bit energized by her answer. "So, you would say Mrs. Craig has not extended step motherly warmth to you?"

"Objection."

Judge Egan hesitated. She wasn't sure what to say. But she remembered her father said, "When in doubt, don't."

"Denied."

Lloyd restated his question for Crystal, "Would you say you and Mrs. Craig are not close?"

Crystal said, "Probably. But it's due to both of us. We tried. But we don't have a lot in common."

Attorney Lloyd said, "You have a business in common, your father –"

Crystal said, "We don't discuss either."

Another note against her calf. Burke quickly looked down. Thank God her eyes are good. *Maybe she has Asperger's,* Jackie wrote. *Not emotional.*

Burke motioned by her calf for the pen. She wrote back: *Christopher Lloyd is cute.*

Transfer of pen. Jackie wrote back: *I thought you liked Lawyer Gene.*

Transfer of pen again, this time by the ankle. Burke knocked the paper against Jackie's knee under the bench.

Jackie read: *At this point, fidelity is not germane.*

They both looked up only to see Judge Egan eyeing them.

They suddenly paid studious attention.

Lloyd said, "Thank you Ms. Craig. You may cross examine," to Attorney McGuinness.

* * * * *

Crystal Craig was a big girl and must have liked Attorney McGuinness standing so tall over her. He began kindly, "I don't mean to be indelicate, but don't you have a history of suicide?"

Ms. Craig said, "I do not have a history of suicide. No one does. I wouldn't be here."

Attorney McGuinness gallantly replied, "My mistake. I'm sorry. I meant attempted suicide."

Ms. Craig replied, "No, I don't."

Attorney McGuinness looked briefly at Mrs. Craig, herself, who was watching attentively.

The writer must have got something wrong, Burke thought.

McGuinness continued, "Were you surprised when your father left everything to Mrs. Craig, your stepmother?"

Ms. Craig said, "Yes, but he was not one for including me in much."

McGuinness said, "Still it must have hurt, you as the sole heir. He had no other children."

Ms. Craig said clearly but not melodramatically, "It did, yes."

McGuinness continued, "So you did not get the publishing firm and I understand you are an exemplary employee, good at the business, a place where you shine, after a life of being kept from any spotlight, and here you get nothing there. Do you think perhaps you would like to see your step-mother guilty?"

Maura raised her eyebrows.

"Objection," said Lloyd. "He is leading the witness."

"Sustained."

McGuinness didn't know where to go with this Crystal Craig. He was trying to raise suspicion that Crystal could have set Maura up. It was like playing tennis with someone who never hit back. He stood there and thought and then, as if he simply decided to let well enough alone, said, "No further questions."

Judge Egan said, "Thank you, counsel." She turned to the jury, "We will be having a short day today, all of us, since I have an appointment that I must go to this afternoon. My apologies. And we will all reconvene tomorrow. Enjoy your afternoon off."

Jackie said, "I hope she's not ill."

Burke said, "I agree."

And then the lawyers stood, and Judge Egan stepped down and left.

* * * * *

All the other jurors got up at that moment. There seemed a bit of gaiety to all of it since it was true, an afternoon off on a sunny, pretty day seemed like they'd just received a gift. But poor Too Tall Paul could not ask pretty Belinda to lunch or a walk in the park. It was sad. Burke noticed him look at Belinda. She smiled back.

Burke thought, "They'll just have to wait till the case ends." Then she realized she must talk to Jackie when they were alone to see what she thinks of the recent proceedings. That whole testimony was a bit confusing. What was the point?

Dangerous Dan was staring at Burke. She looked away quickly. What did he think? She would go to a hotel room with him for the afternoon? God.

Fatty Arbuckle was already on his way out. To luncheon no doubt.

Burke signed to Jackie that she would be in touch.

"I know it dearie," Jackie said and then she too got up to go. "Mary Poppins calls. Where's my umbrella?" she laughed.

Burke soon found herself walking down the hall. And there were those two lovebirds again, talking on one of the benches in the hallway. She slowed herself down so she could hear SOMETHING.

McGuinness was saying, "Remember those St Patrick's Day parades? They were something weren't they? I wish they'd been on a day like this. Sometimes it was so damn cold."

Maura said, "Did you ever notice Maureen O'Hara attended?"

Burke thought these two looked as relaxed as if they were at a Coney Island picnic.

McGuinness said, "Yes she even walked with us."

Maura said, "She was so beautiful, even old. It was grand, as they say."

She didn't mention that it still irked her that Maureen O'Hara was selected Grand Marshall over Maura. Her only response was to write a novel, *Killing off the Grand Marshall.*

McGuinness replied, "My family was always too mixed up to attend. I didn't want my father there any way. He only knew how to make everyone's life miserable."

"I remember hearing your father died. So sorry. Maybe *you* weren't sorry."

"I wasn't. I was glad to get rid of him. He made it into his nineties, and never once did he mention my success. Didn't mind taking the odd bits of money from me I can tell you that."

"I don't remember seeing a service for him," she said.

Maura, as she kept fiddling with her alleged broken shoe heel, thought, "So Gene has his own demons. Well, I will love them away."

"I had him cremated and buried at sea, so to speak. I just didn't want him buried with my dear mother at St. Raymond's. "

"What sea?"

"I took his sorry remains in a brown paper bag, very officious of me, and tossed them off the Staten Island ferry with only the Statue of Liberty to witness."

"Poetic, McGuinness, poetic," she said, appraising him.

He smiled. "Yes, into the seedy waters where he belonged. Good riddance, daddy dearest."

He laughed bitterly.

Burke and Maura, in their different places, both said, "My god."

"Well. I didn't have it so bad," Maura said. "My mother was heartbroken all her life, raising us, but she did come out to see me walk at those parades."

"Well, you were quite the belle of the ball. I was always proud to march with you."

Maura nodded. "They were simpler wonderful days, weren't they?"

"A lot of them, not all." McGuinness was silent a bit and then said,

"Maybe things are simpler when you're younger. But I wouldn't say they were better days for me. Not at all."

How long could Burke stall? And why is she hanging around, she wondered. Is she waiting to hear him ask her to marry him? Doesn't he know the state does not approve conjugal rights? She bent over her shoe.

Maura was waxing on, "They were simpler days for me. No husbands and no company to run, no murder trials – "

"Maura, there is plenty still good before us. We don't have to walk in a parade to enjoy ourselves. You'll see."

* * * * *

That afternoon, Burke stopped off on the way home and saw a film. It was British and old fashioned about the upper class and, even though, she was Irish, she rather liked the pomp and circumstance. Marvelous looking people. The romantic lead was a wonderful Irishman, kind, witty, integrated into the British aristocracy, and she wished, she just wished something like that would happen to her. In the film, he met the woman he falls in love with, incorrectly thinking she is a maid, but she is a rich orphan, and so on and so on. Never happens to teachers. Jane Eyre was a teacher. Always dreary people are teachers.

Jackie thought she had the day off from nursing, so she went to the theatre and tried on some costumes for her debut. Maybe the case will be decided by the time she opens, and all the jurors could come. Too Tall Paul and Belinda could come; could be their first date. Even Lilian Edwards wasn't so bad, she could come, too. They could all have a drink after which got Jackie thinking about drinks and so, once she got to her apartment, she emailed Burke and suggested they meet.

This time they decided on a bar in White Plains. Jackie said she would wear a disguise in case anyone saw them.

* * * * *

Burke was a bit embarrassed as they sat at their table. It was highly unlikely she would ever be having a drink with a Hassid, but she guessed Jackie hadn't thought of that. Jackie had on the black hat, the curls, the suit, even those hanging thread things. She truly looked like a small man.

"You know," Burke said, "I don't think Hassidic people drink."

"Oh, I think they do," she said.

"Well, they wouldn't be sitting with an Irish Catholic girl, I can tell you that."

"I'm unhappily married."

"Well at least your rabbi won't see you here."

"No," Jackie said, and almost hiccupped her martini. It was fun play acting.

Burke said, "What do you think about the case?"

Jackie said, "What do you mean?"

"Well, that Crystal today," Burke answered, sipping her white wine.

"She's an odd one. Can't see she and the stepmother together. Your tall boyfriend managed to get us all suspicious that she might be the murderer, what with being unstable and all that."

"Yes, but what would Crystal get by murdering Maura's second husband?"

"She gets the company if Maura is sent away. Maybe even Maura's royalties, I don't know. If Crystal is a murderer, she should have killed her father, not St. Claire, for making all those women look like her mother. It was sick."

"I know," Burke said. "I don't think Crystal is the murderer. The attorneys were too easygoing with her. You know what else is odd?"

"What?"

"I just read one of Maura's novels and Maureen O'Hara gets killed off."

"So?"

"I heard Mrs. Craig just mentioning her."

"You and Mrs. Craig were speaking?"

"No, I was listening to her and Gene talk."

"Now he's Gene?"

"Soon he will be."

Jackie decided to change the subject. "That Judge Egan should be on the Supreme Court, she's that good."

"She's better looking than Judge Judy, I'll tell you that."

"Yes, without as many face lifts."

"Yes, Judge Egan has a way of being strong and gentle at the same time, it's interesting," Burke said. "I'd like to emulate that."

Jackie didn't reply.

"I wish I'd been a judge or something," Burke continued. "Teaching is so tiring and not remunerative. I have a Ph.D. in psychology. I should do something else. A new career."

"Well, you'll have plenty of time to think about it at court. There's quite a bit of downtime."

"Well, Rabbi, we should go," Burke said.

"Why? What are you doing tonight?"

Burke said, "Maura wrote a book a year, so I have a lot of reading."

The bill came just then, and Burke laughed, "You should pay. You're the man."

"Alright," Jackie said sweetly. She pulled out her money and left it on the table.

"You're the first rabbi who ever carried a handbag," Burke said.

They got up to go and as they began walking through the bar, a man passed them and said, "Shalom."

"Shalom," Jackie replied, wondering if she should give the sign of the Cross to really confuse him.

Once they were in the parking lot, Burke suddenly abruptly said, "Split! Now."

"What?"

They just then both spotted McGuinness in the parking lot. He was walking towards the bar door.

Jackie left, while muttering, "And here I bought you a drink..."

And now McGuinness saw Burke standing at the door alone. They both knew they were not supposed to speak.

He looked at her a bit confused that she was there, and she gave him her prettiest smile. She really wanted to wink, but didn't. Yet the way she smiled had the same effect.

He looked at her deeply and then silently went into the bar.

CHAPTER

Seven

The next morning, Burke had insisted her hairdresser open early so she could have her hair specially done before court. Hours later, she sat in her juror's chair, hair shining and lustrous, wearing a periwinkle blue silk blouse which made her eyes, she had been told, strike to the very core of a person. After all, Gene had looked directly at her last night in the parking lot. Didn't his silence, that very pregnant silence, the intensity of that silence, presage a momentous love affair?

The answer is, Yes. Let him see her glow in her juror's chair, like an angel in the courtroom, as he cross examines today. He won't be able to avoid her.

Jackie came in, "Well aren't we the movie star today. Move over, Maura Craig."

Burke smiled. Good, she thought.

"What happened in the parking lot after I was forced to return to synagogue last night?" Jackie asked.

"Nothing. He looked at me very intensely and that was it. He's not allowed to speak to me, you know that."

They both looked over at him, Burke a touch more adoringly than Jackie did, but neither of them missed that he was totally engrossed in his client. They also noticed that today Mrs. Craig was wearing, of all things, a periwinkle Chanel suit.

Jackie said, "Great minds dress alike."

Once court had been formally called to session, Christopher Lloyd got up and called to witness, "James R. Long."

Burke and Jackie's head swiveled to the back of the courtroom. In walked a tall man in an ill-fitting dark suit. He wore Trotsky like glasses and had a sensitive face, even behind a scrappy goatee.

"Please be seated, Mr. Long."

Mr. Long swore to tell the whole truth and so on.

Christopher Lloyd said, "Would you please tell the court your profession?"

"I am Mrs. Craig's personal attorney."

"Thank you, Mr. Long."

Attorney Lloyd began, "You encouraged Mrs. Craig to have Mr. Guy St. Clair sign a prenup, did you not?"

Mr. Long crossed his long legs. "I did, along with her accountant."

"When Mrs. Craig found out that her husband was authorizing money to go to a woman in Newark, what did she say when you told her about it?"

"She said she could just kill him."

The courtroom erupted as the judge slammed her gavel saying she would clear the court if this outburst continued.

Mrs. Craig raised her eyebrows as if it was ridiculous.

Attorney Lloyd once again looked victorious.

"And what did you make of her incriminating statement?" he asked the witness.

"Objection," from Attorney McGuinness.

"Overruled."

Mr. Long puckered a wry smile, like he had been preparing for this moment. "Counsel, my wife is constantly telling me she could just kill me. I didn't take Mrs. Craig's oft-said expression the least bit seriously."

"I understand your point of view," Attorney Lloyd said, and then turned dramatically toward Mr. Long and said, "but in this case there was an actual murder."

"And I am saying I didn't at the time and I don't believe as we sit here that Mrs. Craig meant what she said literally. Women often say that kind of thing."

Jackie whispered, "And well we should."

Cristopher Lloyd decided to change tack. "In your opinion, who would want Mr. St. Claire dead? Not the Sister from the orphanage. Not anyone at the publishing house. Who then?"

This was such a stupid question that Attorney McGuinness didn't even bother to get up to say Objection. How is her personal lawyer supposed to know who wanted St. Claire killed?

Mr. Long replied, "I have no idea. I am an estate, marriage and will lawyer, not a detective."

Attorney Lloyd said, "Was Mr. St. Claire upset at having to leave his wife without any assets?"

"If he was, he would not have told me."

Attorney Lloyd said, "Who would he have told?"

"That is not my privy."

Jackie whispered, "This lawyer must have been top of his class. He's tough."

Burke thought this was another going nowhere testimony. How many were they going to have to hear? Attorney McGuinness stood up and said, "No questions," thereby signaling to the jury this was, as Burke thought, a going nowhere testimony.

Mr. Long stepped down and, as he walked out, his eyes could not help but go to Burke, whereupon he gave her a slight smile. She cringed. Definitely not her type.

Then the two court attorneys seemed to signal to each other. Attorney Lloyd said, "Your Honor, may we address the bench?"

"Certainly," Judge Egan said.

Both attorneys stepped up to where she was sitting and began talking in hushed voices to the judge.

Mrs. Craig glanced over at the jury and smiled. Combover Ken, by the sound of his growl and his shifting to sit up straighter, obviously thought the smile was directed at him.

She looked down to her table, then back up at the jury and smiled again. This time Lilian Edward's knitting needles seemed to click in delight, at the base of her handbag, at such a prestigious person smiling at her.

Jackie raised her eyebrows in amusement and whispered, "Such an impartial jury."

The lawyers were still avidly talking at the bench.

Burke asked, "I wonder what they are talking about."

"You," Jackie said. "Why you chose today of all days to get your hair done."

Now the lawyers returned to their tables, both with very serious expressions on their faces.

What was most of note to Burke was that Gene did not smile, as he usually did, at Maura as he sat down. He looked a bit disturbed, angry even.

Burke whispered, "Did he just hear irrevocable proof she did it?"

Attorney Lloyd said, "We call to witness Dr. Nikolov."

The jurors once again looked to the door. In came a tall doctor, with attractive dark hair, a nice smile, a gentle manner about himself.

"Dr. Nikolov, do you swear to tell the whole truth and nothing but the truth, so help you God?"

"I do."

Jackie whispered, "My type."

"Too bad," Burke said. "He is married."

"Dr. Nikolov," Attorney Lloyd said, "you are Mrs. Craig's personal physician."

"I am."

"What kind of drugs do you prescribe for her?"

The doctor began to list a bunch of pills that Burke was pretty sure only Dangerous Dan would recognize. He probably deals them.

"Would any of these have the effect of changing her personality? Make her do something she would not know she is even doing?"

"Medications affect different people differently, Attorney."

"I know that is true but that is not an answer to my question."

"I do not prescribe medications to change anyone's personality."

"Then what are these medications for, Dr Nikolov?"

"High blood pressure. Strengthening her bones, she has a small frame. Some valium to help her sleep when she has too many nights when she cannot."

"Would you say Mrs. Craig is a stable personality?"

"She is an artist, Attorney. They tend to be a bit bipolar."

"Meaning what?"

"They go to extremes of excitement or despair. They get an idea and then they are all excited and the planets align well for them. They get a rejection and they feel meaningless. Although Mrs. Craig has not had much experience with rejection."

"So, you would say then that she is in a permanent state of excitement, due to her success?"

"Objection," from Attorney McGuinness, at the same time that Dr. Nikolov said, "I never said that."

"Sustained."

Nikolov took the aggressive role, "And what would be wrong if she was in a permanent state of excitement? There would be nothing wrong with that."

"There is something wrong since your patient is in court for an alleged crime," Attorney Lloyd said.

"She could be in a state of excitement at once again becoming a widow."

"Objection," said McGuinness loudly. "That is outright absurd."

"Sustained and," Judge Egan said, "Mr. Lloyd it is time for you to sit down or you will be accused of being in a permanent state of excitement yourself."

"Thank you, Dr. Nikolov," said Attorney Lloyd. "You may step down."

Judge Egan said, "Jurors and everyone, we will now break for lunch. Meet you back here at 1 pm. Court adjourned." And then she stepped down.

* * * * *

Burke looked at Jackie and just shook her head, as if to say, Who knows what is going on? They, along with the other jurors, began to file out of the courtroom.

Burke wished she had an extra hour for a movie. She had been listening to the testimony but, in truth, she had had a terrible time taking her eyes off McGuinness. She just liked looking at him. She liked his brown suit today, his white shirt, his cream tie. She is sure he is the one. It has to come to pass.

She stepped outside into the sun and decided to do something she had not done for years.

Burke had gone to Aquinas High School. She had loved the school, even Laura Bush had come to visit. Burke's stepmother had gone there and arranged for Burke to attend. It had a lovely chapel and Burke's high spirits had made her a bit of a favorite with the nuns, not that the ones who taught her were still there. But she is an alumnus and allowed to go into the chapel at lunch hour if she likes.

She is going to pray that McGuinness falls in love with her. In fact, in her opinion, the whole reason she is on this jury participating in a most bizarre legal case, was an act of God so that she could meet McGuinness. Once Attorney Lloyd puts Mrs. Craig away, McGuinness can raise his clever brown eyes toward her and life can begin.

She rang the convent's door.

Sister Augustine, whom Burke had met at a fund-raiser year back, opened the door and said, "Oh Ms. Burke, please come in."

"May I say a quick lunch time prayer, Sister?"

"Of course, dear. You know where the chapel is."

Burke smiled and already felt a sense of wellbeing, and her own past youth, as she walked over the blue tiled floor to the chapel. There were girls like she had been herself in little white veils, kneeling, in their pale blue uniforms, while a few nuns were in prayer stalls at the side of the chapel. Much fewer than when she had been there. Maybe women don't become nuns anymore.

Burke stayed in the back and knelt down.

She didn't have to ask for McGuinness' hand, so to speak, since that was already known to God. She actually just took in the chapel smell, and the peace and quiet there, and the sense of goodness and let herself feel that the right thing would happen for her.

God's will, which would be the right will.

At that thought, she sat back onto the wooden bench and closed her eyes. It seemed a long way from Dangerous Dan and Combover Ken and the other jurors. Jackie would even like this peace herself, she thought. Jackie is a kind person, that is clear.

Events would unfold and they would unfold for the good, she told herself. And at that, she got up, left the chapel, went to the entryway, thanked Sister Augustine, and walked toward the courthouse, after stopping for a caffe latte and a caramel macaroon at a café nearby. She loved those.

Men looked at her as she walked, a message from the universe, she thought, that McGuinness would eventually too.

* * * * *

Jackie had also left the courthouse, but she decided to go shopping. She liked department stores; she was one of those people who relaxed shopping and somehow intuitively knew how to navigate a department store to where the sales were and to the designers she liked. This talent of hers resulted in her owning way too many blouses she never wore since if they were marked down low enough, she would buy the same blouse in different colors and then forget she had done so. This habit was an annual boon for Goodwill.

She was rather enjoying this jury duty, after all she had made a truly good friend, someone she could laugh with, but someone who seemed stable and a person of values. Burke obviously likes that tall attorney who obviously likes the murderess, but, as in all great plays, there can be reversals. In fact, there will be. She could feel that, she thought, as she paid for yet another caramel-colored turtleneck. The saleswoman wrapped it in tissue and handed it to Jackie, to go with the other twenty caramel- colored turtlenecks I have, she thought.

* * * * *

Belinda wished she could talk to that Paul pharmacist but they're not allowed. When they start deliberating the case, they can talk, of course in the jury room. That is where she will show him her smarts, as well as her best outfits. She sat outside at a nearby café to the courthouse, and her blonde hair shone in the sun. The waiter kept coming over and repeatedly asking her if she wanted anything else. She didn't. Then he handed her the bill for her salad and iced tea. She looked at it and, scrawled in large letters, was his phone number. She looked over at him and could swear he was wearing a wedding ring. Men! She put down her money and ripped up the bill, leaving the torn pieces with her cash. Paul the pharmacist would not be the type for this kind of stupidity, she was sure. She knew he wanted to ask her out, it was in the way he seemed to wait for her when they left the courtroom, while saying nothing. Like he was a sentry or bodyguard. He's certainly tall enough. She can't wait till this case is over although God knows where it's going. But she just felt God had ordained this case should take place so she could meet the right man for her.

* * * * *

Dangerous Dan had followed Burke to the convent from a distance. The fact is Burke is very attractive, he thought, and the kind of woman he would like to be with. He knows he can't be. He lives in one room in an SRO. Not the kind of place to bring a tasteful showgirl redhead. But look, if the numbers strike, or he sells one of his paintings, that's what he did before he got into betting, made paintings, and many people think he's very talented, a lot of people he's met, and he likes to do it, who knows someone might buy one for a grand and then he could ask her for dinner, once this dingbat case is over, even though he knows enough about women to know she won't go. She wants a type like the lawyers. Straight arrow guys. Sometimes women like the bad boys like himself when he was younger but they really like the straight arrows better. Bad boys have a shelf life, he thought. She's gone into the convent, I hope not to sign up or something. That would be a waste of womanhood. He turned around, and took a walk to save on money, and had himself a cigarette, sat down on a bench, and pulled out his Daily News racing form.

* * * * *

Too Tall Paul was across the park studying. He'd look up every now and then to see if Belinda was walking back to the courthouse. He'd get a glimpse of her if she is, not that he doesn't get glimpses of her as she tends to sit two seats over to his left. Better than if she was to his right which would mean his looking over at her would be more noticeable. To the left, it can almost look like he's fixing a crick in his neck. He likes to notice things about her: what she's reading (Anna Quindlen), her shoe heels (sturdy but heels, nonetheless), bracelet (gold hearts), earrings (pearl drops – maybe her mother's), her ring (class ring but he can't see from where.) She does wear ivory stockings, maybe in preparation for nursing. Oh, there's Dan walking toward the courtroom, it must be time to go in.

* * * * *

Burke was walking back, like all the other jurors, to the courtroom. Walking down the hill from the convent, she felt moved by it all. It is good to have a base to come from, she reflected. What could be Maura's story? Rich men, rich publishing firm. Talented, let's face it. Very beautiful. But why is she sitting in a docket for the second time for murder? What happened in her life? She has everything most people would want. A gorgeous house. She even had a gorgeous husband. Is this kind of overabundance of wealth and beauty and fame destined for tragedy? Every time you open the news, a lot of famous people are in some kind of trouble. Talent is not some insulation from disaster. And she doesn't even seem nervous as she sits there listening to people be interviewed about her. She is only too confident, it seems, she will not be convicted. Is that because she is innocent or because she is a hardened criminal? It's true that someone as delicate looking and refined as she seems to be the antithesis of what one would expect from a criminal. But twice? Yet they haven't heard anything to show beyond a reasonable doubt, that's for sure. They haven't really showed anything. Oh yes, she was at the crime scene when he was killed. That's not nothing. Lloyd, who should be hammering that home, is bringing in all these irrelevant witnesses. Strange. Is Lloyd in love with her too? Maybe they'll all get serious now.

* * * * *

That's when she saw Lilian Edwards, once again, watching her as she walked down the hill. Burke smiled at Lilian, she does seem a nice woman, even if she is knitting a bikini for an elephant or whatever it is. Lilian Edwards was wearing a black pantsuit, with a white blouse underneath. Her cropped short hair blew in the breeze and Burke thought she could be very pretty if she wanted to be. But she didn't wear makeup, or anything, yet her brown eyes had a kind of striking intensity. They nodded to each other, both rather sweetly.

"Who knows what is going on," Burke thought. "Where is Jackie when I need her? Maybe together we can figure some of this out. It takes a woman, sometimes. The attorneys don't seem to be getting anywhere."

CHAPTER

Eight

About five months before our favorite jurors and attorneys were meeting in court to decide on the murder trial of Mrs. Craig, Guy St. Claire had been sitting in a low life bar in Newark, lamenting his recent fall from grace.

He had loved Maura, and she hadn't actually come out and said what specifically made her throw him out. She couldn't possibly think that there was another woman. He had been nothing but devoted.

Yet, why, he asked himself, sipping his scotch, a single malt, she had been the one to introduce him to single malt, and there's no coming back from that, he sipped again, but there was going to have to be a coming back from single malt; he'd even lost his job. She had screamed that night, "I don't want you in my company either," and immediately called the head of HR and told her to please get him off the payroll. He was not to come in anymore.

When the head of HR said there were legalities in firing someone, Maura had yelled, "Irreconcilable differences." The head of HR could see Mrs. Craig was too angry to tell her that expression was solely used in divorces, or had been; instead, the head of HR decided it a good idea to find some way on her own to get rid of Guy. Shame, he was a good worker and his employee reviews were all good. She'd have to find something. She'd call their corporate lawyer.

Maura, on her part, may have unconsciously known Guy was not the type to fight her. Anyway, Maura was in the moral right.

As Guy sat there with his drink, he asked himself, why hadn't he told her the truth about Sister Maureen at the beginning? That would have solved this. He took another sip. It was obvious why he hadn't. Then he would have to have revealed his rather unprepossessing past and she might have thrown him out for misrepresenting who he was to her and her company in the first place. That would almost be a worse indignity. He was in a no-win situation. He was either a liar, a phony or an adulterer.

He began his own defense at the bar. He was a romantic and he had hoped that their love would win out. Isn't love supposed to conquer all? Evidently not.

On top of which he had signed a prenup where he was left with absolutely nothing. What kind of love had that been on her part? It was positively cruel to do something like that. She wouldn't consider doing something like that to her maid, Patricia. Oh no, Patricia she treated like Polish royalty, if there is such a thing. But he, her husband, gets no severance pay.

He ordered another drink.

What is he going to do?

* * * * *

Meanwhile two seats over, Ernie Burleigh, a slim, pasty eyed man was eyeing this very expensively dressed handsome man. Could be a matinee idol, he thought. Not that he'd attended many matinees, he imagined them full of old ladies sitting alone, eating their chocolates; old ladies who didn't have enough money for him to bother robbing them.

He also ordered another drink.

And then Ernie had another one of those coughing attacks. Damn, when would they end? Well, according to the doctor, they were going to end alright, at the same time that Ernie was scheduled to end. Which, he thought as he hacked, is going to be very soon.

Guy looked over at the coughing man, sadly. Poor old guy.

Burleigh finally stopped coughing, caught Guy's eye and said, "Lung trouble."

"Sorry to hear it," Guy said politely.

"Yes, and only a daughter to leave behind."

"That bad?" Guy asked, a bit appalled.

"That bad."

"Well, I hope your wife takes good care of you."

"I haven't seen Betty in God knows how many years. Nice girl. But I was not for the marrying life. Some men aren't you know."

"Yes." Peculiar character, Guy thought. The type of guy Maura would find intriguing for one of her novels.

"You have a wife?" Burleigh asked him.

"Yes, that's why I'm here. She threw me out."

"Oh well, good riddance. They can be so problematic, let's face it," Burleigh said, sidling up with inner joy. There's opportunity here, although he couldn't see it yet. "But I always sent money to my wife. Not lately, of course, what with my health slowing me down."

"You're English, right?" Guy asked, relieved to take a break from his own troubles.

"Yup, born in London but met my wife when I was on shore leave in New York. I was in the British navy stationed in New York –"

"In New York?"

"Security attached to the embassy."

"I see."

"And I guess I got Betty pregnant and I married her. But I had to go back to England when they changed my posting, but I always sent her money and cards to Kathleen, my daughter. Once I got out of the Navy, I came back to the USA. I could become American, you see, since I was married to a Yank. But I didn't go back to home and hearth, no, not for me, thank you very much," and then he coughed again.

"I see." Guy turned to the bartender, "Hey, give him another drink."

Guy shouldn't be spending money, he thought, but hell, when you're broke what's 5 dollars here or there? And he had a tiny bit put away. Actually, he had been sending money to Sister Maureen and she wanted to return it to him now that he needed it. Always kind, that woman. She thought he could use it as he started over.

"What kind of work did you do when you got back into civilian life?" Guy asked.

"Well, I did a variety of things, a super, a bank guard, that paid off later, I can tell you, but I wasn't so good at a normal job. I was always getting fired. I think I just wasn't cut for a normal life. Some people aren't you know?"

Guy nodded. He supposed he wasn't either, but he certainly had enjoyed a normal life in Tuxedo Park. A beautiful wife, an interesting career, unlimited money and vacations and shopping. Yes, he was cut out for that. Who wouldn't be?

Burleigh was back to talking. "I found it easier to panhandle, to be frank, and then got into some petty crime robbing stores and finally banks."

"Well, that must have taken some skill," Guy said.

"It does and I loved it, did I love robbing banks, even when not being that good at it, because I was in and out of the slammer enough times, but there is nothing like robbing a bank," he said, sipping his scotch. "You must try it," Burleigh said. "It's a real high. And you looking like you'd own a bank, you might be quite effective."

Then he coughed again.

"No, can't say I want to rob a bank," Guy smiled. This Brit, he thought, is right out of a novel. Raymond Chandler would pay to meet him.

"Crime *does* pay," Burleigh went on. "Don't let the old adage fool you. You can make a damn good killing on a crime. "

"Well, I'll keep that in mind," Guy said laughing and ordered another drink.

Actually, this was turning out to be a rather unexpected, pleasant afternoon.

"Did your wife know you were up to these kinds of things?"

"Let me tell you about women," Burleigh said. "They can be very forgiving if there is money involved. Women love money. Everybody knows that. I never saw her and the kid again after I went back to England but Betty wrote me that she told Kathleen I was at sea and would return. If the girl is as smart as her old dad, I doubt she believed her mother. But anyway, Betty must have sensed I was not in a traditional career when she would get payments from me in large denominations of cash. Not that she ever offered to return those bills, let me say. Oh no. Women love money."

"That's quite a story," said Guy, who still thought with his publishing mind.

"Although I must say, you know, I'm not long for this earth and I would like to leave my daughter some money. But I just can't do a hold up anymore. Too ill, frankly."

Guy sipped his drink.

Then Burleigh asked, "What happened to your wife? Why'd she chuck you out?"

Guy pointed at their two glasses and motioned to the bartender to fill them up. This is better than confession, he thought.

"I think she thought I was having an affair."

"Were you?"

"No. I was sending money to a nun."

At this, Burleigh started coughing because he thought it was a joke. "Yes," he hacked," and I have a bridge – "

"No, it's the truth. The nun was the only mother I ever had. I was left out on a doorstep by my birth mother. At least I imagine it was she."

Burleigh had enough sense to stop joking. He stared at the bottles behind the bar.

"Maybe your wife just wanted out of it," Burleigh posited. Could be true. "Women get bored easily you know. What she look like?"

Guy was getting a bit unsteady on his legs now, what with how much alcohol he'd consumed, but he managed to pull out a picture of Maura from his wallet. He was fairly sure Burleigh was not a reader and wouldn't recognize her.

"Good looking woman," Burleigh said. "Very good-looking woman. You must have made a handsome couple. "

"We did. But you know," Guy said, "she just dumped me with nothing. Threw me out with the clothes on my back and the car I got in the marriage."

"Well," said Burleigh, used to tougher times, "that's something."

"No, she's a very wealthy woman and—"

At the word wealthy, Burleigh's ears seemed to triple in size.

"Very wealthy, did you say?"

"Yes, and she just treated me like I was a handyman she'd fired. She'd treat a handyman better."

"You have to get back at her," said Burleigh, warming up to Guy. There's opportunity here, Burleigh thought once again. If I can just figure it out.

"You should make her pay for her terrible treatment of you," Burleigh said.

"I know. But I don't know how."

Burleigh took in the expensive watch. The camel haired jacket. This man has money somewhere.

Burleigh did something he rarely did, "Let me buy you a drink and we'll think something up."

After this many scotches, Guy might have agreed to becoming a bank robber himself. What did he have to lose?

She'd taken everything away. Lifted him up with love and made him feel secure, something he had never had, he'd given his life to her and his heart, and then, on a whim, as if he was a piece of paper in a typewriter, tossed him out. Over a supposed infidelity. She, a crime writer, never bothered to investigate. She must have just used it as an excuse. She was done with him. She was tired of her boy toy. She'd thrown it into the old toys pile. Ready for the salvation army to pick up. A toy drive.

Burleigh was talking but Guy was barely following, lost in his own thoughts, but he tuned in now.

"Yes, these women get on their high horses I'll tell you that. You have to discipline them. Show them who's the boss."

"Why not scare her a little bit?" Burleigh added.

"How?"

"I dunno. Something to show she's not so high and mighty."

* * * * *

Burleigh was getting creative now. Theatrical. Maybe it's the British blood, we're marvelous at theatre, he thought.

"You could sort of set up a false crime that she would look guilty for."

"To what point?" Guy asked.

"She would be guilty, and the courts would make her PAY you for your damage. And her reputation would be tarnished. And…" he went on," she would see you could outsmart her. And," he continued, on a roll, "she'd see how smart you are. You said she's a crime writer. I can't think of a better trick to play on her than to involve her in a crime."

Guy was a bit dizzy about all this, but it did sound pretty good. He was tired of being the pretty boy, the plus one, the joke, she was the star, and now he'd been discarded. And her having to pay some recompense was no small attraction, either.

"I see," he said.

Burleigh was feeling no pain and getting more and more excited by his own cleverness. "We could have her accidentally shoot you in the leg, you know, it looks like an attempted murder, nothing serious a graze, makes her look less like an angel and listen, she would have to pay you something of note for that."

"How would you get her to do that?" Guy asked.

"No, no I would do it. I'd dress up as her. You've got that picture. Drive her car, graze your leg…"

"Well how good are you with a gun?"

"Excellent," he lied.

"Really?" Here Guy sobered up a bit. "Where did you learn?"

"In the Royal Navy, young man, the Royal Navy."

Oh, Guy thought, he must be good.

The yellow Cadillac, he thought. This man could drive it. Dress as her, he probably knows where to buy a wig and rent a coat, and then they would arrange a place –

"You know you could be getting out of your car at the bank or something," Ernie elaborated.

They looked at each other and nodded.

"Alright listen," Ernie said, "you think about this some more. And call me. Here's my number. If you're serious. It would cost about ten grand for me to do this."

"Ten grand?"

"Yes, well I am risking a lot here myself, if I got caught.... So, this requires real know how. You're paying, Guy, for real know how."

Guy had to agree. "Yes, I see."

He sat deliberating rather slowly, thanks to the single malt.

"Alright, I'll reflect when I'm a little more sober and call you."

He fingered his jacket for where he put Ernie's card. He had it.

"Alright then, let's have one more drink to celebrate the downfall of these uppity up women. They can't just toss us aside." Actually, Ernie was referring to his own current girlfriend who had been speaking a bit too often of tossing him aside if he didn't come up with the rent. He's a genius. He had just done it.

"No," Ernie continued, "they must not toss us aside."

* * * * *

Ernie didn't have to wait too long. Although with the way his lady friend was harping, five minutes was too long. Two days later, he answered the phone knowing it was the rich guy. He moved into the other room so his girlfriend could not hear. After his saying hello, this is what she would have heard:

"Okay I'm in. I need the cash up front."

"10-grand in small bills. "

"Okay when do you want this done?"

"Where shall I do it?"

"Where do I get her car? No, I can hot wire it, can't I? Oh, you have an extra set. Good."

"What? What do you mean? I'm a pro. I don't miss."

"I know. I know. A graze. I'm not a killer."

"Yes. I hear you. Okay it's your funeral. Just a joke, just a joke, my friend. Just a little assassination humor. Lighten up pretty boy."

"Okay. Let's go over this. I have to go through the woods in Tuxedo Park. Take a yellow caddy convertible out of your garage, drive past the front gate wearing a black wig, fur coat, glasses and gloves. Very kinky. I like kinky."

"Oh. So, there will be a gun in the glove compartment? I like to use my own gun."

"Of course, you're right. Her gun. It's a frame up. Come to think of it, this should be worth more than 10 grand."

"Okay we agreed on ten – cash in the car."

"So, I wait outside the bank making sure the car is seen, shoot you as you come out of your car, then return the car. Perfect. Any fool could do this."

"Make sure the money is on the front seat. You know it's going to snow again?"

"Yes, won't be that bad at 4.30. I agree. I'll be there."

"I know. Take the wig, and stuff and make sure the gatekeeper sees me."

"Nice doing business with you. Cheers."

* * * * *

Once Ernie put down the phone, he clicked off his tape machine. He always taped these kinds of discussions. You just never know when they might come in useful.

He decided to go back to sleep. He lay in bed and thought a bit. It is a pity when you think about it to set up such a pretty woman like that. He remembered Guy's photograph of her. And is ten grand really going to help Kathleen that much after he goes? I mean so this writer woman got tired of her boy toy. Big deal. He should have been smarter all along and protected himself. Or he should have expected it. Nothing lasts forever. Look at himself. He's found out personally just how temporary everything is. No, Kathleen needs more money than 10-grand. So, this Guy is going to make a payday on his miserable ten grand and here old Ernie is, taking the risk. Something's off about this. Come on, Ernie, think smarter.

Maybe he shouldn't do this to this innocent woman. I mean what about the fact he is about to meet his maker. He's already got a bit of a battle in front of him convincing his maker he's not a bad guy. Although all he did was a few bungled bank robberies. But how's it going to look setting up what seems like quite a sweet woman? No, he shouldn't do it.

But 10- grand. He needs money. There's the rent. But after that, what's left for Kathleen? Not a helluva lot.

Ernie, you must be smarter about this.

He began to close his eyes. He'd come up with something in the morning.

CHAPTER

Nine

Burke just could not get over how relaxed Mrs. Craig was as she sat waiting, along with all of them, for the next witness to be called. Is she innocent? It was so confusing. And really, Burke was starting to miss being at work. What were her kids doing? Yes, they exhausted her but now, rather than be looking at yet another colored Chanel suit every morning, she missed little Anthony with his gap-toothed smile asking her the most bizarre questions, like "How do you make a lychee martini?" She'd had to say," Anthony, I don't think that is quite what my job, to prepare you to be a bartender." To his credit, he giggled.

Yes, she would miss seeing Eugene McGuinness but she already formulated a plan of how to see him once the case is finished, so really, why don't they get on with it?

Even Jackie seemed a little bored.

Attorney Lloyd was now nearing the end of his witnesses. Soon it would be the tall guy's turn.

Attorney Lloyd called, "Patricia Lawzarkewica."

Jackie mouthed, "Who?"

An attractive woman, with short cropped blonde hair, walked up to the witness box wearing, oh not again, a Chanel suit, one that was very reminiscent of Mrs. Craig. Are these women not getting the memo that Prada, Michael Kors, Marc Jacobs are all out there, too – there are lots of designers for them to choose from.

Jackie turned to Burke. "Chanel?"

Burke rolled her eyes.

Patricia Lawzarkewica sat down and swore to tell the truth and nothing but. As she did this, she did two things: she corrected the pronunciation of her name to *Pa-tri-cha* and she also gave Mrs. Craig a warm, friendly smile.

Attorney Lloyd said, "Please tell the court your occupation."

"I work for Mrs. Craig as her personal maid or maybe assistant," she said, in a heavy Polish accent.

"For how many years?"

"Ten."

"So, you know Mrs. Craig very well?"

"I do," said Patricia L.

"Did Mrs. Craig express to you her upset with Mr. St. Claire and his sending unauthorized money to a woman in Newark?"

Patricia shook her head, wisely. "Of course. No woman likes to find this out."

"Can you be more specific, Ms. Lawza--?"

"Lawzarkewica."

"Ms. Lawza – you understand whom I am talking to."

"Yes. You are talking to me. Mrs. Craig upset, it affecting her writing, and she thought he was happy husband like she a happy wife, and she no want to be with some man who is misbehaving. So, she tell him to go."

"Did he refuse?"

"He protest. Then he does what she want."

"Did she have much bitterness once he left?"

"Noooooo," she said. "She seems happy. You know smart women don't need men much. Just for some things. Otherwise hold you back."

Judge Egan was making a very serious effort to not smile.

"Please go on," said Judge Egan, finding herself enjoying this diversion.

"Well, Mrs. Craig is a writer," said Ms. Lawzarkewica. "She need story ideas. I tell her not to worry too much -- this make good story."

"What did she say, Ms. Lawzarkewica?" asked Judge Egan. Both Jackie and Burke were impressed how Judge Egan didn't mangle the name.

"She said story of man going off with other woman done before."

"Many times," Judge Egan agreed and turned to Attorney Lloyd. "Back to you, Counselor."

Mrs. Craig was nodding, very affirmatively with everything the witness said.

Burke leaned into Jackie, "Is this a murder trial? Are we in the wrong court?"

Judge Egan shot Burke a glance.

Attorney Lloyd said, "Did you see Mrs. Craig get into her yellow Cadillac the night of the murder?"

"I did not."

"Were you even there that night?"

"I was not."

"It would be hard to see her then if she had."

Ms. Lawzarkewica did not answer.

"Was it common for Mrs. Craig to go out in her car at night in a snow storm?" asked Attorney Lloyd.

"It is not my job to keep track. You should ask guard of the estate."

"A Yes or No will do, Mrs. Lawzar -"

Mrs. Craig looked so amused, it was as if she was watching an *I Love Lucy* show.

Jackie whispered, "They can't get any facts on her."

Burke said, "Except for being at the crime with a gun."

Jackie kept quiet, because she had forgotten about that fact. Too busy watching all these Chanel suits. Must make one go brain dead, she rued to herself.

Attorney McGuinness was also watching all this, as if he, too, was faraway and it had nothing to do with him. Either these two are madly in love, madly being the operative word, Burke thought, or something is going on in this case that they have not revealed yet.

Jackie leaned over toward Burke, "Maybe Judge Egan did it. She seems to have a low opinion of men."

Burke smiled.

Attorney McGuinness stood up and said, "Ms. Lawzarkewica, would it be fair to say you are more than a personal maid to Mrs. Craig."

Mrs. Lawzarkewica said, "Yes I am grateful for her many kindness ...."

Mr. McGuinness said, "In fact didn't Mrs. Craig take you with her on trips and even give you some of her clothes as you are about the same size?"

"Yes, we travel all over world. She very generous. This one of her suits I am wearing."

Jackie and Burke nodded to each other.

Mr. McGuinness said, "Would it be fair to say you would do anything for her?"

Attorney Lloyd stood up. "Objection. Leading the witness."

Judge Egan said, "Overruled. Get on with it, Counselor."

McGuinness said, "Thank you, Your Honor." Then he turned to the witness, "Did your friendship allow you to drive her car?"

Lloyd stood up, "I object to this line of questioning."

The judge said, "Your objection is noted. Continue, Mrs. Lawzarkica. "

"Yes, we went shopping together. I often drive. I like to."

"So, you're about the same size as Mrs. Craig and drive her car."

Lloyd again, "Leading the witness."

Judge Egan, "Sustained."

Jackie said, "I am finally waking up."

"Did you like Mr. St. Claire?" Gene asked.

"He too young for her. I tell her many time. He pretty boy after her money. I tell her."

Mr. McGuinness said, "Mrs. Craig seemed to do so much for you. Would it be fair to say that you in turn would do anything for her?"

"Yes, anything," and she looked meaningfully at Mrs. Craig.

"Did you know that Mrs. Craig kept a gun in her glove compartment? You are under oath, Mrs. Lawzarkewica."

"I did not. I never open glove compartment."

"Where were you on Wednesday, Dec 4th about 4 pm?"

Not a sound could be heard in the court. And then came Mrs. Lawzarkewica's voice, "It was my day off. I take train to New York to see my cousins."

"Did you take Mrs. Craig's car to the train station?"

"No, I walk to train. Polish used to snow."

"Did you kill Mr. St. Claire for your employer?" asked Mr. McGuinness.

Lloyd jumps up, "Objection."

The judge sternly said to the jury, "Please disregard that comment from Mr. McGuinness."

Patricia began to scream, "No, no Mrs. Craig, she wouldn't do such thing. She love him. She is a wonderful woman. Yes, I would kill for her. He bad man. He let her down. But I didn't do it. I swear on my mother's grave!"

"Thank you. No more questions at this time. I wish to reserve time to reexamine this witness. Please sit down, Mrs. Lawzarkewica. Thank you again."

Judge Egan said, "Granted. Cross, Mr. Lloyd?"

Attorney Lloyd stood up, a bit angry, "Not at this time, Your Honor."

Attorney McGuinness went to sit down next to Maura. Maura also seemed a bit annoyed.

"We're getting down to business now," Jackie said.

* * * * *

"Our next witness will be Mr. Senegal Mabre."

In came a very handsome young, black man.

Once he was sworn in, Attorney Lloyd asked, "How long have you been employed as Mrs. Craig's security guard?"

"Three years while I have been going to school at Rockland Community College."

Burke, Mrs. Craig and Attorney McGuinness nodded approvingly.

"What are you studying, may I ask?" Attorney Lloyd asked.

"Law."

"Well," said Attorney Lloyd, "then you well understand the severity of a murder trial. Did you see on the late afternoon of the murder Mrs. Craig driving out in her yellow Cadillac?"

"I did, yes." He looked sadly at Mrs. Craig.

Unbelievably, Mrs. Craig smiled at him encouragingly.

What next? thought Burke. She whispered to Jackie, “Maybe she *wants* to go to jail so she ’ll have more time to write.”

Jackie nodded.

“Can you describe how Mrs. Craig looked as she drove her Cadillac?” Attorney Lloyd asked.

“She had on her signature gloves, dark glasses, and a fur coat.”

“You would say that it was her?”

“I would. Yes.”

“Did you see her come back in?”

“I did,” said Mr. Mabre.

“What time was that?”

“Around 5 pm. I had it logged.”

“The shooting took place at 4.30 pm so that meant Mrs. Craig had—”

“Objection,” from Mr. McGuinness.

Judge Egan hesitated, then said, “Sustained.”

“So the driver returned by 5 pm.”

“Yes,” answered Mr. Mabre.

“So, in essence, you saw the defendant on the snowy night of the murder in her Cadillac and return to her mansion – and the time that she was not at her abode was the time when the murder took place.”

"It seems so," Mr. Mabre said.

Attorney Lloyd sat down, and Mr. McGuinness rose to his full height.

"Was Mrs. Craig wearing a scarf?"

"I did not note that."

"Would you say the fur coat was her fur coat?"

"She drove quickly by me so I didn't study the coat, but it didn't strike me as not being her fur coat."

"You will be a good lawyer," smiled Mr. McGuinness.

Burke was feeling so softly towards the tall guy. It's inevitable they are to be together and he does occasionally look over at me, she thought. She pushed out of her mind that he also occasionally looked over at Lillian Edwards and Combover Ken. He did not tend to look over at Dangerous Dan. She has seen him smile at Belinda, but in a paternal way, if she thinks about it, which she is. She –

She had lost her focus on the case and, when she looked back, the young security guard was returning to the courtroom, Attorney McGuinness and Mrs. Craig sharing their usual ease about everything, and Attorney Lloyd had just called in Ms. Lisa Winkler.

A small older woman, wearing a blue print dress, with longish dark hair which gave her the aspect of an artist, came up to the podium.

Jackie said, "What a name. She sounds like a toy."

Ms. Winkler was sworn in and began to look admiringly up at Attorney Lloyd. In short, she was enjoying this moment on stage.

"You were at the scene of the crime on November 26, 4.30 pm in

Monticello, New York?"

"I was. I was getting some last-minute groceries for my home, given we were having a snowstorm."

"Can you tell us what you saw?"

"I was standing on the street, debating with myself whether a storm requires Bullitt bourbon or just plain shelf, when I heard a car backfire. I looked up and it was not a backfire at all. A man in a very nice camel haired coat, a tall, kind of glamorous man whom I now know is Mr. St. Claire, was getting out of his car when a bullet, not of the alcoholic kind, hit him and he immediately fell down, not to get up. I surmised now this was a gunshot. I had previously noticed a yellow Cadillac with a woman driver parked right next to me while I was deliberating my purchases because let's face it, a yellow Cadillac is unusual. Once the shot went off, the yellow Cadillac tore out from right in front of me heading south. "

"Are you sure there was a lady driving it? "

"Yes," and here Ms. Winkler pointed to Mrs. Craig – "that lady."

"Why do you think that the driver of the yellow Cadillac is the killer?"

"Well, the shot came from my side of the street, where the car was, directly across the street to Mr. St. Claire's car. It wasn't like Kennedy, the shot coming from a roof or somewhere. This shot was a direct hit from across the street, which is where the yellow Cadillac was situated. And, the way it pulled out so dramatically, rather than being curious and all, like I was, looked suspicious."

"Did you call the police?"

"I did but a lot of people who were around at that moment did, so they were there almost as I was taking this all in."

"Thank you very much, Ms. Winkler. Your witness, Mr. McGuinness."

The tall guy stood up and came toward Ms. Winkler who immediately began smiling.

Jackie whispered, "No matter what age the girls seem to like your McGuinness."

"Did you see a gun, Ms. Winkler?" he asked.

"No, sir. I did not."

"Did you see the actual shooting?"

"No, I did not."

"Essentially you saw a car move out at the same time as the shot."

"Exactly –"

"No further questions."

* * * * *

Attorney Lloyd now called, "The DA now calls Michael O'Block."

A small man with a brush cut of gray hair came to the stand. He seemed a bit uncomfortable in the courtroom, but on a mission to tell the truth.

"A crusader type," Jackie whispered.

After he and Attorney Lloyd went through the requisite oath taking and then ensuring he was at the crime on the right night and so on, they got down to the nub.

Attorney Lloyd began, "Where were you standing on the night of the murder, at the time of the murder?"

"I was out shopping for some last-minute supplies. I wanted to get some hamburger for my dog, Falstaff."

He stopped.

"Falstaff is a corgi and terrier mix," he added.

"Yes? Thank you." Attorney Lloyd began again. "Do you remember where you were standing on the evening of the crime?"

"Oh yes. I was on the same side of the street as the recently deceased Mr. St. Claire. I was quite close to Mr. St. Claire's car because he had a nice Ferrari and I am interested in cars. Across the street was an old yellow caddy so that also caught my interest. I thought what a town that all these fancy cars are around, even on a snowy night --"

"Did you see anything strange?"

"Not really. But I did see a gun come out of the window of the caddy and shoot at Mr. St. Claire as he was getting out of his car."

"How do you know it was a gun?"

"I have lived a long life, Mr. Lloyd, and been around guns. Not all of my life has been what you call squeaky clean. I know a gun when I see one. It was a small pistol, a lady's pistol. It was a shot dead on," he said knowledgeably.

"Were you frightened standing there?"

"Of course. I didn't know if this lady was some kind of mass shooter like everyone nowadays, so I crouched down behind Mr. St. Claire's car, after the first shot. Once she sped away, I got back up."

"Can you describe the driver of the car, holding the gun?"

"It was a good-looking lady, dark hair, sun glasses, a fur coat. It was this woman sitting there," he said, pointing to Mrs. Craig.

"Are you sure?"

"Yes, I am."

"Why are you sure, Mr. O'Block?"

"I know ladies, like I know guns. When I see a good-looking lady, I commit it to memory."

"Thank you, Mr. O'Block. Your cross, Mr. McGuinness."

Attorney McGuinness stood up. "You have done time, have you not, for thievery?"

"Yes, upstate."

Attorney Lloyd stood up, "Objection. This is Mrs. Craig's trial, not the witness."

Judge Egan said, "Objection sustained. The witness has served for his crime, Counselor. No need to bring this up."

Attorney McGuinness then said, "Mr. O'Block, are you sure that the driver was Mrs. Craig? I mean a snowy night, sunglasses, a split-second vision, it could have been anyone."

Mr. O'Block replied, "Not anyone drives a yellow caddy. But aside from that, as I said, I know a good-looking woman when I see one, and this driver and this woman are the same person."

"Thank you, Mr. O'Block, you may step down."

And he did and Burke and Jackie looked to Mrs. Craig, who watched with interest, as Mr. O'Block left the witness box and then made some notes on her legal pad. As usual, she looked unperturbed.

"I have to tell you," Jackie said, "Your boyfriend did not do a good job of proving the thief wrong."

Burke hated to admit it but she couldn't disagree.

Well, no one is perfect. And it is Mrs. Craig who is in the hot seat. And Mrs. Craig being put away suits Burke fine.

By this time, it was 3 pm, nearing the end of the day. To some extent, the jurors may have been thinking that deliberating this case might not be too hard. I mean the car was there, the security guard saw her leave, there were witnesses. It doesn't seem too circumstantial. It seems that this renowned, beautiful, talented writer had been seen offing a husband.

Burke looked over to Crystal, the step-daughter, just to see how she was taking this news. Her eyes were glued to Mrs. Craig. Burke leaned over to Jackie and under the bench pointed to Crystal. "That is not a look of love," Burke said.

Jackie nodded. "She must be wondering if Mrs. Craig offed her father. The woman seems capable."

Burke said, "As long as she doesn't off my attorney."

"I think she has to be married to off them."

"We don't know that beyond a reasonable doubt, "Burke smiled. "Seems in this court room anything is possible."

Burke looked at her watch. "Boy this has been a long day. It's almost time to get out of here." That's when she looked to McGuinness and saw him wink at Mrs. Craig.

What is going on? she thought. He winks just when two witnesses testify saying she is the one who did it. Are they planning on living together in jail?

At that moment, a very young man in an immaculately pressed suit, as if it just came off the rack, entered the court and headed to the defense table. He whispered something to McGuinness and then handed him a note.

Burke said, "Now what?"

Jackie said, "I can lip read. It's part of acting. That young man said, 'I got the paperwork. We got it. Here. It's over.'"

After giving McGuinness his folder, the young man hurriedly left the courtroom.

Judge Egan peered out over her glasses. "What's going on now? Up to your old tricks, Mr. McGuinness?"

Mr. McGuinness looked intently at the paperwork, seemingly checking it for what he wanted. He stood up. "Your Honor, if it would please the court, it has been brought to my attention through various sources that there has been a constitutional violation with respect to some basic rights of the defendant."

Judge Egan raised her eyebrows. "Are you looking for a mistrial, Mr. McGuinness?"

Judge Egan had hardly got the word "mistrial" out when Attorney Lloyd leapt from his seat shouting, "Your Honor, Sidebar!"

Judge Egan slammed her gavel, drawing the immediate and fixed attention of the tiring jurors and those sitting in the court. The press also raised their eyes, since they were all busy scribbling notes as to how Mr. O'Block said he saw Mrs. Craig and the gun.

Judge Egan turned to Attorney Lloyd and said, "I will give you and Counsel opportunity to speak your peace, but I must have before me claims made by McGuinness before you approach the bench."

Attorney Lloyd sat down while saying, "Thank you, Your Honor."

Judge Egan now turned to Mrs. Craig's counsel. "Now, Mr. McGuinness proceed, although I find this very unusual for a mistrial in this court. Yet I am well aware that in the past you have been known to pull unorthodox stints wasting the court's time. I hope that is not what is going on now."

"I assure you Your Honor that the evidence I will present is meritorious and irrefutable," he said, deferentially, but still taking advantage of the gravitas his height gave him.

"Proceed, Mr. McGuinness."

"Your Honor, if it pleases the court, I have been led to believe that the prosecutor or his office has been directly involved in a constitutional violation."

Lloyd jumped up again saying, "What? Your Honor, I strongly object."

"Sit down Mr. Lloyd, your objection has been noted. Ball's in your court, Mr. McGuinness."

"Your Honor," he continued, and one could not hear a sound in the court, "my allegation is based on the constitutional laws that a person is innocent until proven guilty and entitled to a hearing by a proper jury of all evidence and that said jury be composed of peers of the defendant. Your Honor, I truly appreciate the high level of your judicial intelligence – "

"Get on with it, Counsel. I'm fully aware that I am not just a pretty face."

This brought a chuckle from the court room and the jury.

"You are wasting the court's time and my patience," she added.

"I believe, Your Honor, that this matter should be heard outside the presence of the jury as this undoubtedly will influence this jury."

Burke and Jackie shared a glance as if to say, this should be good. Go get 'em, big Mac.

Then Burke almost got up and started dancing, since McGuinness' eyes traveled to her for a split second.

I love this man, she once again thought.

Judge Egan, in her quiet authoritative tone said, "Mr. McGuinness and Mr. Lloyd, the jury has already been influenced. Bailiff, please escort the jury into the jury room while this matter is under consideration."

So, within minutes, the jury found themselves sitting round a utilitarian, old fashioned room, waiting. The sun came in through the slats in the windows. Ms. Edwards pulled out her knitting, Dangerous Dan his racing forms, Jackie her script, Belinda her nursing studies, Too Tall Paul his pharmacology books, Combover Ken his Ian Fleming and Fatty Arbuckle, *The Secrets Of Great Chefs*.

There was silence, the jurors had been trained at this point for that.

* * * * *

The lawyers were now in Judge Egan's chambers, which contained a highly polished mahogany desk, three walls of law books, an overstuffed leather couch with a magnificent painting of her ancestral home in Galway Bay. Above her door was a green plaque stating, An Irish Blessing To All Who Enter Here And Love Justice.

"Well?" she said to McGuinness. "I hope this is good."

"It is. Let me explain. Being the friendly guy I am," McGuinness said, "I've had the good fortune to converse and hob knob with all sorts, some of whom are connected to our esteemed DA's office. But I am sad to say that one night, after a few Guinness stouts, I learned of a possible jury tampering."

"Can you prove this?" she asked.

"I would be delighted to," he said.

Attorney Lloyd looked totally confused.

"Now," she said.

"I have a witness."

"Back to the mines," she said.

* * * * *

Judge Egan and the two lawyers reconvened to the court. The jury was called back to their places.

As Eugene strode back to his table, he smiled at Maura, reassuringly. She would be out on the street in less than an hour. It doesn't matter what all had been heard, fixing the jury prevents a new trial.

* * * * *

McGuinness stood up and loudly recalled, "Police Officer Williams." The middle-aged officer, dressed in his uniform, once again stepped up and swore to tell the whole truth.

"Can you recount specifically what were the duties assigned to you regarding jury selection?" asked Mr. McGuinness.

Police Officer Williams answered very directly, "To obtain a list of all valid county jurors and submit the list to the commissioner of jurors."

"Did you follow these instructions?"

"Yes."

"As given?"

"Yes, sir."

"Can you explicate what you mean by 'As Given'? Remember you are under oath to tell the truth."

Police Officer Williams seemed a bit nervous.

McGuinness repeated, "The truth."

"Well, I was told to leave out the names of any citizens who'd purchased books by Mrs. Craig. We had two police officers go to the local bookstores and collect names."

The jurors all looked at one another.

Burke and Jackie raised their eyebrows. Burke then said, "I told you we were all illiterates."

Jackie laughed, "Well Fatty Arbuckle sure is."

"Objection your honor," said Lloyd, as the courtroom began buzzing with comments.

Judge Egan banged her gavel again and again trying to restore order and calm in the courtroom. The press were busy flashing their cameras, making it seem like it was the fourth of July.

"Thank you, Police Officer Williams," Judge Egan said. "You may step down. Attorney Lloyd, I think you should have a very serious chat with the Police Chief who ordered this. It is not something that should go on. Do you have a plan for this?" she asked him.

"I do. I was unaware of this," said Attorney Lloyd.

"I hope so," she said.

McGuinness gave him a hooded look, as if to say, he was not so sure Attorney Lloyd was unaware of this.

Judge Egan then turned to the jury. "Looks like you can all go home now and enjoy your lives. You have been a very attentive jury, if a little talkative," and here she, not so surprisingly, looked at Burke and Jackie. "I thank you all for your service and you are now dismissed. As am I."

But the jury just sat there, a bit stunned. There was something rather insulting for all of them to have been selected for their reading choices or lack of them. Like they were a Confederacy of Dunces, a rather good book, perhaps they would not have known of it.

Jackie said, "Well you can go after unowho now."

Burke said, "Yes."

"You won't have to get so dolled up every morning either," Jackie said, smiling. "But most importantly, we can meet for drinks in peace."

Burke said, "Yes."

Jackie turned to her, "Now the real crime can take place. The case of

How You are Going to Snag Him."

"Very funny." Burke then added, "I know you are going to miss Combover Ken."

Jackie laughed. "Well, I *am* going to invite them all to my play. I must get their emails somehow. Perhaps you can ask your new boyfriend to the play."

Burke smiled.

Jackie said, "Now Lilian Edwards can finish her coverlet."

Burke looked over and there was Lilian smiling at her again. Burke smiled back. What does it mean?

"All's well that ends well," Jackie said. "Not to mention look how smug the murderess looks. She got off again."

Burke said, "I'll be glad not to have to look at another Chanel suit, I can tell you that. I was starting to get sort of immune to them."

Judge Egan said, "Clear the court, please. No more pictures," she added for the press.

Crystal got up and Burke saw her shaking her head and mouthing something. Burke elbowed Jackie to lip read. "What is she saying?"

Jackie looked over. "She's saying 'Unbelievable. Totally unbelievable. How does she do it?'"

Burke replied, "I can tell her. A crime writer would be the very one to know how to do it."

* * * * *

Maura looked up at McGuinness as he began packing his briefcase.

"You're a genius," she said, "Not that I didn't know that when I chose you."

"I am," he said. "It pays to drink Guinness."

"I had an ace of my own too, you know," she added.

"Oh?" he said. "What?"

She smiled prettily and said, "I'll tell you" although she wasn't sure she would tell him, now that she thought about it. It's good to hold your cards till you need them. "We can talk about everything over a romantic dinner. On me."

"How can I," he asked, snapping his briefcase shut, "say no to such a perfect offer?"

And soon they both were ready to leave the courtroom together. The press was in the hallway, ready for countless questions and photos, since this case had garnered headlines everywhere. A murder and a pretty face. It will do it every time.

It was now so late in the afternoon, the sun was going down, signaling to the attorney and his client that this might be the perfect time for celebratory pre-dinner cocktails.

Burke was still watching and, McGuinness and Mrs. Craig leaving like that, smiling and intimate, was to no end annoying to her.

Jackie could see her thinking. "Well onto our next adventure," she said. "Your pursuit of Mr. McGuinness. I just hope it doesn't involve murder."

Burke smiled, "It doesn't." And the two left together, and no one will be surprised that they too decided that the afternoon darkness, past the time of the gloaming, was indeed the right time to stop off and have a pre-dinner cocktail

CHAPTER

Ten

Since Maura and Gene were in the mood for a big celebration, they decided to go into New York City. Eugene knew of a restaurant in the West Village that was quiet, old fashioned, with a fireplace and big windows, and a skylight, but small and romantic and unlikely to be a place where the press would find them. New York is good about sheltering its famous.

Maura made it a point to always be well dressed, even when she was writing at home on her own or, as it turned out, on trial for murder, so there was no reason for them to stop at her Tuxedo Park compound so she could change. Instead, she was to be chauffeured right away into the city by her childhood friend, protector and hero, Gene.

So much had just transpired in their lives that, at first, once they closed the car doors, they just sat in silence, ruminating on all that had happened. Then Gene turned around to the backseat. He kept a bottle of Absolut and stemware in the car pockets in the back for clients and thus poured a double for Maura so she could sip as they drove along. Gene had given up drinking the hard stuff twenty years ago when he spent an hour trying to find out where he parked his car. The Guinness he allowed himself since, as we have seen, can prove useful.

Maura chug-a-lugged the vodka down as if it were tap water, just now realizing how much stress she had been under.

Gene broke the silence asking, "Million dollars for your thoughts." In her case, judging by her book sales, that might be an accurate dollar number to pay, he laughed to himself.

Maura coughed and said, "Do you know anyone who would be interested in buying a yellow caddy. Cheap?"

They both laughed.

Gene pulled out of the courtroom parking lot leaving photographers in his trail calling out nonsensical questions. Maura covered her face with one hand and held her glass in the other. Once they escaped the paparazzi, she took another sip. The vodka burned but she needed it. Gene wondered if this magnificent jewel sitting so close to him knew how much he worshipped her.

They sped into New York, and with each mile, she relaxed some more. They chatted a bit about the past and then she asked, "Did you notice that the red head in the jury was fixated on you?"

He had but he said, "Well they all tend to watch the defending attorney. They think it will help them know if the defendant is guilty."

Something, in truth, he wouldn't mind knowing himself, but he was too much of a gentleman to ask.

"No, I think she really is taken with you, Gene," Maura said.

He liked that she was showing some jealousy. Being a gentleman, he didn't respond, but of course he knew the redhead was fixated on him. In truth, that Burke young woman was very attractive. He'd have to be blind not to have noticed her. But right now, he was with the woman he loves so what difference does it make if the red head was watching him?

"Can you imagine," he said, "that the DA's office chose people who had not read your books. Fascinating."

She said nothing.

"Even more fascinating," he said, "is whether Lloyd knew they had done that."

"Somehow I don't think so," Maura replied. "Christopher Lloyd seems essentially a decent person."

At this, Gene kept a bit quiet because now he was feeling a tad jealous himself.

"And, Gene," she laughed, "not everyone has read my books. I frankly didn't even understand what difference it made if they'd read my books."

"It was just a legal ploy," he said, "for me to use. They were skewing the jury."

"Brilliant," she said, although she still wasn't sure why reading her books or not made much difference to deciding if she was guilty or not. Maybe it's because, she thought, everyone assumes novels are true. So, if she writes about murder, she must be a murderess. It annoyed her that people read so much into her work.

"That must be it," she said, out loud.

"What must be it?"

"Did they think that they would get hints on how I would murder, if I did do it, from my own books?"

"I suppose," Gene said.

She sighed, thinking, "People are so stupid. I can figure out how to murder someone without reading my own books." (Perhaps the vodka was taking a bit of a toll on her.)

"Well, I have to admit," she continued, "a lot of them did look like they wouldn't read a book if they're life depended on it. Looked more like they should appear in crime books."

"Yes," he laughed.

"The red head does look like she reads, though," Maura said. "I bet she did end up reading some of my books."

"Probably. She was not into following the rules. I saw she and the British woman next to her, the nurse, out having a drink together during the case when they were not supposed to be. The Brit was disguised as a Hassidic Jew. It was pretty funny."

Maura laughed.

"In fact, if that mistrial idea didn't work out, I could have used those two's antics, their chattiness and so on as some kind of excuse for a mistrial," he said.

Maura nodded her head. "They sure seemed to find a way to make the whole thing fun for themselves."

"It's rare for jurors to become friends but I think they will be," he said.

"Can I, as a defendant, become friendly with any of them?"

He looked over at her and thought what an odd question. "I don't know. It's rare. I don't think there's some legal argument against it."

They arrived at the restaurant. He parked on west 12th street. They got out and walked into the Beatrice Inn. The maître d' knew Gene, it was a place he liked to decompress in solitude, and immediately took the couple to the back room, near the fireplace. The high ceilings made it seem palatial. "Shall I choose dinner for you, Sir?" asked the sartorially dressed maître d, who looked like the uncle we would all like to have.

Gene turned toward Maura, and she said, "Of course," although she had no idea what the maître d was going to serve. But he brought pate, a lovely white wine for Maura, then they shared a cote de boeuf that was magnificent, and the maître d brought a wonderful red wine for Maura, and even Gene had a few sips from her glass, after all, this was not just a celebratory dinner for freeing her of a murder case, it was, he hoped, the beginning of more than a beautiful friendship. He almost wished he could procure a diamond ring from his jacket pocket. It was the right atmosphere, especially with the flambé dessert and ice cream.

They laughed quite a bit during dinner, God bless the Irish, and he felt, *this* is how I want the rest of my life to be.

"Somehow I might be able to use that redhead in the next book I write," Maura said, musing.

"Why not write about the woman who knitted all the time? Mme. Defarge. That was a bit unique," said Gene.

Maura did not say it, but she always hated when men felt they should give her ideas. She doesn't give legal advice. Her broker liked to give her story ideas. She always wanted to hang up. She doesn't give him stock advice. Why do they all think they have book ideas?

"I'll think about it, "she said sweetly. She was not unaware of the fragility of the male ego.

Yet in truth, she knew Gene was an extraordinary man. Loyal, loving and brilliant in his own right. Perhaps she had been marrying the wrong men. She would not be the first to have done that.

She put her hand across the table so he could take it.

He did gracefully and with the firmness of all his ardor. They smiled deeply at each other, knowing they were crossing over from being friends who marched in a parade together to being far more.

Maura thought, I don't really have to worry about that red head, although she is quite attractive. But she can't possibly have my brains which clearly mean something to a man like Gene, nor could she share a history with him as she does.

The bill came, and Gene gallantly reached for it.

"Shouldn't I pay," she said, "as the client?"

"No," he said, "you are no longer my client. I am firing you. I am thinking of offering you a different position in my life."

And her heart, as the cliché goes, skipped a beat. What woman would not?

"Let me get the car," he said. "You can relax. Being up for murder can be a trifle tiring," he joked.

"Yes," she said, "it can." But not as much as you think, she thought. I had an ace in the hole to be proved innocent. But she kept that to herself.

But Gene had of course noticed that she had never worried about being found guilty. In some ways, he found that odd.

Well, time reveals all, he thought, as he went out to the West Village streets to get the car.

* * * * *

Senegal, the gatekeeper, jumped up to let Gene's silver S class Mercedes into the compound. He had been a bit nervous about his job, given that he had fingered Maura in the courtroom as going out in her car the night of the murder. He was pretty sure he was going to be fired.

But as they drove in, she leaned over Gene's shoulder, and said, "Hi Senegal. Nice to see you again. Have you had to fight off a lot of press?"

"You're not kidding. They're lined up down the street."

"God, you'd think they'd need sleep," she said, laughing.

"I think they sleep in their vans," he said, getting rather excited inside that she did not seem to be holding anything against him. In fact, she seemed in a fabulous mood. Well, she'd just gotten off, but still she was positively giddy.

"Well, we both know news travels fast in a small town. They'll get bored eventually –" she said.

He nodded and said, "Hi, Mr. McGuinness, good to see you, too. I am so glad about the acquittal, Mrs. Craig."

"Thank you," she said, and Gene said, "Thank you Senegal," and then Senegal saluted the car and. Maura put her silk hanky to her eyes and wiped away a tear. It was indeed good to be home.

They drove past the magnificent clubhouse and boat ramp heading for Maura's lake side home that mirrored the club's Gothic structure.

Both driver and passenger were wondering if he was going to spend the night. On her side, it would be nice but she was so tired and just wanted a bath and good night cocktail. On his part, he wanted badly to hold her but the lawyer in him also badly wanted to ask her if she did it.

Patience, Gene, told himself. Patience on all fronts.

Gene said, "Listen, this has been a spectacular night, but I can bet you're exhausted beyond belief and maybe our first night should not be tied to a murder trial in our memory. Let's separate them out a bit. How about I take you somewhere wonderful this weekend? I'll think of a surprise."

Truth be told, Maura could use a little downtime. It had been ages since she'd actually had a normal life. He was right to separate their love affair from the trial.

Even though she knew she would not be convicted, it had been tedious to hear herself discussed like all the time and have that jury stare at her like she was some kind of rare she-cat on display.

"I appreciate your sensitivity," she said. "You're right, let's make a fresh start."

"It was a wonderful dinner anyway," he said. "I could not keep my eyes off you. It's been a long dream of mine, Maura, to be with you. I've held fast to that dream since childhood."

She looked up at him and was moved, but also, she was thinking maybe she should put that line into her next book.

Well, murderess or not, he leaned over and gave her a kiss. It felt funny to kiss someone you'd known since grade school. As if, maybe the teacher would catch them. Oh, that's ridiculous, he thought, and he loved that her lips were soft and she felt so delicate in his arms.

Maybe, they both thought, quietly to themselves, dreams do come true.

* * * * *

Once Maura got into the mansion, she was glad to see her old friend, Patricia, had waited up for her and met her at the door with a martini and her slippers.

Maura slipped into both. "Come sit down with me, Patricia. What a time."

"I know, you must need rest."

Patricia disappeared to get her own martini and then sat down across from Maura.

"No more these husbands, Maura. If you get new one and something tell me you already interviewing for post –"

Maura smiled, like a little girl.

"If you marry tall man, no more murder trial."

"I'll try," Maura said, joking.

"Just write one," Patricia said. "Since I have less cleaning, I made some plots for you."

"As long as you didn't buy any in a cemetery."

Patricia looked at Maura suspiciously. She didn't get the joke, but no one likes the word "cemetery."

"You want listen?" she asked.

"Not right now Patricia. By the way," she leaned forward, "did you mean what you said when you told them you would do anything for me?"

"Of course." Both women pulled their legs up onto the couch.

Patricia said, "You have given me much, Maura. Clothes, money, home, help family in Poland – my life belong to you –"

Maura smiled and went onto describe to Patricia her date with Gene, with all the flourish of a fiction writer, that by the time she'd finished her tale, Maura had convinced herself that she and Gene should get married by the end of the month. Her story telling ability astounded even herself.

She looked over at Patricia and was a bit chagrined, but amused, to see her good friend was fast asleep.

CHAPTER Eleven

Attorney McGuinness had just ripped up the bill for Mrs. Craig's case and was about to go into another partner's office to discuss his possibly taking on a divorce case, the grounds for divorce being politics. He didn't like divorce law and saw no reason for him to be involved but he would listen to his partner discuss the pros and cons and appropriate recompense for a wife who was holed up with her TV station, while the husband was holed up with his. Was that really grounds for divorce, wondered McGuinness.

He was about to leave his office when his phone rang. He picked it up.

"Mr. McGuinness? This is Nora Burke aka Juror number 2. From the Maura Craig case."

"Hello, Ms. Burke," he said gravely and formally. Why would she be calling him?

"I was wondering," she said a bit nervously, "did you ever think about hiring a psychologist, which I happen to be as you know, to work with you in jury selection and help you to calm down your clients?"

Gene said, "I already have someone to assist with jury selection. I am curious, though, what would a psychologist do, in your opinion?"

Burke thought, Sell yourself, girl.

She straightened herself up on the chair she was calling from. "Well, the right person would be equipped to profile potential jurors. You know separate the wheat from the... ill-informed. Assess the right kind of mental state for the case, and so on."

"I understand but I have a profiler, as I mentioned," he said. He was almost beginning to find this funny. Where was she going with this?

"Oh yes, that's true. I wondered why you selected a jury of people who never heard or read any of Ms. Craig's books. Now I see you had an ace up your sleeve.... Clever of you," she said softly.

He squinted his eyes. "I did not focus on that selection criteria, the DA did that. I was unaware of his antics."

That's even more interesting, Burke thought. How would he have even won without the DA's finagling?

"Yes, "she continued, "now, I remember. But since you have a profiler, I was thinking I could help maintain the state of mind of your defendant, assist with the mental anguish the typical defendant may go through."

He said nothing, listening.

Burke now got a little looser. "I mean, Gene, Mrs. Craig was an emotional wreck. A good psychologist like me would know how to work with her on how to respond to the questions from the prosecutor, you know, how to win over the jury."

If this Ms. Burke thinks Maura was an emotional wreck, she can't be that good a psychologist, he thought.

"Look, Ms. Burke, I've been doing this for twenty years. I think I understand the juror process pretty well. And I know how to keep a defendant relaxed or on his or her toes, if necessary. Are you just looking for a job?"

"Well now that you mention it – "

Burke thought, "This is tougher than I imagined."

She continued, "May I call you Gene?"

"It seems you already have."

"Okay please call me Burke. Nora seems unprofessional."

Had she had a cocktail or two? She wasn't totally making sense. "Well, Burke, "he said, "I thought you were a teacher, speaking of profiling. That is what you said you do for a living. Why do you need a job?"

"I like to look at other options and I want to use my psychological acumen."

"I see. Do you usually contact potential employers this way?"

"Only handsome ones," she replied gaily.

Oops! she thought. Oh God what did I say. That chocolate martini might not have been the right thing to get my courage up.

"Listen, Burke," he said, ignoring that comment and now thinking it best he get off the phone before she embarrasses herself although he did somewhat admire her bravery, "call our HR department and see what they have. Maybe there is some position open in the firm."

Then she blurted out, "Just one more thing, am I wasting my time... and yours of course?"

Gene stood up at his desk. What is she really asking? "Of course, as you know, time to a lawyer is money. And, unfortunately, I am now expected at a meeting. So yes, we are wasting time somewhat. Now if you'll excuse me, I must get to work. I appreciate your call and wish you luck in your search."

"I understand. Thank you for listening, Gene," she purred.

"You're welcome and I hope you find something," he said.

They both put the phone down. He shook his head and ran off to see McGregor down the hall with his cantankerous divorce case.

Burke sat back and took another sip. I have found something I like, you idiot. I found you. She remembered he last time she saw him when he'd won the case with that suspect mistrial. He and Maura looked so enamored with each other. It was ridiculous. She didn't want to be catty but, in her opinion, he and Maura look all wrong for each other. He towers over her by fifteen inches. Whereas I am tall. Also who would want someone with ice cold blue eyes like that woman has? Doesn't he know they could be a sign of early onset madness?

But ah how handsome he looked with his smirk of confidence on his Irish face as he realized he had won the case. And he had winked at her, Burke. Winked.

Even Jackie had noticed it, although she had been busy decoding, like Morse code, Crystal Craig's lip movements. Burke didn't know why she needed to. Anyone could see deep down Crystal Craig hated Maura no matter how smoothly Crystal had acted on the witness stand.

Who is the damn killer of Guy St. Claire? Burke wondered. Maura? Crystal? Patricia? And why are all the suspects women, Burke suddenly thought. Not like a woman to kill a handsome man. There are so few of them out there. Or could my Gene have done the dirty deed? He certainly had a motive: extremely blind adoration.

Oh well, she thought, as she now dialed Jackie. We'll see what she has to say.

* * * * *

Two hours later, Burke and Jackie were sitting in a neighborhood bar that had a kind of steak house, men's bar feel. They both liked that.

Jackie had just added highlights to her dark hair which gave her a more sophisticated look.

"Why did you do that?" Burke asked, pointing to Jackie's hair. "I mean it looks nice but why? Did Christopher Lloyd ask you out?" she added, joking.

"Not yet," Jackie said. "I just felt like a change. You know how it is."

"Yes. Speaking of which I called the tall one about a change."

"What do you mean?" Jackie asked.

"I thought maybe a change from my job where I would be his profiler of jurors. Where I used my psychology degree to assist the legal profession, namely him."

"Really? You would leave all your school benefits for that?" Jackie, being a nurse, thought any job where you got summers off was nothing to turn your back on.

"My school benefits come with a lot of curses. Like the parents. And, anyway, obviously my intention was to get closer to our dear Eugene. "

"I take it, it didn't work."

"No, he says he has a profiler. He was very unencouraging. Frustrating," Burke said, looking round the room. Why didn't things go easily for her in the men department?

"Hmm," Jackie said.

They both were quiet as they sipped their drinks.

"Were you off today?" Jackie asked.

"Half day. School holiday."

"Well, you do get SOME perks. Nurses never get time off. "

"I know."

Again, they both stared off.

"Look, dearie," Jackie said, "you have to find a way to get McGuinness to go for you."

"I know. I gave him an opening," Burke said. "But he didn't take it."

Jackie applied her most snobbish British accent and said, "Don't be so defeatist. It's so middle class."

Burke looked a bit shocked. "What did you say?"

"Don't you watch Downton Abbey? If not, there's something wrong with you. That's what Countess Violet Crowley would say."

"Oh, thank God, I thought you were insulting me."

"No. Never. "Jackie paused and then said, "Why don't you apply for a job working for Maura? He's bound to be around there, what with their being friends or whatever they are."

Burke looked at her. "Work for that murderer?"

"You don't know. You might find out who the murderer is and solve the case. That would be sure to enormously impress him." Jackie sipped her drink, "A bloody good strategy on my part, if I do say so."

Burke bit her nail, ruminating.

"And," Jackie continued, "you'll be around a lot and he may fall for you. You ARE younger."

"What would I do for the illustrious Mrs. Craig, then?"

"Call her up and say you're a psychologist, as you are, and you could help her with research and character analysis. Apparently, people like James Patterson and who was the one who wrote, Hawaii?"

"James Michener," Burke said.

"Right. They all have people working for them doing research and so on. You can't think her maid Patricia is coming up with all the ideas, do you?"

Burke said, "No."

"And if you are working there, he will see you. He will be so relieved to see someone not in a Chanel suit that he'll fall in love based on that alone."

Burke laughed.

"It's an idea. Do you think she'll hire me?"

The waiter came and they reordered. He was tall, with dark hair hanging over one eye, and had a sort of rag round his waist.

Jackie said, "He should be in an O'Neill play, don't you think?"

Burke was not interested in this line of conversation. "Go back to why she would hire me," she said.

"She was looking at you during the trial and she is curious. I could see that."

"True."

"You need to plot out your McGuinness plan," Jackie said, taking a sip.

"What do you mean?"

"Well, he is obviously intelligent. So be very intelligent. He is witty. Be witty. You're tall. So be tall." Jackie hesitated. Where was she going with this? That young man was distracting.

"Yes?" Burke asked. "What is your point?"

"I am trying to remember," she said. "Oh, I know. Get some info on him from Maura. You know, their childhoods, important stuff and then..."

"Yes?"

Jackie was thinking.

"I had no idea," Burke said, "you're such a strategist."

"Oh yes, I know what I was thinking. When you have all the info you need, it's easy. Engage him in conversation. Make him feel understood. Men love that. And then that's that. Also, as I said, be good if you solve the case for him. He must deep down wonder if she did it. It's not exactly pillow talk, is it, for her to say, 'Oh darling I did murder my last two husbands, nothing to worry about dear. Just don't argue too much with me.'"

Burke laughed. "You *are* good in the theatre."

"Of course," Jackie continued, "you better be careful. I mean if she sees he *does* like you, your life is in danger, isn't it?"

Burke sipped her drink, "Thanks for those encouraging words."

Jackie smiled when the waiter returned with the bill. Maybe there is a part for him in one of the plays she's in. Then Jackie looked at the bill. "You might as well pick up the cheque seeing as you might not be alive the next time we meet."

And then they both laughed and Burke, kindly, did pick up the bill. After all, she thought, she would call Maura and see if there was a job there. It was a brilliant idea.

Burke pulled out her purse, "Jackie, dear, you're worth every penny!"

* * * * *

That night Burke looked up information on all of Maura's books, and then read some latest analyses of the trial in the press. She was already showing signs, she thought, of being an excellent researcher. None of the papers had any idea who committed the crime. They all, however, thought that McGuinness was the guy to have as a trial lawyer. Most articles lauded him for getting a mistrial. She would not disagree; he had done his research.

* * * * *

Maura's books were more revealing. Clearly, the one about the murder of a publisher (written long before Mr. Craig, the publisher, "fell" off his floating flotilla or whatever it was) was her unconscious or conscious desire to get rid of the husband. She had to give it to Maura here. Who wouldn't want to get rid of him? He sounded pathological.

* * * * *

Maybe Eugene will see her appearing at Maura's as a way of saving his life. And, if she does save his life by forestalling his murder, he will then see her true value. Burke's not Maura's. Maybe that is why she wants to get this job. Clearly, by looking into all Maura's books, Burke did feel

Maura has a rather avid interest in murder, as a subject. It does show a kind of perversion, when you think about it.

This new approach to the job where she would be saving Eugene's life gave her the courage to immediately write Maura a letter, c/o her publishing firm.

Dear Mrs. Craig,

I had the honor of being a juror at your trial and I am so happy you were almost acquitted. By the mistrial, I mean. You had an outstanding attorney and, for this, I commend you also.

I have a degree in education as well as a Ph.D. in Psychology, from Fordham. As one alumna to another, I would like to propose my services to you, on a part time basis, since I still teach special needs children, as a research assistant. My psychological acuity could also help when you are building characters, especially villains. Not that I know many villains, but I have studied the various psychological illnesses – schizophrenia, bipolar disease, borderline diseases, not to mention jealousy or avarice – that can lead to, your favorite subject, murder.

I would be happy to meet with you at your office or home, at your convenience.

Yours truly,

Nora Burke

* * * * *

Burke very carefully chose what stamp she would affix to the envelope. Burke had a great love of stamps and part of her joy in life was seeing the latest designs. For this letter, she chose Eleanor Roosevelt. Woman power never hurts.

She went to the kitchen and poured herself a celebratory glass of wine. If she gets the job, she will find out who the killer is or isn't and maybe be able to help Eugene. She sat back and let herself dream. Maybe he will make her his assistant researcher, once he sees how good she is. Then she can switch to working with him. They would be a husband-and-wife team, like Madame Curie and whomever she was married to.

She went to her email and fired one off to Jackie: *Mission accomplished. I wrote Maura.*

Jackie replied, *Jolly good.*

Burke lay down and what should she do now? Watch a romantic film? One where a lawyer gets the girl? Usually, the lawyers are tricked by some femme fatale. That would be Maura, Burke decided. Perry Mason didn't even have a girlfriend. He had Della Street. When had a woman solved a lawyer's case?

She heard her text messaging ring.

Jackie: *Don't get her jealous. I don't want to lose a good friend.*

Burke: *Hah.*

Jackie: *No, I'm actually worried. This is not a joke.*

Burke: *Your worrying is a joke. I can take care of myself.*

Jackie: *Guy St C probably thought the same.*

Burke was thinking what to type when the ping went off.

Jackie: *What if it's Eugene himself? He seems to like the defendant. Nothing like getting rid of a husband to clear the way.*

Burke: *Impossible. He's too decent. Think Jimmy Stewart. Think Jimmy Carter.*

Jackie: *I don't want to think Jimmy Carter, thank you.*

Burke: *Don't worry, Jackie, I'm perfectly safe. People don't murder people with red hair. We're known for our tempers.*

Jackie: *Well, I can see you're not known for logic. Good night!*

Burke: *Sweet dreams.*

And so, our two jurors went to sleep that night, coddled by the winning combination of good friendship coupled with a plan.

CHAPTER

Twelve

Maura tried to focus on the resume she was supposed to be reading. Patricia was sitting nearby on a simple brocade chair, to the side of both women. Burke was across from Maura who was on a gold couch. They all were in Maura's well-appointed living room since matters that had to do with Maura's novel writing took place at her home, not at the publishing firm.

Burke surreptitiously glanced around and was impressed by the Tiffany lamps and the assorted velvet couches (why hadn't she herself thought of buying one?) and the oriental rugs and the overall tasteful affect. She noticed a signed Picasso and even a De Chirico.

She turned back to Maura who now began talking, "Well this is quite a surprise, Ms. Burke. I admire your drive in seeing an opportunity whilst attending my trial."

Burke said, "Well not an opportunity, Mrs. Craig. I just thought you might need a researcher and I am good at that sort of thing, and we're both Fordham people, and ..."

Maura said, "No need to sell yourself. I understand."

Actually, Burke thought, she is quite nice, not to mention drop dead beautiful up close.

Maura turned to her, "You may be a bit psychic. I had thought of doing a novel where there are jurors as main characters. We don't really know if the defendant is guilty or not and the jurors' personalities are equally as interesting as the murder trial."

"I see."

"Be a bit hard to pull off," said Maura, looking off into the distance as if there might be answers there, and then turning back to Burke, "but I believe one should always try new things, even if the publishers hate that. On the other hand, since I own my own publishing firm, that is not too much of a problem for me."

Burke smiled. So, she has a sense humor.

"What do you think? "Maura asked.

"Well," Burke said, "I am not a creative type. My friend Jackie is, she was another juror – "

Maura smiled. "Yes, I remember you two chatting quite a bit. I almost thought you two would get me a mistrial—"

Burke chuckled. "As Judge Egan put it, we like to serve."

Now Maura chuckled. "Are we going to end up friends," Burke thought, "but we're mortal enemies." We both are destined for the same man.

"Now," Maura said, "you would have to do character studies of jurors and some research on trials, once I assign what the trial is."

"That would be fine," Burke said.

"You would share all this with me of course and with Patricia."

"Patricia?" Burke asked. She was too polite to say, you mean your cleaning lady?

"Yes, Patricia has an excellent criminal mind. I do the writing, of course, but I like to bounce ideas around with Patricia."

"Oh. Sure," Burke said, thinking, What? Did they kill St. Claire together? It's obvious. They dress the same. Maybe her first research paper should be a note to this effect to Gene. No wait, Burke, get more information.

"I'll be delighted to share," Burke said again, smiling at Patricia, who nodded back to her. Share with Gene, I mean.

"This job will be temporary Ms. Burke, you understand that? "Maura said.

"Yes. Well, I have a job as you know as a teacher."

"Doesn't that keep you very busy?"

"Not all the time," Burke replied, even though, in fact, it kept her horribly busy, but the path of true love is never smooth. She has to be here to see McGuinness.

"You will have to sign an NDA," Maura said. "Meaning you can't talk about our work together."

"That is fine."

Maura studied Burke and then said, "And you don't need to be so dressed up when you come here. We all just work at home."

Burke got what she was saying. Don't be too attractive. That must mean he comes here.

"I understand."

"Okay, I suppose with your teaching, you would want to be here weekends."

"Ideally or after school."

"That is fine with me. How about Tuesday at 6 pm. We can work a few hours before dinner."

"Thank you. "

"I will pay you," and she listed an amount per hour that shocked Burke. It was more than she made as a teacher. Well, they always underpay us. Perhaps I can get that winter coat with the fur trim I've been longing for. "Thank you, Mrs. Craig. That works."

"See you then next Tuesday. "And, with that, Burke got up and left the house.

* * * * *

Maura said, "Well what do you think of her?"

Patricia was just handing Maura a tuna fish sandwich, "Odd contact you. But you famous. Maybe she smart. I think she will be excellent. She not seem princess."

"No, "Maura said, a tad distressed, "she doesn't."

Patricia then went off to clean the kitchen and the downstairs dining room. Maura sat back and stared out the window. She was just getting readjusted to normal life, now that the trial was over. Not that she had ever thought she was going to prison.

She shook her head at how easily life had worked out for her, then she looked over at the watercolor of the Irish countryside her grandmother had painted. That generation did like to paint. But really what made her eyes go over there was she knew that the safe behind there held the small package which would have been her ticket to freedom.

It happened so easily. There she had been in bed, so upset over that fool Guy's ostensibly sending money to another woman. Patricia had then brought in the mail. Maura usually never opened the dozens of letters and manuscripts sent to her. On principle, those people should send those letters and manuscripts to her office and not bother her at home. It was intrusive behavior, signifying a difficult writer trying to get published. We can live without that. But that particular day, she'd noticed a package on her tray.

Patricia knew Maura's fondness for gifts. Even though Maura had grown up "dirt poor," Maura's mother often had little surprises for her only child. It may have been just a new toothbrush (always blue to match her eyes), or a comb to adorn her ink black curly hair. It was a gift of love.

Maura had chuckled as she opened the small package between sips of a mimosa in a tall Powercourt Waterford Champagne goblet. She wasn't quite certain of whether she liked the drink or the crystal. She extracted a tape with a note from the envelope.

She got out of bed and played the tape first, for some reason. It was so unusual to get a tape.

What she heard, as she played it, left her chilled to the bone. Two men speaking in whispers. One was her darling boy toy absent of phony French accent asking someone to shoot him using the gun Maura kept in the glove compartment of her yellow Cadillac. Oh, how she hated that car and the man that gave it to her. With the tape, there was a short note written on a bar napkin with the phone number of a man called Ernie Burleigh. Wisely, she had kept that note.

That afternoon, her wheels had spun. A great plot for a novel? But this wasn't make-believe, this was a genius murder plot with she herself being set up as the murderer. Who would think young Guy could come up with a plot like this? She had really underestimated him. But he didn't know what he was up against. After all, she wrote the book.

She listened to the tape again and again and called Patricia for a mimosa refill but this time, she said, "Hold the OJ."

Patricia had given her a funny look and left the bedroom.

The phone rang just one time. Ernie Burleigh, whomever he was, must have been sitting on it. He sounded much like the recording; British and raspy like a heavy smoker.

"What do you want of me?" asked Maura.

And he had told her.

"I'm a dying man me lady, in and out of prison all me miserable life. I only have a short time left. The only good thing I have is my daughter. I left, no deserted them, years ago. I thought that maybe if I could leave a few bucks for my little girl, she might forgive me. She would be about eighteen now and just starting college."

Maura was listening, amazed. She still couldn't get over that Guy would or could conceive a plan that would put her in jail for life.

Ernie explained he'd had a change of heart.

Maura arranged a meeting with the assassin that day. She had the tape where Guy hires Ernie to so-called make an attempt on him and it would be her salvation in case Guy ever did happen to get murdered. Someone with this kind of evil mind like his, trying to set her up like he did, definitely was the type to have it backfire on him. No court could involve her in any murder now. Could they?

Maura had placed the tape of the conversation with Ernie and her husband Guy in her wall safe. Gene, that darling, wasn't going to have to work that hard to get her off. He just never found that out since, it turned out, he was quite smart himself.

And now this funny thing with this Burke woman showing up. Never a dull moment.

After Maura's rumination, she began paying some bills.

* * * * *

On Burke's next late afternoon, after her school day, she did indeed dress down. A simple maroon dress which was a creative selection, given her red hair, and a dark cardigan. She wore flats, but she still towered over Mrs. Craig, disproving, Burke thought, that taller people make more money.

Maura had Burke sit down at a separate desk, an antique one in her living room, with enameled markings. Burke felt like she was a French countess. I should have worn my hair up, she laughed to herself. With fancy combs. I must tell Jackie about this.

"Alright, Nora –"

"Burke, I prefer my last name."

"Why on earth would you prefer that? Nora is a romantic name –"

"Would you really in all honesty name a character Nora?"

"No," Maura said, "it's been used for ever..."

"Precisely. Call me Burke, everyone else does."

"Alright...Burke, now I would like you to make a list of 12 jurors, give them all jobs and then look up the characteristics of people with those jobs. Particularly their failings."

"Do you think they list failings?"

"You're the psychologist researcher. Maybe you can track that."

She's probably right but where on earth would I find those, Burke thought. Suddenly, she could hear Jackie's voice, like an angel, "Make them up, love."

But what if Mrs. Craig wants sources? "Do you need sources?" Burke asked, innocently.

"One thing good about writing novels," Maura said, "is you don't. You just need imagination."

Burke said, "I see," and thought, Good. I have that.

Maura excused herself and off she went.

After a half hour, which Burke found to be quite fun because, naturally, she wrote out profiles for Blender, Too Tall Paul, whatever happened to them she wondered, Dangerous Dan, Combover Ken, Fatty A and, of course, Ms. Edwards and her knitting needles. She pondered about Jackie. How would Jackie feel being in one of Mrs. Craig's books? She might not like the depiction and then blame Burke for it, not Maura. Better not to, she decided. As she was thusly musing, the doorbell rang.

Patricia said, "I'll get it."

And then like a dog whose ears pop up at the sound of its beloved, she heard Eugene saying, "Nice to see you, Patricia."

"You too, she getting ready upstairs. You going to opera?"

"We are."

"We have great music in Poland."

"Yes," he said, "you do. Chopin. But I don't know any Polish operas. I am sure there are some."

"My grandmother told me they play Chopin on loudspeakers on the streets of Warsaw after war," Burke heard Patricia say, "because the city was ruin. And the peoples."

"No, I did not know. Interesting."

Gene had now come further inside and looked to his left at a figure there.

Burke turned and smiled at him.

"You?" he said, "Here?"

She felt her heart in her throat. She suddenly felt all girly and embarrassed. Where is her wit? All she could do was blush. "I—" she stammered.

He smiled, seeing that.

"It's alright, Burke. But what are you doing here?"

"I am researching —"

"Researching what?" His eyes twinkled at this odd new development.

Suddenly she got ahold of herself. "Mrs. Craig's new book."

"Employing your psychological talents, are you?" he teased her.

"I hope so," she flirted back. Now she was on game. After all, she thought, this is why I am here.

"It's a book about jurors. I am going through all the jurors' psyches. Giving descriptions."

"What you wanted to do for me," he said.

"Yes."

"Well," he laughed, "glad you found employment."

"Yes. I guess," she said, "we'll be seeing a lot of each other."

"Yes," he said.

"Are you representing Mrs. Craig on something else?" she asked.

"No."

"Oh." Then why is he here all the time?

Just then Patricia whisked in. "She right down."

"Oh Patricia, I forgot." He handed her a brown bag. "I brought you some perogies. There's a place near me –"

"So kind, Mr. McGuinness." She took the perogies. "Mrs. Craig, she finishing up with accountant."

"Upstairs?"

"She has extra office. You know."

"You must know Burke," he said, pointing to Burke. "She was one of our jurors."

"She working here now on new book. Maura thinking good ending."

"What kind of ending?" McGuinness said.

"The lawyer, the lawyer, he do murder."

"I know she runs things by you, Patricia. But that seems far-fetched," McGuinness said.

Burke wanted in on the fun, "Well lawyers do have a bad reputation, let's face it. Nobody trusts them." Then she smiled flirtatiously, "It helps when you look so honest like you do...but Patricia I like that idea."

Patricia smiled.

"Yes," she said, "the lawyer did it."

And then Patricia left the room.

Burke teased him, "Did you? Are you the killer of St. Claire? You can tell me," she joked. "I don't think you can be charged now. Some law against that? Double indemnity or something..." she turned to her notepad and wrote it down. "I must look that up."

"I'll leave you to figure that out yourself, Burke. After all, I would have had a motive."

"Which is what?" And then she understood what might be his motive. Ugh. Why did he have to bring that up? Now he was looking up the stairway as Maura was coming down the stairs.

Maura looked lovely in a black velvet dress with embroidered flowers on it. Very form fitting which showed off her petite figure. Her hair was a bit longer than it was at the trial which made her younger looking. Her hair of course was not as nice as Burke's, never could be, but still he seemed to not notice Burke's hair.

"Hi Burke, dear," said Maura.

“I just finished up your profiles.”

“Oh, wonderful thank you. You can go now since we are leaving too. Do you want a lift anywhere?”

“No thank you, I drove here.”

“Well why don’t you come here on Wednesday after school and we can continue working together.”

“Okay thank you I will.”

Patricia was holding Maura’s fur coat. Which McGuinness took and held for Maura.

Patricia then came with Burke’s cloth coat, which McGuinness also took and held for her.

Well, now we’re talking, Burke thought, as he stood there holding her coat open. She did swirl her red hair outside the collar for effect. “Thank you, Gene,” she purred. His fingers touched her shoulders as he helped her put it on. He looked a bit consternated while this went on, as if confused by Burke’s attractiveness.

She has a shot! She has a shot!

She has to get him alone.

* * * * *

Next Wednesday, Burke was at Maura’s door when Patricia opened it.

“Mrs. Craig in office upstairs. You go up,” Patricia smiled. “I take coat.”

“Thank you.”

Burke climbed the circular long staircase, feeling like she was in a

1940s movie, and heard Mrs. Craig on the telephone. She knocked and then went in.

Maura, looking pretty in a clingy print dress with long sleeves, waved her in. Burke sat at the adjacent desk and saw that she had been left an assignment: *Burke, select the right murderer from the jurors and then do a character analysis of the lawyer representing the female defendant. Yes, you can model it on Eugene.*

She took off her coat and put her bag by her side.

Maura was off the phone now.

Maura, looking perky, and as if she found all this funny, said, "All set?"

"Yes," Burke said. "But...I might have a few questions."

"Shoot."

Burke joked, "I guess we shouldn't use that word."

Maura nodded.

"What..." Burke began slowly. "What were the lawyer's beginnings?"

"Gene?" she smiled. "Oh, he went to an elementary school where he was secretly in love. With me, you see. He was studious, and even a bit heroic then. He always made sure no one bullied me. He had a brutal father, drunk and very cruel to Gene, and sometimes cruelty engenders cruelty, but not in Gene, although apparently, he did cremate his father when he died, and put the ashes in a paper bag and dropped them off the Staten Island ferry. The only attendee at the funeral being the Statue of Liberty. It doesn't exactly sound like a Roman Catholic burial, does it?"

Burke said, "No." Suddenly Burke thought maybe she should make

Maura suspicious of Gene. That may be one way to get him. "Well, it does sound a bit cruel. Maybe he has secret pockets of cruelty. You know..."

"What do you mean?" Maura asked.

"I mean sometimes people who have been abused are quiet abusers. You know this lawyer in your book, maybe he is the murderer, frightened of not being loved, I mean you did marry two other – I mean your characters marries two other men. This might secretly enrage him."

"Yes, I see what you mean." But Maura wanted to continue talking about Gene. "Gene's mother was browbeaten by his drunken father, but she had one pleasure beyond raising her brood of children and that was playing the piano left in the parlor by a former tenant. His mother took her precious time out to play a few happy tunes much to the delight of the neighborhood."

"Does Gene play?"

"He was never allowed to take piano lessons from his mother as his father deemed it a waste of time and money. Instead, Gene was always collecting cans, walking dogs, cutting grass and washing cars. College was not a goal of the poor, you know. A civil service job like a postman or a cop was the best way to ensure a future and a pension. At least that's what his dad said."

"So how did he get so successful?"

"He sort of made his own path. He lived in his family's attic. They called him the shadow. That was his solace. He tried to stay out of sight of his father. He says now that he only regrets not punching his father when he slapped his mother about the beer not being cold enough or the meal a bit late. Anyway...he went to school on the GI bill."

"What happened to his mother?"

"She died on her 40th birthday never got to see her son graduate law school or her other children excel. Maybe the difficulty from the father and the love from the mother gave them strength," Maura said. "Who knows?"

"Oh."

"The father never gave Gene the least bit of acknowledgement even though he did live to see Gene's success."

Just then Patricia came in wearing designer jeans with a duster. Burke noticed her feet were quite large. Where did she get her high heels to match her hand-me-down Chanel suits? Probably a cross-dresser shoe store in Manhattan.

Burke then looked to Maura. Her feet were tiny. Like one of those Chinese women who had bound feet. Interesting combination.

While she was busy musing on these important facts, Gene walked in. Boy, he is here often, Burke thought.

He walked right into Maura's bedroom. That's quite intimate, Burke thought. And Patricia hadn't let him in.

Burke blurted out, "We're working here, Gene."

They all looked at her. Why did she say that?

Maura gently said, "It's alright, Burke. He can come in here, any time."

Gene seemed cheerful and was just taking off his tie.

Good God, Burke thought. She slipped off her heels in some kind of automatic response.

He undid his top button to his shirt.

She undid her top button.

He looked over at her for a second, then back to Maura.

"Anything you would like to do tonight, honey?" he asked.

"Why do I put myself in these horrible positions," Burke thought miserably. "I took this job to see him, fine, but not to see him romance Mrs. Craig."

McGuinness looked amused. "By the way, Maura, Ms. Burke here can tell you it's not really in the profile for a defense attorney to murder someone."

"Even if he wants to get rid of the defendant's husband?" Burke asked.

"Exactly," said Patricia, agreeing with Burke.

"You two are out of your mind, there must be something in the cleaning fluid," Gene joked.

"But," Patricia said, "you marry so quickly."

"Who got married?" Burke asked, terrified.

"Mrs. Craig, I mean...no more. Mrs. McGuinness..."

"You're married?"

Gene smiled, "Yes, Ms. Burke, we got married a weekend ago in the side altar at St Patrick's by our friend the Cardinal. Maura's other weddings were Justice of the Peace quickies so we decided on a Catholic wedding. Quiet thing. What with the press being all about..."

"Why didn't you tell me?" Burke asked.

"Was I supposed to?" he asked. "We've been keeping things very hush-hush given the press, as I mentioned."

"Oh," she said, her voice breaking a bit. "But how do you know Mrs. Craig, I mean your wife, is not the murderer of Mr. St. Claire?"

Maura was spell bound by this interaction.

"That's an odd question, Ms. Burke, "he said.

"Do you think I am the murderer?" Maura asked, cheerfully.

"No one.... knows," Burke said, "definitively."

"Well, "Maura said, getting up to go to her dressing room. "I suppose it all doesn't matter who the murderer is anymore."

"Don't you...care that your former husband was murdered?" ventured Burke. So, what if she is making a fool of herself? Now that she knows he is married. She's never coming back here again, that's for sure.

Maura gave Burke a hard stare. "That is not something I wish to discuss with you."

Burke looked at Eugene. "Don't you care that she doesn't care? Doesn't that worry you?"

Eugene gave her a look that was gentle. He had compassion for her. "Are you concerned about my welfare, Ms. Burke?"

"Actually, I am. How could you just get married like that?"

"I have loved Mrs. Craig – my wife – all my life. That's how."

"I see," Burke said. "Well, congratulations."

"Thank you."

Maura had gone into the other room.

"I guess I should go," Burke said.

"See you Monday," Maura yelled.

Burke didn't reply. But then she thought she shouldn't burn any bridges too quickly. "Yes...and ...Congratulations on your marriage."

"Thank you, dear," Maura yelled out.

* * * * *

Burke got into her car and immediately called Jackie.

"Guess what horrible thing happened?"

"Dearie, I am at work. Can we speak later. Hard for me to talk. Working ICU these days."

"Okay. Call me when you get home."

* * * * *

Burke put the car in gear and began driving down the long driveway. Which was not that easy because tears were obscuring the windshield. She'd really believed that she had met the man for her. It's so rare to meet a man and feel he is the right one. She just sensed it and sometimes she thought he sensed it too, even if that woman had drugged him or something into being her husband slave. It just isn't fair, she cried. Why can't she have a husband like everyone else? Why does she have to be alone? She'll never find someone more right for her than Gene.

* * * * *

That night over a cocktail, Jackie listened to a longer version of Burke's lament. Once Burke had finished, Jackie sat in silence.

Jackie then said, "This is the moment my Dad would have changed the subject by asking, 'How's your drink?'"

"Meaning?" Burke asked.

"Meaning time to move on to another subject."

Burke said, "I know."

"There are other fish in the sea," Jackie said.

"They're mostly pike."

"It was a long shot, let's face it dearie. A long shot. He was clearly taken with her. That's a difficult situation to win."

"I know."

"Why not just take to drink?" Jackie said joking.

"I am considering it."

They were quiet.

Then Jackie said, "You never know. There might be a new development."

"Like what? She's too old to die in childbirth."

"No, something. The case is still unsolved. Or a tall dark stranger could waltz into this bar. Or you could ask Dangerous Dan out. He likes you."

Burke smiled in spite of herself.

"We could get Ms. Edward's knitting needles and have her stab Maura," Jackie continued, trying to distract her friend.

"I liked Ms. Edwards in the end," Burke said.

"Combover Ken? Any interest?"

"Not on a cold day in..."

"I wonder if Belinda and Too Tall Paul got together," said Jackie.

"They probably did," Burke said. "Everyone gets together except me."

"Look at me. I'm cheerfully single. Who needs all this *sturm und drang* with men? I like my drama on stage, not in my private life. Anyway, there's enough at the hospital. One can live a very happy life without a man."

"I already know that. The only males I meet are 8 years old at my school."

"Plenty of men look at you when we go out. Smile at them or something."

They were still silent.

Burke said, "You know what Jackie? I am not giving up. I don't believe in giving up. A wife is just a small hindrance if true love is there so ..." and now Burke seemed a bit more chipper, "I am not giving up."

CHAPTER

Thirteen

Who would be calling me at midnight? I must get caller ID, thought Burke. She picked up the phone, hoping the school hadn't burned down or something.

"Hi lovey, it's Jackie."

"Jackie Enright, do you know what time it is? I need my beauty sleep... badly."

Burke pulled the phone closer to her ear and snuggled into the blankets.

"I know you do, love. But this is important. Sit up now, dearie, and listen closely. And you better hold onto your knickers since you won't believe this. Or perhaps you don't wear knickers in bed. Don't tell me. Remember I was telling you about one of my patients in the ICU unit that was an ex-con?"

"Yes, he was let out on a humanitarian thing."

"Well, I don't remember that but anyway I was checking his IV and he said he wanted to see a priest and confess his sins. I guess he knew his time was up. He was really badly off, poor bugger."

"The point of this call?"

"My, aren't we impatient..." Jackie laughed.

"It's late, Elizabeth Jacquelin Enright."

"Okay you will quite get the point of this call when you hear what my patient said about that sod Maura Howard Craig."

Suddenly Burke sat up, and even switched on the bedside lamp.

"I'm wide awake."

"Well dearie my patient told me that he killed a man. The man he killed was Craig's husband."

"So, the bitch was innocent after all," Burke said.

"Wait, it gets craftier. This bloke, by the way, his name was Ernest Burleigh, born in London like me he was."

"Yes..."

"He said he met Guy St. Claire in a seedy pub in Patterson. St Claire was a little too well dressed for this pub. Anyway, he said St. Claire had one too many top shelf Dewar's, but he was buying, so Ernie became his best friend. Ernie told St. Claire that he was dying, one month to live in fact, and had nothing to leave his daughter but his bad name. Then, as they got to sharing, St. Claire went on to tell him his own hard story. His rich wife was going to divorce him leaving him without a quid and no job. He then offered my friend Ernie a deal. He would give him $10,000 if he would shoot him in the leg using his wife's gun while driving her car. Ernie agreed thinking this would be a nice bundle to give his daughter."

"You mean St. Claire hired this ex-con to kill him? It doesn't make sense."

"No, silly. The deal was that he would take Maura's yellow Caddy out of the garage, drive to the bank in town and use Maura's gun that she kept in the glove compartment, shoot him in the leg, return the car and the gun, cleaning up all the traces."

"But not kill him? The car must be one of a kind if Guy was so sure that would indict her."

"Right. He just wanted to be wounded, not killed. So, Ernie would drive the car back to the garage and replace the gun. Everybody in town apparently knows that yellow car. I'm sure it is the only one in a hundred miles. That way the wife would be the prime suspect and Guy would be recompensed for this egregious crime."

"So, Guy just wanted to frame Maura for attempted murder and your British pal killed him instead?"

"No, now it gets interesting. The poor bugger found religion and had a change of heart. Ernie realized this would be a worse legacy for his daughter."

"A change of heart? About what?"

"Framing Maura. He'd taped the conversation with Guy and sent a copy to Maura. That way his conscience was clear. She invited him to her mansion in Tuxedo Park. He said for a classy lady she had quite a potty mouth. Do you want to know what she called St. Claire?"

"Spare me Jackie. I almost feel sorry for her."

"Maura apparently told Ernie she now realized that her toy boy—"

"It's boy toy," Burke said.

"Alright. She realized her toy was only after her money and was a worthless piece of trash. The tape Ernie sent her proved it."

"I still don't quite get it."

"You must be tired. St. Claire concocted a murder plan where Maura would be accused of attempted murder and sent to prison, and he would have it all since they weren't divorced. Anyway, what's now far more important is that Ernie and Maura made a deal of their own. Maura would set up a trust for his daughter for 100K and Ernest Burleigh was to kill the fucking louse. Oops, I told you she had a potty mouth. Maura, being a first-class mystery writer, twisted the plot. She would provide gloves, a wig, sunglasses scarf and her mink coat. Ernie could easily drive past the security tower. The guards of course know her yellow car. St Claire had originally set the time at 4, it would be getting dark."

Burke gasped. "Good God, didn't she know she would be the prime suspect?"

"Yes of course, you twit, but she had the original tape so it looks like Guy is the one who set up the hit, but it just went badly. She would get away with murder, maybe for the second time."

"Yes, I get it now."

"But you can't con a con. Especially one who got to learn his tricks in the big house. Ernie taped Maura and himself talking. He took the hundred thousand from Maura and made another tape for his daughter confessing the real dirty deal and telling her how sorry he was that he wasn't there for her. He was going to give the tape of Maura ordering the hit to Kathleen."

"Did he tell you where the tape of he and Maura is?"

"Yes, in a locker in Grand Central station."

"Boy he told you a lot. Did you give him sodium pentothal?"

"People get honest before they die."

"You'll never find the tape without the number."

"I have it. He took a liking to me. I sang some of the old English songs mum used to sing to us. I think it gave him a little comfort and you know how I'll sing at the drop of a hat."

"Yes, Gypsy Rose Enright, queen of stage, crime, and neighborhood karaoke."

"Ha-ha. Anyway love, he told me his life story including where he put the money along with a note and a tape for his daughter Kathleen. He made me promise to give them to her when he passed."

"What are you going to do?"

"That's why I'm calling you. The poor bugger died and gave me the locker key he kept on his rosary beads. We need to go to the locker tomorrow morning and find everything and then see Kathleen. She is in a small Catholic college, you see."

"So, we are going to a small Catholic college," Burke said.

"We are. But you're missing the big point."

"Which is?"

"You can give that tape to lover boy, the one with Maura initiating Guy's murder, and show him who his wife really is. And live happily ever after the annulment."

* * * * *

Naturally Burke called in sick that day and the two former jurors were scurrying at rapid speed through Grand Central. Jackie kept stopping to remark on the grandeur of the building, repeating twice, "It was the other Jackie, Jackie O, who fixed up this building, you know."

"I know," said Burke. "Let's find the locker."

They learned the lockers were on the lower, lower floor. Burke was on a mission but Jackie kept wanting to stop and look at the stores in Grand Central. "This place is so interesting," Jackie said.

"Not now, Jackie. Let's go."

Eventually they went down three flights of stairs and found the hidden lockers and Jackie pulled out the paper with the lock code. "Ernie told everything as it is," Jackie said, as they opened it to a shopping bag with a tape and an envelope of money for Kathleen. Also, a letter for Kathleen.

"Sweet really," Jackie said, "that he would think of his daughter so much. That he would do a crime so she could have some cash."

"I am sure he did crimes all his life. I wouldn't get too sentimental."

Burke popped the tape into the tape machine she had brought, put in ear phones and began listening.

"Oh my god," she said, "it's all here. It's Maura and this cockney. She's telling him she received the original tape of Burleigh and Guy talking about the attempted frame up... Now he's saying he's had a change of heart, he couldn't do it to such a pretty woman. Give me a break," Burke threw in. "Here he goes, get the violins out please, he was going to do it for Kathleen. Oh, Jackie, you should hear Maura. She's furious Guy was going to do this. Here it is, here it is. 'I could just kill him,' she says."

Burke stopped the tape. Jackie looked at her. "Go on, lovey, go on."

"I'm just catching my breath."

Burke put the earphones in again. "For how much?" Burleigh asks....

Maura sounds a bit flustered. "Hundred thousand," she says angrily. "Oh, I shouldn't do this," she says. "I'm the one doing it," Burleigh says, "Your husband deserves it.... Just his artery, the original plan. It's just a lesson," Maura says, "They agree. Same plan as he had with Guy. Different instigator... I'll keep this tape, Burleigh," she says, "You mean the one between your husband and me?" he asks, "Yes." She says, "if you want the money..." "I do," he says. And he must have given it to her because now she says, "Thank you...." "I guess you mean I'm framed," he says, "and you're clear...." "Yes," she says, "Well you're dying anyway, you say. So, what difference does it make...?" There is a silence and then Ernie says, "Where will the money be?"

Burke was quiet and listened some more and then finished the tape.

Jackie said, "Let's get a proper pot of tea and tell me what else was said."

* * * * *

Burke had a fruit salad and Jackie a muffin while Burke explained, "The rest of the tape was just the plan. Ernie was to be checked through the Tuxedo Park security gate disguised as a cleaning woman. Patricia was off that afternoon. She gave Ernie a ten-thousand-dollar cash deposit. The rest would be in the car. Off he went with the cash but obviously he'd surreptitiously taped his conversation with her."

"We Brits are clever," Jackie said.

"Yes."

They both sat thinking. Burke said, "With Maura now in, she could provide the right fur hood, dark glasses and large sunglasses, hers. She just didn't know Ernie would have made this stop at the long-term locker in Grand Central station."

They both looked at the shopping bag with all the cash, the tape recording and a sweet letter to his daughter.

Jackie said, "He told me it had been hard to do because he was coughing up blood. He only had 2 weeks to live at that point, poor sod."

Burke said, "He must have had to trudge in the snow over a half hour through the back woods in the falling snow."

Jackie added, "He said the mansion was lit with thousands of Christmas lights. He also said the caddy was a great car in the snow. Men always talking about cars."

"It's pretty fool proof," Burke said. "Maura would get off scot free. Guy would die by his own foul deed and Ernie's darling Kathleen would have a future."

"Yes," Jackie said, "but what is interesting is that Maura only wanted a graze. Something went wrong. Although she did say 'I could kill him.' Maybe he took her literally."

"Well, if you're coughing and ill, how good is your aim going to be?" Burke said.

They nodded.

"Poor Guy," Jackie said.

"All he did was send money to a nun."

They smiled at each other.

Jackie said, "Let that be a lesson to you!"

And they laughed again.

Burke said, "No wonder she was cool as a cucumber. But this tape means we've got her! I've got McGuinness finally. I knew it wasn't over."

Jackie gently took her hand, "They are married. You keep forgetting."

Burke smiled, "He's a decent sort. He might put up with snoring, a lack of thriftiness, but not attempted murder."

* * * * *

They both started walking through Grand Central. "Be careful with that money," Jackie said. She let Burke carry it since she was taller and more formidable.

"Yes, that's all we need to lose her inheritance."

"Now we've got to go off to St Francis, the school she's at. When are you free?" Jackie asked.

"Let's go on the weekend so I don't miss school."

"Okay."

"You realize," Burke said, as hundreds of people passed them, "that we solved the case. You did really, with your singing in the ICU."

"Yes, only good comes from a stellar performance."

CHAPTER

Fourteen

The closer Jackie and Burke got to Loretto, PA, the colder and snowier it became. They arrived at St Francis University, got out of the car, and looked around at the peaceful campus and rubbed their arms and body to keep warm. The air was clear and pristine, like they had just landed on a glacier. They could almost blow smoke rings as they began walking down a path to one of the buildings. The temperature was below freezing but the brightness of the sun felt so close, they felt like they could touch it.

They trudged along but, in truth, they were both enjoying this good will adventure. It's always fun to be in a car with a good friend but they also were happy that they were delivering something that would make this young girl happy.

The first part of this adventure had been trying to track Kathleen down. With Ernie's deathbed confession, that was one of the few facts that had been overlooked. But finding Kathleen, of course, hadn't been too difficult thanks to Facebook which Jackie steadfastly refused to use. Burke had been the one to take on the assignment since there is one thing to say about 8-year-old students. They might not want to spell, "Czechoslovakia," but when told to find "Kathleen Burleigh" on social media, they were like race car drivers. They came up with three names within seconds, and one was a woman of 40, another was living in Peru on some kind of mystical search and the other was a young girl attending a Catholic college in Pennsylvania.

As Burke explained to Jackie, "A no brainer."

They wrote Kathleen that they had news of her father which they did not want to post but would Kathleen please get in touch with them, and give them her number?

She did, and they told her their mission. Kathleen sounded a bit taken aback by their call but was very open to meeting the two women. It confirmed for both Jackie and Burke that no matter how missing in action a parent is, a child is always curious and longing for that connection.

And now here they were, glad to be fulfilling a dying man's last wish. It felt important and ordained and it wouldn't be too sad, really.

Kathleen's father was dead, true, but it's not like Kathleen would miss seeing him. On the other hand, he had died a hero of a sort, at least to his daughter, and they were bringing her good news, not in the religious sense, but just plain good news. Some financial freedom and also the news that her father did love her. Kathleen would know that she was what mattered to him at the end of his life. Nothing else.

This journey made Jackie and Burke happy because they were two women, after all, who had built their lives on doing good, one a teacher and the other a nurse. This trip of bringing joy and comfort was up their alley.

They looked around at the curated grounds, the big trees on the campus, the clean pathways, and took it all in.

"St Francis of Assisi would have loved the peace and solitude of this campus," Jackie said.

"All it needs is an assortment of animals to complete the picture," Burke added.

Jackie laughed. "A couple of donkeys, you mean? I happen to know a few."

Burke nodded, "Don't we all?"

The university buildings were up a hill, and once they got there, they took a moment to take in a breathtaking view of Shenandoah Valley. They looked down at the frozen lake and saw the co-eds spinning around on skates. Their laughter and screams echoed off the hills and they could hear one of the girl's iPad's playing Christmas rock music.

Jackie and Burke both smiled.

"They'll soon be off school for winter break. Good we came now," Jackie said.

They kept walking and passed a bell tower in the center of the lawn which began to peel. They checked their watches as Jackie said, "It must be noon or they've had a polar bear sighting."

Noon it was.

Jackie added, "Was it Poe who said it 'tolls for thee?'"

"I teach 8 years old. I can't remember." They kept walking looking for the administrative building where they could ask for Kathleen.

"Oh, I remember," Jackie said, "John Dunne."

Burke said, "Impressive, Ms. Enright, impressive. Maybe you can enroll here."

Just then a priest in a long brown robe rushed across the quad to a building that seemed to bear the name of their all-American basketball player, Maurice Stokes.

The friar looked like a speed skater the way he confidently avoided the ice on the footpath. Suddenly spotting the two women, he changed course and headed in their direction.

"Good afternoon, folks. Are you here to visit one of your children?"

That was a crushing blow. Do we really look old enough to have a college age child? Burke thought in fear. Guess so, she answered herself.

"I'm Father Bede," he said. "I teach English literature - or try to. May I ask the name of your student?" he asked cheerfully.

"Well, Father Bede, is it? We're just here looking for a friend's daughter. Maybe you know her, Kathleen Burleigh," Jackie said.

"Oh yes, Kathleen -we're a very small school here and a close community at SFU. I know Kathleen very well. She is sweet and as sharp as a whip – She's here on scholarship, you know. Yes, a very nice young lady. May I ask what's your business with her?"

Jackie wanted to say, it's none of your damn business but didn't, since saying so might put her on a faster track to hell, since she was pretty sure she was going there anyway.

Burke cut her off while catching a quick glance at the snow-covered toes of Father Bede. My God, she thought, he's wearing sandals in this snow!

"Father Bede," Burke said, charmingly, "Kathleen lost her father a few days ago and we are here to deliver a message from him."

Jackie chimed in, "Yes I was Mr. Burleigh's ICU nurse. He seemed to be very troubled knowing that he had a short time to live. I called for a priest but there wasn't enough time. He gave me a key to a safe deposit box. His last request was to tell Kathleen that he was sorry he wasn't there for her and we have the tiny contents of the safety box for her."

"What a sad tale, I'll say a mass for his soul. I'm sure the dear man died in the state of grace."

Jackie lifted her eyes to the sky, "State of grace, um, can't say I'm sure—"

Burke jumped in again, "Father Bede, would you mind directing us to her dorm?"

"Kathleen should be in class right now. Does she know you're coming?"

"Yes, she does, Father."

"I would then suggest checking in at Doyle Hall," Father Bede said, "so the university knows who you are. These days one cannot be too careful, can one?"

Jackie muttered under her breath, Who the bloody hell does he think we are? Instead, she said, "Oh sure, we'll do that. Where's Dudley Hall?"

"It's Doyle Hall named after our past President and founder, Father Timothy Doyle, F.O.R. He was a good holy man. Some say a saint."

Then Bede took an ice-cold breath as Burke asked, again graciously, like she was royalty, "Doyle Hall? And where would that be, may we ask?"

"It's the red brick building behind Alpha House. You can't miss Alpha Beta Phi. The boys painted it bright green with yellow trim. Something about the rites of Spring. Those Alpha boys are full of good fun. When I was in the seminary – "

"Thanks, Father," said Jackie, adding, as she began moving away, pushing Burke along with her, "I'm a nurse, dear, and do put on some socks and knickers. Keep moving so you won't feel the cold. And mind the ice, love."

They started walking quietly and Burke remembered her own college days in New York and taking the subway to Lincoln Center. The air was not fresh like this, she thought, that's for sure.

"Oh, there's the green Alpha house. Cool!" Burke said.

"Thank God there's a shoveled path around the back," Jackie said." These boots are made for walking but not in knee high snow."

"There it is, Doyle Hall," Burke said, looking up at the inscription.

Doyle Hall turned out to be an impressive field stone building reminiscent of City Hall in the Bronx or, as Jackie pointed out, the entrance to Sing Sing prison. Unfortunately, they immediately noticed that the steps were a sheet of ice. Jackie wondered if the good Friars had spikes on their sandals.

Up they went, cursing every step, hoping and trusting the administration office was open.

Another brown robed priest sat at a small desk seemingly in a meditative state. He was fast asleep and snoring at a high decibel sound.

They slammed the heavy oak door twice to wake the Friar.

"Jesus Mary and Joseph, you could give a man a heart attack."

I like this one, thought Burke. Very round and jolly with the mandatory shaven bald spot on his otherwise coal black hair. He's like Larry of the Three Stooges.

"What can I be doing for ye?"

For ye? He speaks my language, thought Jackie.

"Say Padre," Jackie began, "you could use a dash of salt on those bloody steps."

Brother Timins paused, smiled with all his Irish charm and said, "Oh that's above me pay grade, heh heh."

Wonder if he plays Santa Claus to the neighborhood kids? Burke thought.

"Father?"

"Brother Timins will do."

"Brother Timins, my name is Nora Burke and this is my friend Jackie Enright. We're here to see one of your co-eds, Kathleen Burleigh. We want to give her a message from her dad who died a few days ago. She's expecting us. "

"Oh. I see, you're not family?"

Jackie jumped in, "No Brother, just messengers."

"Oh, I know Kate," he said, sitting back in his chair, "an honor student you know. She works in the Dean's office to help pay some expenses not covered in her five-year scholarship. This gives her some pin money, poor soul. She applied for a custodial job but her talents are best served in the Dean's office on a computer rather than washing dishes. Well then, please sign on the visitor's form and don't forget your license plate number."

The two women did as told, and Brother Timins then called up Kathleen's dorm and announced Burke and Jackie's arrival.

He put the phone down. "She'll be here any second. You three can go to the small living room over there with the couches and everything to have your unhappy chat there, then. In fact, make yourselves comfortable and I'll send Kathleen in."

"Thank you, Brother," and as they turned to go, Burke turned back and shocked Jackie by asking, "How long do you think it takes for a Catholic to get an annulment?"

Brother Timins looked shocked too. "Well dear it's not something that I actually have a lot of experience in, being a kind of custodian in a girl's school, but I would say from a religious point of view, maybe a few months. After all, don't annulment requests have to go to the Pope?" He stroked his rosary beads here, thinking. "I am not sure, dear. Why? Is our Kathleen secretly married?"

"No, no, no, no," Jackie said. "My friend is just curious."

"How long the law takes is a whole other thing. I just don't know," he said. "I would say try and be careful, dear girls, in whom you marry. Then you won't have to go through that."

Jackie said wryly, "Thank you for that kind information, Brother."

"Thanks," said Burke, and then she and Jackie turned toward the living room.

* * * * *

As they waited, Jackie said, "I wonder if this money we've got affects Kathleen's scholarship."

"It's in cash. It can't."

"Right."

Just then Kathleen walked in.

She was a pretty girl with long straight blonde hair, a little plump, with a sweet smile. Jackie explained meeting her father in the ICU and his love of her and how he had left her this paper bag here with money and a note for her. They did not go into how he got the money, even though she probably knew her father was hardly a corporate businessman.

They handed her the bag, which Kathleen at first almost looked frightened of, but she seemed to get used to it, with nothing odd jumping out of it.

"And how is your schooling going, Kathleen?" asked Burke.

"Well, I'm getting mostly good grades. I have to. I am on scholarship."

"Yes, we know. What subjects do you like?"

"It's funny," she said, "I think I like criminology."

They both looked up.

"Yes," she said, "I would like to study crime."

Jackie said, "Not to do it but to catch them you mean?"

Kathleen laughed. "They don't teach you here how to become a criminal –"

Then they all laughed, and Jackie said, "No I guess they wouldn't."

"I might be a criminal lawyer or detective, we'll see."

"Good, good," said Burke. "And what about your mother? How is she doing?"

"Oh, she's alright. After dad left, she became a book-keeper so she keeps herself busy –"

"A bookie?" asked Jackie.

Burke said, "No, a book – KEEPER."

Jackie said, "What is that?"

Burke looked to Kathleen, "These English are odd, aren't they? Her mother handles people's accounts in their businesses and such."

"Oh."

Jackie looked back to Kathleen and could see she kept fondling the bag they'd given her. She must be anxious to open it, Jackie thought. I would be.

"Well, we should be going," Jackie said.

"Yes, thank you so much for doing this," Kathleen said.

Burke and Jackie stood up and Burke said, "Let us know if there is anything we can do for you. Here's my card. Let me write down Jackie's info too," which Burke did, as they both watched her, and then handed it to Kathleen. "Feel free to call us at any time."

As they were leaving, Kathleen asked, "May I ask you a question?"

"Of course," Jackie said.

"Are either of you his girlfriend?"

Burke said, "I never met your father but Jackie, here, well," she turned to Jackie, "were you?"

Jackie said to Kathleen, "She's only joking. No, as I said, I only met him in the ICU as his nurse and believe me he was in no state for a girlfriend."

"I understand," Kathleen said, "well thanks so much for coming out."

"Our pleasure."

Jackie said, "You know your father was English and so am I, so I guess there is a bit of comradery there, after all, dear, always keep in mind you are half English. You should go and see England," Jackie went on. "Marvelous people. I mean your father may not have been a good father, but you know the English were never that good with children –"

Burke looked at Jackie in amazement. What is she doing?

Jackie continued, "It's a fact. They're of the children should be seen and not heard school and that children should be on their own from about 5 years old on, emotionally. But, on the other hand, we English are a rugged, principled people, even if we did dominate the world for a long period of time, but we brought great education—"

Burke said, "What are you doing, giving a British lecture..."

Kathleen laughed, "I'm enjoying it."

Jackie went on, "Yes, she's enjoying it. So, as I was saying, you come from sturdy stock. Never forget that. Your father might have not been the most responsible man, but it's still sturdy stock and here he was at the end of his life, trying to do the right thing. Never forget that. Which is very English."

Kathleen smiled a bit sadly. "I wish I'd known him better."

Jackie said, "Well don't be too sure about that but he did love you. And love is all that matters. Burke here will attest to that."

They all laughed and then Jackie said, "Let me give you a hug goodbye dear even though Brits are not the best at that, but I have been duly Americanized."

And so, they hugged and Kathleen went off with her knapsack of money, or if the truth be told, her knapsack of ill-gotten gains, and Burke and Jackie left the "living room."

Brother Timins was still there. "I have a surprise for you two ladies."

Jackie said, "And what is that? You got my friend an annulment certificate?"

"No, I put salt on the stairs."

"Excellent and thank you," said Burke and Jackie at the same time.

As they walked through the University commons, Jackie said, looking fondly at Burke, "You do have to admit that Maura's bizarre trial was indeed the beginning of a beautiful friendship."

Burke laughed and hugged her friend. And then, as she shivered, she said, "If only we were in Casablanca right now."

* * * * *

As Burke drove them back home, Jackie said, "What are you going to do with the tape implicating Maura?"

"I have to let Gene know. Never mind my own interest, but he should at least know the truth. After all, I think that's why people are interested in the law."

"Well, aren't you the naïve one."

"Not really, but let's face it, he should know," Burke said, "that his wife is a murderer. It's not going to make him that comfortable if they have an argument. Plus, he will never trust her."

"He may already know she is," Jackie said, looking out the window at the highway and all the different types of exits in New Jersey. "I must say I'm glad you're driving. I find all these highways thoroughly confusing."

Burke nodded.

Then Jackie said, "So how will you do it?"

"Mail it to him and then call him. He may want to talk to me. Find out how I got it and all that."

"True. Being a lawyer, he definitely will. As you say, they never trust anything."

* * * * *

The next morning Burke wrapped the tape up in bubble wrap for safety and put it in an envelope. She included a note in her best penmanship on a thick piece of ivory paper. It practically looked like a wedding invitation.

Dear Eugene,

My friend Jackie Enright, also on the jury, as you know, is a nurse at St Mary's Hospital. She was working in the ICU and I will be happy to tell you in person about how she met this gentleman, Ernie Burleigh, who was on his deathbed and confessed to a murder. He had been paid to do it and he wanted Jackie to deliver the money to his daughter (which we did.) The victim of the murder was Guy St. Claire. Once you listen to the tape, you will see how the actual murder came about. It may shock you.

My number is 917 543 5698, since I suspect you may want to talk to me after you hear it. You probably will also want to have a serious talk with someone else.

Affectionately,
Nora Burke

* * * * *

Once the kids' classes were finished for lunchtime break, she scurried out of the school and drove to the post office because she wanted to send the package registered mail. This was one item she did not want to get lost. This tape, with Maura in her own voice condemning herself was, in its way, Burke's dowry.

Once she'd mailed it, she got back into her car and sat there for a minute. She felt somehow her life was about to change. There was no question that one has to take action for change. Or maybe that change presents itself, such as the strange serendipity of Burleigh, the tape, and Jackie coming together. It was almost novelistic. And now, the man she knows in her heart belongs to her, will have to make his own changes. She put the car in gear and thought, I hope he is up to it.

Just then there was a rapping on her passenger window. She looked over and there, of all people, was Dangerous Dan, dressed, she noticed, in one of his most dangerous outfits. A black leather jacket (or is it plastic? she wondered), skinny black jeans that really would suit his son more if he has one, and, oh no, that can't be a tattoo on his neck. Where's his motorcycle?

She brought down the window.

"Hello," she said.

"Ms. Burke, that's it right?"

"It is."

"I just saw you, looking lovely as ever."

"Thank you." Is she supposed to be chatty and polite? One is supposed to be kind. "And how are you doing?" she asked.

"Well, I am enjoying not sitting on that boring case, I can tell you that. We still don't know who did it although I have my theories."

"Oh yes, what are they?" she asked. This should be funny, she thought.

"The policeman who only chose people who hadn't read her books."

"Oh yes? What motive would he have?" She hopes his OTB betting picks are not this bad. He must be destitute.

"I dunno. But usually in these things, it's the least likely person. You know on Perry Mason or whatever."

Good God, she thought.

"Well good to see you," she said, "I have to get back to my school."

"Where is that?" he asked.

"I can't quite remember the exact address," she said.

"I was wondering you know if would like to you know go with me sometime on a date? I could take you to the track, it can be fun, you might make some money, you never know –"

"No, uh, no. Thank you for asking."

"You're not involved with that woman you were always talking to?"

"What woman?"

"The English one."

"No, I am not... But I AM seeing someone."

"Well, figures, a girl with your looks."

"Well good luck with everything, "she said.

"You too," he said, and she pressed the button to pull the car window up and drove out so quickly she almost hit a Cadillac.

At least it's not yellow, she thought. The policeman. My God. Thank God there *was* a mistrial.

CHAPTER
Fifteen

Gene stood up in his office and put his hands in his pockets and stared out his floor-to-ceiling glass window. If he looked far into the distance, he could see the Hudson River. He tried to put his focus on the familiar buildings facing him and the water behind them, to calm himself, really, and thought, Yes, that "Burke" delivered a bombshell.

At first, he'd thought the tape she'd sent was a hoax, but even he would admit that was wishful thinking on his part. It was obvious that Ms. Burke found him attractive, but he didn't think she and her British cohort would create a phony tape, although one of them is allegedly a part-time actress. Kooky as those two women might be, they were not criminals and sending a tape that frames someone for attempted murder is a lot more diabolical than "kooky." And, damn it, it is definitely Maura's voice. The right inflections and the actress would have no way of knowing that.

He'd listened to this Ernest's deathbed confession over and over, a man who turned out to be very "earnest" in his last moments. Gene remembered a law professor who seemed a bit kooky himself who thought there was something to names. Princess Di did die. The professor gave other examples which Gene could not remember right now. Gene had other things on his mind, like the fact Ernest had told Maura he'd had a change of mind about framing her for Guy's murder at Guy's behest.

Gene kept replaying the tape. Yes, his lawful wedded wife was the one who asked for the murder. Now Gene inexplicably remembered another joke. Black Adder saying "awful wedded wife," rather than lawful wedded wife. Why is he thinking like this? He doesn't want to face the facts, obviously. His Maura, his newly wedded wife, the love of his life, took Ernie's change of mind and convinced him to murder her boy toy husband, for a better price.

Since Ernie was dying, whom did he care was hiring him? He only cared how much he got for it. He was the one who would be deemed guilty, if anyone ever found out. But he had taped Maura's conversation. Why hadn't she seen that coming. She knew he had taped Guy's conversation (patterns, patterns are the engine of the law), which had let Maura in on the first diabolical plan. Maybe Ernest thought his beloved daughter might want the new tape to blackmail Maura.

Gene had to admit Burke and Jackie did the right thing by sending the tape implicating Maura to him. They didn't even give Kathleen a chance.

He sat back down at his desk and looked at Burke's fancy note for her telephone number.

She picked up the phone instantly.

"Miss Burke?"

"Hello Mr. McGuinness."

"Hi. I...uh...got your package."

"You mean," she said, "the one with the tape where Maura Howard Craig hired a man to kill her husband. I had a feeling that might get your attention."

"I should ask you a few details. Let's meet in my office in White Plains this afternoon."

"Too far," she said. "I have a school meeting."

"Okay. Do you know the Piermont area near the Tappan Zee Bridge?"

"Sure."

"How about Slattery's at 7 pm? My cell number is – write this down -- 830 288 8228."

"Slattery's at 7 tonight. I'll be there. My meeting is over at--"

"Sorry, Ms. Burke, I have to rush right now –"

"Good-bye then, Mr. McGuinness."

"You can call me Gene."

"And you can call me anytime."

God, this woman is indomitable. "Alright, see you later."

She put the phone down. Boy, do I have courage, she thought. But loving someone, she justified, brings the lion heart out in you. It also makes you wonder what you should wear to Slattery's, she thought, as she jumped up to look in her closet.

* * * * *

Eugene, on the other hand, went to his safe, unlocked it, and slipped in the recording, the recording by the killer of Guy St. Claire, to be given to his daughter after he died along with a fist full of new hundred-dollar bills, the recording that implicated his wife.

He locked the safe and thought, I'll figure out what to do with this later. Perhaps on my own deathbed.

Then he called Maura. "Darling, I'll be back a little late tonight. I have some investigation on a case I have to do."

"Totally fine," she said. "I'll have the cook have something ready for you. Love you," she said.

"Yes," he said. "See you later."

Maura put down the phone and said to Patricia, "He sounds a bit distracted. Must be quite the case."

* * * * *

That night Burke sat waiting in Slattery's, wearing a silk deep purple dress that enhanced her figure. He came in with his briefcase, tall and handsome, but clearly, sad.

He sat down and could barely smile.

"You could use a drink," she said.

"That I could," he said, and he was the type of man who rarely said that, thanks to his father's predilection.

The waiter came and she said, "I'll have an old fashioned."

Gene said, "A gin and tonic. Light on the gin."

Burke decided to be cheerful but stay on point. "I still can't get over that not one juror read any of her books. Seems strange since she is the queen of mystery novels. On the other hand, I can say first handedly, since I am a teacher, that people are less and less interested in books."

Eugene was hardly paying attention to this prattle.

She was a bit hurt at his lack of enthusiasm. After all, didn't she and Jackie solve the case for him? They should get an award or something.

"Well," she said, retaliating, "I thought it duly proper that you should know that your wife conspired to kill her husband."

He looked over at her soberly.

"Or," she said, "did you know that already?"

"Burke, I am sure you can understand that I am not going to discuss what I did or did not know about the case. But I would like to know," he said, taking a sip of his weak drink which, he worried could get him drunk, since he so rarely drank, and this whole thing had made him forget to have lunch, "how you got this tape."

"I told you," she said, prettily crossing her legs, "Jackie Enright works at St Mary's ICU and it so happened she was taking care of Ernest Burleigh. He was at the end. He was British, like her, so they got chummy, apparently, she sang old Navy songs for him, and he confessed to the whole thing, the murder, where the tape and money was, and asked that Jackie get the money he'd left Kathleen to her. Which we did, by the way, and he wanted us to give his daughter the tape, but we thought you should have it. Naturally. It is a strange synchronicity, he and Jackie meeting, I'll give you that," she said, "but it's what happened. "

"It's so unbelievable," he said, "that I believe you."

She smiled. "Well, aren't you glad that at least the case is solved?"

"Burke, you must understand that it has other implications for me."

"Indeed, I do." Indeed, I do, she said to herself gleefully.

He went back to being professional. "Jackie can of course swear to this and so on."

"She can."

"There's no need for me to meet the daughter. I might have to have proof Mr. Burleigh was in the hospital."

"I am sure Jackie can get you those records or tell you whom to ask."

Burke then asked, "Do you need the tape verified or something?"

He was quiet for a moment, took another sip. "Sadly…no."

She wanted to ask him, "What are you going to do?" but even she knew it wasn't her place. She could see he was heartbroken. She wished she had some decent information about annulments. Surely the Pope lets you get out of it if you find out your wife is a murderess. I don't think you can try a person again, she thought.

"Well," he said, trying to be polite, "and how you are doing? You are no longer working at the house, I see."

"No," she said. "I especially do not want to know. I hope she doesn't put a hit out on me," she said jokingly and saw, looking at him, that the joke went flat.

"I wouldn't worry about it," he said, thinking he might put a hit out on her, himself. She'd just ruined his life.

"Well," he said, "I'd better go. I'll probably see you again since you have a habit of popping up everywhere."

For once, he smiled, and the skies, once again, opened for her.

"Yes," she said, smiling kindly and she did mean it kindly, "I hope, Gene, we do see each other again."

* * * * *

Eugene now had to go home to Tuxedo Park. His fingers nervously tapped, up and down, the steering wheel as he drove. How does he handle this? Oddly, he was discovering, that when you love someone, nothing stops the loving, even when finding out your beloved is part of a murder plot. By rights, and he is a man who has made a life of upholding the rightful law, he should hate her. But he doesn't.

Well, one thing he does know, he thought, as he parked the car, the way to get through things is to face them head on.

Patricia let him in, gave him her usual smile. I wonder if she knows, he thought. Here I go, signing up for a lifetime of suspicion.

He jumped up the stairs to Maura's office.

There she was, always at her desk, this time wearing a white t shirt and silver pleated skirt. She was so engrossed that, when she finally understood that he was in her office, she turned around almost befuddled, just now leaving another world, the one in her laptop.

"Oh Gene, darling," she said. "There you are."

He nodded, scratching his neck.

He sat down. She noticed this, since he didn't normally do that.

"Tough day at the office," she asked. "Difficult case?"

"You could say that," he said.

"Me too," she said. "I can't make this plot work," she turned to the laptop accusingly, as if it was the laptop's fault. Then she turned back, "I can't make these jurors bad people."

Well, he thought, she gave me a segue way.

"I see your point," he said. "Look Maura, I have something we need to talk about. Just so our marriage can go on transparently. I don't want secrets."

She looked at him quizzically.

"I was sent a tape –"

Maura was smart, she knew immediately that the tape had to do with St. Claire. But how could that be? SHE had the tape. So, what tape? And here, unbelievably, was the first time she considered that that cockney might have taped HER. He hadn't seemed particularly mechanical and she didn't see a tape. But cons, Maura, she suddenly thought, cons are clever. Their business is deception.

"Oh?" she said, "What kind of tape?"

"A tape of you speaking with some man who apparently is now dead, and left this tape to his daughter, but it is a conversation where you hire him to shoot St. Claire. On the tape, you can hear him tell you he'd had some change of heart, I think about being paid by St. Claire to attempt to shoot St Claire, and to look like you he did it. St. Claire was trying to frame you and apparently this rather unsophisticated hitman did not want to frame you for it. I know you know all this –"

"Gene—"

"Let me finish."

She began biting at the nail polish on her fingernail, a habit she had when she was nervous.

"So, to make a long story short," Gene continued, 'you were so outraged that you said YOU wanted St. Claire killed, and you offered Burleigh such a good price that he could not say no. Why you two decided to use your car I do not know. If you wanted St. Claire dead, let him kill the guy, and he would have died before ever going to prison. Why, Maura, and this I have wracked my brains to understand, would you set up a murder and frame yourself?"

Gene did not know about HER tape, to defend herself, where anyone could hear Guy hiring Mr. Burleigh to frame her. But Gene had a point, she thought. Why did they have this whole subterfuge? Burleigh would have just been the murderer. They didn't need her car to do that or dress him up as her.

She found herself at that moment not worrying that her husband may think she is a murderess, but, what seemed even worse to her, if she was losing her touch in concocting murder stories. It seemed that was almost more important to her. Why did she and Burleigh frame herself? Oh, she remembers, so that Burleigh's tape, the one *she* has, made sense.

"Well," she said, "there is a reason. It's the same reason I knew you could get me off."

"What?" he said.

"I have the tape where Guy hires Burleigh to play me and make the assassination attempt."

Gene listened. It is one thing, he thought, to have to listen to this kind of chicanery in his office, another to have to listen to it in his own home.

"I see," he said.

They were both silent for a moment, thinking, what do we do next?

"So," he said, "I have the tape implicating you and you have the tape implicating Guy. The difference is Guy wanted it to be an attempted murder, your tape is asking for a full-on murder. Which is precisely what happened. Not that either of those ideas were good ideas. But yours is more deadly, particularly in a court of law."

"You and I both know I cannot be tried in a court of law."

He did know that, but he asked, "Why not?" just to see what she would say.

"Because you can't testify against a wife," she said, cheerily. "And I don't think someone can be tried twice. Can they?"

"No."

"Well then, "she said as if they had just made dinner plans, "nothing's the matter then."

He looked at her. "I wouldn't say that exactly. The whole thing makes me a little ginger about having an argument with you. Your reprisal could be a bit over the top."

"Oh Gene, very funny."

"I wasn't being funny. I am wrestling with the whole thing of being married to a woman capable of instigating murder. I've loved you all my life, Maura, you know that, but this puts an interesting dent in the whole thing."

He looked at her and he could see she was now, uncharacteristically, struggling with herself. She looked cornered but also as if she had something else to say.

Now she took the offensive. "What would you have done if you found out that someone was framing *you* for a hit? Wouldn't it have enraged you?"

"Yes, of course it would have. But I am not sure I would have put an attempted hit on the person. I would have found legal ways, which you had in your possession, since you had a tape showing his malintent. That should have been good enough. You should have paid this guy just for giving you the tape. You didn't have to up the ante, Maura."

She said nothing.

"You know, Maura, marriage only works where there is respect. I've avoided the whole damn nuptial thing because I couldn't find anyone I respected as much as you. And now," he ran his hands through his hair, this really was absolutely unbelievable to him, he who prided himself on principles, "now, I have to consider you are like a helluva lot of the lowlifes who come into my office."

She sat there like a little girl being reprimanded by her parent. She was listening attentively, because, well, you never knew when she could use this in a book.

"You didn't need to murder this guy. Personally, I never liked him," Gene continued. "I never understood what you saw in him although when I did my depositions and discovery, he wasn't that bad a guy. Had a hard life, but he seemed, in essence, sort of a passive type of guy. I don't think he seduced you for money, I think he really loved you. He was sending money to a nun for God's sake. We'd have to search for a long time to find another Catholic rushing to do that. He was ashamed of his roots, with his phony French, but that's not worthy of being murdered. You didn't bother to find out whom he was sending money to. Instead, you murdered him. What, Maura, does that say about your character?"

She sat there taking her lecture.

"And what does it say," he went on, "about the future of our marriage? If I can't admire your character, how do I live with you for the rest of my life? Are we to have one of those horrible marriages where we look good socially yet there is an intense coldness at the core of our union? Do I not trust your ethics for the rest of my life, while smiling at you at your book parties? Is that the deal, Maura? Because," here Gene started to get angry, "Maura, I am not Guy St Claire, willing to live in your shadow, and an ugly one at that. I am not the type to follow you around and be patronized. I am a different man—"

"I know that Gene."

He sat back. "I am...just horrified. I am... in some ways, Maura, destroyed. I am in love with a woman who has committed a murder. A woman who makes irreparably evil decisions."

"Actually, it wasn't like that," she said.

"What do you mean it wasn't like that?"

"That's not what happened."

"I have the tape, Maura."

"But there's more to it, Gene."

CHAPTER

Sixteen

Maura had gone to bed the night before Guy St. Claire's murder and slept badly. She lay awake most of the night, thinking about this ridiculous thing she had done with this strange Cockney man. By the time she got up, she was in a bad mood and thought, Oh Guy. He and his stupid ideas. And now she had got herself mixed up in one of them. Guy's attempted murder on himself. Now she might be the one who finished the murder off.

But this really could end up being real, not a story.

Patricia brought breakfast into Maura's room, opened the curtains, had put the mail onto Maura's tray and fired up Maura's laptop for her, which sat ready for Maura beside the breakfast tray. Maura drank her coffee, had her fruit and then took her laptop and, before she knew it, between issues at the publishing firm, and issues about the house, and issues with her literary agent, and issues about translations of her books, and problems with her cell phone, and appointment rescheduling due to some other meetings being rescheduled, it was now, unbelievably, 1.30 pm in the afternoon.

She got up, put on a blue wool dress and that was, in a way, when she came to consciousness. She had to stop this Burleigh guy. It was truly the most insane thing she had ever done.

"Patricia," Maura yelled, "I just did something crazy because I was so angry at Guy. I've got to find him and stop him."

"Who?' Patricia came into her bedroom.

"That man who came yesterday."

"The strange one?"

"Yes, the strange one," Maura said. "Oh, I know what to do, I have his phone number with the tape –"

"What tape?" Patricia asked.

Maura ran to her painting, took it off the wall, and there was the safe and she didn't even care that Patricia saw her opening it. It was the first time Patricia knew Maura had a safe, or at least that is what Maura assumed.

She hurriedly got out the tape and the letter with it. "Oh, here it is."

She ran to the phone and called Burleigh. No answer. "No voice mail, either," Maura said.

Maura put down the phone, worried.

Patricia said, "Well he maybe buy supplies for snow storm. I go soon, too."

"He doesn't seem the grocery type," Maura said, hardly listening. "Maybe he's at a pub." She ran her hand through her hair. "Maybe he is warning Guy and Guy will murder me."

"What are you talking about?" Patricia asked. "You take many sleeping pill?"

"Never mind, never mind," Maura said, walking around in circles.

Patricia left the room. "Where are you going?" Maura asked.

"To make you drink."

"Good idea." Maura called out, "What time is it?"

"3.45."

"I'll keep calling."

Patricia arrived with a drink. "Why not go write?" she asked.

"I can't concentrate. I have to stop a murder."

"In book?"

"No, not in the book."

Patricia shook her head and left the room. Her mother had always said that writers were a bit off. She was going to put her things together so she could leave.

Ten minutes later, she came back to Maura. "I leave early. Snow storm coming."

"Yes, yes that is fine," Maura said distractedly.

Maura kept watching the clock. Every half hour she called Burleigh. Nothing.

Patricia returned with another drink. "This help before I go. See you tomorrow."

"Yes," Maura said, "thank you. See you tomorrow."

Maura took a sip and sat down. She didn't know where he lived. What was wrong with her, setting up an almost hit? There must be something to this whole notion of an Irish temper.

That Burleigh guy may do it even if she tries to stop him; he needs the money. I will tell him I will pay him double if he doesn't do it, she thought.

She kept calling every ten minutes but no answer. Where is he? she wondered frantically. He can't be out in this weather.

She finished her drink. Should she warn Guy? No. That would be strange. But she could warn Guy not to be where he is supposed to be to be shot. Yes, she'll tell Guy to never drive into the town where the hit is supposed to take place. Guy would know which town.

He'll wonder how she knows about it but who cares?

Now she began calling Guy's cell.

No answer to that either.

She left a message, "Guy. It's very important you call me."

Why don't men answer their phones?

Then she got the perfect idea. She'll do something so the cockney can't take the caddy. She'll slash the tires. That's what she'll do since she doesn't know how to jimmy an engine or do something to the ignition.

She ran into the kitchen to get some kind of knife and found one that she thought would be sharp enough to puncture the wheels and then ran out to the garage. A snow had just set in.

She got to her garage, the snow wet and beginning to accumulate and she was only wearing slippers but she was so agitated that she did not have time to reflect on that. She pushed the remote to open the garage door.

She looked around frantically. It was about 4.45 pm now. The yellow

Cadillac was gone.

She looked up at the sky.

And realized this murder was taking place right now. Oh my God no, she said, sinking down to her knees.

* * * * *

"What did you do then?" Gene asked, sitting in his chair in her bedroom.

"I went upstairs and, what did I do, I nervously went around each room over and over. I had another drink and then fell asleep because I had drunk too much."

"Then what?"

"Then I woke up, depressed, and...I took a bath and washed my hair," she said. "I suppose I wanted to feel less dirty."

"And then what?" he asked.

"Then the police came."

He sat across from her and stared at her.

The fact is, he believed her.

He stood up and said, "Let's go out to dinner. I didn't have a chance to eat."

"Good idea," she said, immediately getting her coat. She couldn't wait to get out of here. "I wonder where is open this late."

"New York. New York is always open this late."

"Let's go to the Beatrice Inn where we went after the case," she said.

"No," he said, "it will depress me. I felt so full of innocence and hope then."

"Okay, then. Where?" she asked.

"Let's go to Slattery's near the Tappan Zee."

"Are they still serving?"

"Probably pizza. The kids go in late," he said.

* * * * *

In the car, Maura chatted nervously about what she was writing and about Patricia's family and about the neighbors and a tiff Patricia had had with them and about other matters. She wanted things to be normal between them, but Gene wasn't listening.

He was thinking.

When they sat down, the waiter recognized him from when he was there hours ago with Burke. This guy gets around, the waiter thought.

Maura smiled prettily at the waiter and ordered an old fashioned.

"You having a lite gin and tonic?" the waiter asked.

Gene nodded.

"That's an odd thing for him to ask you," Maura said.

Gene didn't say anything.

He hadn't said anything in an hour. This was all overwhelming him. To have idolized a woman for so many years, dreamed of marrying her, dreamed of her as the ideal woman. And now to find out she behaves like some of the people he tries to avoid in the tombs.

He looked over at her, to the sound of the other patrons in the restaurant most likely speaking of normal matters in life. Not attempted murder.

His silence was unnerving her.

"Gene, I tried to stop it."

He just looked at her.

"Well, Gene, do you want a divorce or something? I mean you are acting pretty strangely yourself. I told you. I tried to stop it."

He said, "I don't know, Maura, what I want. I need a little time to think."

She nodded, a bit annoyed.

And then they were interrupted by two young people, a very tall young man, and a pretty blonde with enormous blue eyes. The young woman said, "I can't believe it's you two. We ARE allowed to talk to you now, right?"

At that moment both Maura and Gene realized they were staring at two of the former jurors at her trial. The pretty nurse, Belinda something, Gene remembered, and the very tall pharmacist, Paul.

Maura smiled, "Yes you are allowed to talk to us. But the question is, are you allowed to be talking to each other?" she teased, happy for a distraction from the glumness at her own table.

"Yes, we are now," Paul said, "the case is over."

"And you two met that way?" Maura asked.

"We did," Belinda said, "But we didn't communicate when the case was on. We studiously avoided each other. But.... we knew we would like each other. In fact," and here she gave Maura and Gene a movie star wide smile, "You two are the first to know that we decided tonight to get married."

"Really?" Maura said, glad that this distraction from her rather difficult marriage kept lengthening itself. "How wonderful. When will it be?"

The young couple looked rather excitedly at each other. He said, "We're... we're not quite sure yet. Probably in the spring."

"Great," Maura said.

"Oh, we would love it," Belinda said, "if you would come to the wedding. We don't have details yet of course. But it is because of your alleged murder that we met. So, you would be a real guest of honor, never mind that you're so famous and...beautiful." Then Belinda politely turned to the silent Gene, and said, "You too Sir, it would be wonderful if you came. You were so impressive at the trial. We often talk about how clever you were. You just seemed so relaxed as if you just KNEW you would win the case."

Gene nodded and said, "Thank you. I'll be happy to come."

"And," Belinda went on, "I know it's gossip but we heard... well... that you two got married. I think it was in one of the papers, wasn't it?" she turned to Too Tall Paul, but he looked a bit confused.

"We did," Maura said.

"Congratulations," Too Tall Paul said." So, both of us couples found each other at the trial. How strange."

"Well, we knew each other before," Maura explained, "since childhood."

Belinda said sweetly and giddily, in her new happiness, "Mr. McGuinness, you were so loquacious at the trial. I had no idea you are so quiet in real life."

Maura laughed in delight at this, "That is so funny Belinda... I must say you were quite a bunch of jurors. I met a Ms. Burke after the trial too."

"Oh, the redhead?" Belinda asked.

"Yes, she is also a very interesting person."

"Yes," Too Tall Paul said.

"I noticed during the trial how she fixated on you, Mr. McGuinness," Belinda said. "She seemed to be transfixed by whatever you said."

"Yes," he said, "it would seem. Some people enjoy a trial."

"Do they know, now," Paul asked, "who actually was the murderer?"

Both Gene and Maura went very quiet.

"I think the police have a suspect," Gene said, kindly. "A man admitted to the murder and he has since died in hospital, due to illness."

"Oh. I am so sorry, Mrs. Craig... or McGuinness," Belinda said. "What a terrible way to lose your husband. I am so glad you got another one so soon, you know what I mean but what... do they know the killer's motivation?"

Maura looked to Gene, "Do they?"

"Yes," Gene said, "he did it for money."

Belinda and Paul looked at each other. Obviously, this all was a bit too dark of a story for a night you get engaged.

"Well I am glad everything worked out for you Mrs. McGuinness," Belinda said.

"Yes, thank you. And for you. May we buy you a celebratory drink for your engagement?"

Too Tall Paul said, "No, we'd best be going," at the same time Belinda said, "That would be lovely."

Maura, quite gay now, said, "Welcome to marriage. You will constantly be fending differences of opinions. Who should win this one?" she asked challengingly.

Gene said, "He should," and Maura said, "She should."

Then Gene said to Paul, "Women always win."

They motioned to the bartender. Maura said, "Some Dom Perignon champagne for this lovely couple. Why don't you two sit down?"

Gene was still very quiet, but coming round to some curiosity about the goings on at his table.

The waiter came back with 4 champagne glasses.

Gene let them fill his, thinking he hadn't drunk this much...ever.

"Well to your health and happiness," Maura said, turning to the young couple, who almost looked like angels in their innocence.

Gene said, "Yes, I concur."

Belinda and Paul beamed, although Paul was aware, he had a final tomorrow morning. Well he better get used to things not always going the way he planned.

"Are you writing a new book?" Belinda asked, cozying up to Maura and excited to be intimate with such a famous person.

"I am."

"I know writers don't like being asked what they're writing," she said, "but I just know it will be good."

"I hope so. And where are you two planning on living?"

"Oh, I think we will move to Manhattan," she said. "Maybe to the west village, if we can. I hope to get a nursing job at Mount Sinai."

"Oh," said Maura. "In what area?"

"I would like to be in the children's cancer ward."

Maura said, "That will be tough, dear. Hard on you."

"I know, but also meaningful."

"And you Paul?" asked Maura. "What will you be doing?"

This was the first time Paul had heard anything about living in Manhattan which was clearly too expensive for anyone not in the prime of their career. When had she come up with that?

Gene sat there sort of glassy eyed watching all this, like it was a play going on before him.

"Oh," Paul said, "I will get my degree this May and then I will either work for a chain as a pharmacist or I might..."

Here he slowed his conversation down and looked nervously at Belinda, might as well go for it, he thought, "I might apply to the FDA."

"In Washington?" Maura asked.

"Yes, I would like to work with them. Our chemistry knowledge can help with some of the pharmaceutical approvals."

"We would have to live in Washington?" Belinda asked him. "I didn't know that. What about my family here?" She seemed a little distressed.

"Well, I haven't got a job yet," he said. "It's a thought," he added. "A thought I have."

"Well, you two have plenty of time to talk about lots of thoughts," Maura said, trying to waylay any difficulty between them. "And, Belinda, there are cancer wards in Washington, as I am sure you know."

"But my mother..."

"True," Maura said. "I understand. I am sure you both will work it out."

That was when Gene spoke up. "Just don't ever lose your tempers. It can have irrevocable results."

And the three of them looked at him and all of them said at the same time, "Of course not."

CHAPTER

Seventeen

When Maura and Gene drove home, they were more jovial. The young couple had eased their tension and, perhaps, with Belinda and Too Tall Paul being so obviously besotted, they reminded Gene and Maura of their own love. They decided to go back to Gene's apartment in the city, just for a change. The Tuxedo house carried the weight of all they had been fighting about, and all the responsibilities Maura carried.

They entered the elegant gold and marble lobby of Gene's building just off of Fifth Avenue, near the Metropolitan Museum of Art. They took his private elevator up, and even though they were both much happier now, he couldn't resist asking. Maybe it was the lawyer in him. "One thing plays on my mind," he said. "I thought you were only grazing Guy?"

"Well, I did say, 'I want to kill him.' Which Ernie must have taken literally. Or maybe he just missed his shot. We'll never know," she said, tiring of this discussion. They were now in the foyer of his apartment. "We have to let this all go, Gene. It will be better for us."

"I am intending to," he said. "Just one other thing, I promise. Do you have any proof you tried to call it off?"

"Yes," she said, looking at him directly and sweetly. She put her arms around him and smiled. "My proof, darling, is my word."

He laughed. "And you do have a lot of those!"

She pulled him over to the living room couch and made them sit down together. "Did you know," she said, "that the drawing room is named such because in ye olde England they used to call it the 'with-drawing' room. "

"Interesting," he said.

"I saw it in Ben Johnson's house. In London."

"Interesting," he said again.

"You know we're a perfect match, don't you?" she asked.

"Who? Ben Johnson and you, or you and me?"

She cuddled into him. "You and me," she said.

He lifted her onto his lap and here is where he gave up any hope of ever feeling separate from her. "It's alright, Maura," he said. "I might have done the same if I found out that I was being framed for murder." Actually, in truth, without her on his lap, he was pretty sure he would never have done the same thing.

Yet as he stroked the clavicles of her shoulders, one of his favorite parts of her, he felt that, in a way, he was and would always be her protector. She was right that, as her new husband, he cannot testify against her. And even though that fact had given him pause as to whether that was the reason she married him, he was pretty sure that she truly loved him. That is something you can't falsify. She had her head on his shoulder and he reminded himself that he still adored her and would always yearn for her company.

He said, "Do you want some champagne? I have some in the kitchen."

"Alright," she said. "I see you are drinking."

"Yes," he said, getting up. "I'll even have a Jameson. I've realized I am not really in danger of becoming my father so I can have a drink now and then. If nothing else, this whole episode has taught me that."

He got them both drinks and then went to the side table to go through his mail. She got up and went to the extra office where she kept her laptop. She wanted to see if anything new was going on in her business and then he yelled out, "I'm going to take a shower."

"Alright," she called out.

* * * * *

A few minutes later, the buzzer rang. "Who's that?" she called out.

"Does Amazon come this late?" he yelled, not hearing her.

The private elevator door opened, which was odd, and Maura ran out to see what it was. It must be the doorman, she thought.

"Crystal!" she said, "What are you doing here? Did you just play a concert?"

She was carrying her violin case.

"I'm here to see you, Maura."

Maura was struck by how her step-daughter, at this moment, looked exactly like an angry linebacker. Not to mention, Crystal was glaring at her as if, as if she hated her.

"I can see that, Crystal. But it's so late. And...how did you get up here?"

"I *am* your step daughter, Maura. They let me in."

"Couldn't this wait till the morning? Did something happen?"

"No, this couldn't wait. Obviously."

Crystal was clearly unglued. Her usual stringy hair seemed more so, and her blouse was buttoned wrong. She seemed extremely agitated, unbalanced even.

"Are you alright?" Maura asked.

Crystal fixed blue glassy eyes on Maura and said, "No, Maura, I've been following you. I followed you to Slattery's and I followed you here. I am not alright. Thank you for finally asking. It only took you thirteen years. I am not alright. How could I be knowing you murdered my father and got away with it. I am not alright with you depriving me of a father and a business –"

"I did not murder your father," Maura said.

"You did and you know it. I have eye-witness accounts from people who were on the boat."

"I am sure you paid them to say that," Maura said.

"More likely *you* paid them not to," Crystal said. "Anyway, I am not here to argue who is right and who is wrong because I already have my answers. I've done a lot of research, Maura," and here Maura realized just how unglued Crystal was because, right then, Crystal ferociously unlocked her violin case and pulled out a what looked like a semi-automatic assault weapon.

Maura began to blanche.

"Crystal, what on earth are you doing with that--?"

And Maura, who had written of such scene's countless times, ran to Crystal to pull the gun away from her. She had to because it looked like Crystal was crazy enough to use it.

They began wrestling but Crystal was the bigger of the two and the more out of her mind which gave Crystal additional physical strength.

But at least Maura was able to knock Crystal over onto the couch, but that barely rattled Crystal, even though it stopped her from fingering the gun to use it. "I am doing the same thing as what you probably arranged to be done to that innocent sop Guy," Crystal breathed out as Maura, like a child, kept grabbing at the weapon. "What goes around comes around, Maura," and Maura chose to use the only weapon of her own she had at that point. She dug one of her four-inch Jimmy Choo stiletto heels into Crystal's size 11 foot.

Crystal screamed in pain and Maura seized that moment to get the gun. Maura too was screaming, but for Gene to come, yet she did not hear his footsteps, only the sound of the shower running. Crystal regained herself and took that moment to try and get the gun back, but Maura, being small, was quick and darted back from the couch. Crystal jumped up too and used all her bulk to wrangle Maura down to the floor but somehow Maura was able to keep the gun away from her, just by slithering back quickly. Where the hell is he? she thought.

"Gene," she screamed again.

"Oh, forget Gene. Another sap you've conned," Crystal blurted out.

Maura spit out, "Crystal, I wish you had seen a psychiatrist rather than go off your rocker."

"I am *not* off my rocker, you sociopathic writer," said Crystal, with the two of them slithering around on the floor like a four legged, four armed monster, both focused on the gun.

A moment later, Gene rushed out wrapped in a towel, "What was that?" he said, meaning the huge explosive sound that rang through the apartment. As he said that, he saw the two women entangled on the floor. A pool of blood had already begun to form on the highly polished marble floor.

"It's about time you came out," Maura said.

"What the hell hap —" he said, aghast, as he suddenly focused on the lifeless body of Crystal. He turned away aghast. The body had no head.

Maura untangled herself and stood up, a bit breathless. She left the gun on the floor.

"She was trying to kill me..."

"Maura –"

"She broke in trying to kill me, do you hear me?" she said.

"I do. I do. I am just – speechless."

"Evidently."

Finally, he came to his senses. "Are you alright?" he finally asked, looking up.

"Took you long enough to ask," she said.

Gene finally collected himself. "Come over here," he said, and she did. Her hair was all over the place and she now too was coming down off all the adrenaline. He pulled her to him and just held her.

She was shaking, but he also could not help but notice she wasn't crying.

"Gene?" she finally said.

"Yes," he said.

"You understand it was self-defense."

"Of course, I do, honey," he said, although he could already see the headlines not taking that approach.

"Although," he said, "living with you, maybe I should increase my life insurance."

She laughed into his shoulder and then lifted her head and kissed him.

"Well, isn't this romantic?" he said. "Here we are with a dead body without a head." He suddenly got up and began walking to the phone, returning to his legal self. "I am going to have to report this," he said. "You know that."

"Gene?" she said.

"Not now, Maura."

What a day, he thought, as he picked up the phone. That juror Burke's information and now this.

"911? I have a dead body, uh, at my apartment. Can you guys come over. No, not a murder. Accident," he said, looking at the body. It didn't look like much of an accident. "Yes, you have the right address. Eugene McGuinness. Come soon."

He turned to her and she looked at him and said the most unlikely words he'd ever thought he'd be hearing from her this evening or was it morning now?

She said, "Will you defend me?"

He took a moment to take this in, and then said, "I am your husband now. Not sure if the judge will find it a conflict of interest me defending you again. I will have to talk to Egan."

Maura nodded.

"But it is legal, darling, so I will if needed. Oh...and I better get dressed."

"Too bad," she said, smiling.

The buzzer rang. "I'll get it," she yelled and went to the door and pushed the bell.

A bevy of policemen walked in, the chief whom Gene knew well, was one of them. "Hello Maura. The people at the call desk recognized that Gene and I have worked together before. They informed me." Chief O'Reilly looked down at the headless body.

Gene reentered the room at that moment.

"Chief O'Reilly. Didn't know you were coming."

"They let me in on it."

"Glad they did."

They both looked down at the body.

"It's Crystal Craig, Maura's stepdaughter," Gene said.

The younger rookies who followed him in, first looked shocked, and then the Chief nodded to them. "You know what to do." They began collecting evidence, the gun, and swiping finger prints all over the place.

The chief asked Maura and Gene," May I ask what happened? "

The chief looked back down at the body of a young woman in a beige suit. The suit was soaked in blood.

"Crystal broke in here and wanted to kill my wife. It was her gun. They scuffled and an accident occurred. The gun went off," Gene said.

"I can see that," the Chief said. "Forensics, all that, they're on their way. The coroner too."

"Thanks."

He turned to Maura, "Sorry again, Maura. For your loss and for...this mess."

"Yes," she said. "It's not fun to have someone want to murder you."

Gene looked at her. He thought maybe she was finally going into shock.

"My wife, Chief, is pretty upset. Naturally."

"Of course. Does she...uh... does she have a lawyer?"

She looked at Gene imploringly. "I guess I will be the lawyer for the time being. There's no reason to take her in. I'll vouch for her."

The buzzer rang and more people came in. Soon the coroner and his two assistants were doing their own police work, whereupon they began lifting Crystal into a body bag. Maura watched the whole scene. She is definitely in shock, Gene thought.

He closed his eyes to think.

The Chief said, "You know I have to take her downtown. There has been a murder here, Gene."

"It was an accident, not a murder. We need to manage this a bit."

"Okay, for now," the police chief said, getting ready to go. "I am sure the DA will be in touch. Do you want me to alert the press? It's going to be a field day. Worse than the St Claire murder trial."

"I know," Gene said. He turned to Maura. "We have to deal with the death, darling, the arrangements and so on –" He ran his hand through his hair.

The police chief turned around, "Gene, much as I like and respect you both, I have to take her in. If just for questioning. I would be remiss."

Maura got back into her stilettos. "I understand, Chief. Gene, it'll be okay. I'll go," thinking this would make an amazing novel. What are they going to ask her?

She went over and kissed Gene. "I'll meet you down there. Make sure this gets all cleaned up," she said.

"No, Mrs. McGuinness. It's a crime scene," the police said. "We have to keep it the way it is."

"Oh yes," she said, wrapping her fur around her.

Gene watched all this wondering how she was going to take to the tombs. Well, she's done it before.

"Do you think you should wear that?" he asked. "They'll just take it from you."

"I want to," she said. "It will keep me warm on the way."

"Okay, I'll be down later to post bail."

"I know," she said.

"They're taking Crystal to the morgue," the Chief said.

"Yes," Gene said. "I'll see you later, Maura. You have to be arraigned and then I'll post the bail."

"Yes, dear," she said. She turned to the Chief. "Here we go, yet again."

* * * * *

That night, he sipped a scotch. There was so much to figure out.

First, they needed to arrange the funeral. Maura was in the rare position of being both the stepmother and the murderer. A bit of a dichotomy. Crystal had never appeared with a friend or boyfriend. Who knew who had her will and so on.

Then there is the press. How to keep them in line with some modicum of respect. He should forget about that. They probably have already surrounded the police station and caught Maura walking in. The funeral parlor. They're probably there, too. They must pay off policemen to know what is going on so quickly.

This is overwhelming, he thought. He had only been married 5 months, most of them ecstatic except for this evening. At least he got to know Maura had tried to call off the St. Claire murder. She was innocent, there was no malintent, it seemed, although he'd had some doubts. And now this. Certainly, it was self-defense. But a lot of unseemly deaths certainly do happen around her.

The phone began ringing. Here we go, he thought.

It was the head of PR for Craig Publishing. "I am so sorry Gene. I just heard. I should put out a press release. It was a murder, right? In your apartment."

"I didn't see it so I can't say that. It was self-defense. And I do not want that to be the focus of the obituary. Talk about Crystal's many accomplishments at the firm."

"Nothing about the way she died?"

"No. That is not public information yet. She was killed in an accident, an accident of self-defense."

"To the press, Gene, how she died is very relevant. Crystal was Maura's stepdaughter. And it is of police record, Gene, that Maura is being held for the murder."

"She is being questioned, as is normal in these situations. She is not up for murder. And that is not the focus of Crystal's obituary," he said. "An obituary is usually about the accomplishments of the deceased. Not rumors."

"It's a story, Gene, like any other. People read for a story."

"Yes," he said, sadly, "look we both know the press will have a field day with this, but do we have to assist them?"

"Gene, they already think Maura may have murdered two husbands. She's had plenty of front-page coverage for that. Articles. That her step-daughter now gets murdered -- by Maura, even if an accident – is, frankly, hard copy."

Gene drew his voice into the one he used when making summations at murder trials. He even stood up from the couch to tell this damn stupid woman, "I am telling you, not asking, to write a long, adulating obituary. Maura is going to help with the funeral. Perhaps give it, I guess. Do you have any papers in HR of Crystal's other next of kin and so on? Her personal attorney? Have that person call me."

The PR woman could hear the coldness in his voice. "Okay, I will have them call. And may I say, how sorry I am. For Crystal and for you and Maura."

You should be, he thought, because I am going to have you fired. "Thank you."

*   *   *   *   *

A day later, Jackie called Burke. Burke, at this point, had read The New York Post, The Times, People's rush edition, and Vanity Fair online.

"Well?" Jackie said.

"Amazing," Burke replied.

"It is, isn't it. Sounds like self-defense, doesn't it. I mean Crystal broke in with a gun..."

"But why are there so many murders around this woman?"

"It IS her subject..." Jackie said.

"Knowing Gene and how good he is," Burke said, "I'll bet he's defending her."

"Yes. Odd isn't it?" Jackie said. "Wonder if we can be jurors on that trial."

"Funny. They'll have to find a round of jurors again who haven't read her books!"

"Why do you think Crystal broke in with a gun?" Jackie said. "Maybe she knows Maura DID murder her father."

"That's what the press is alluding to."

"Maybe Crystal is in love with Gene like you are. She wanted to pop Maura off."

"Poor Gene," Burke said. "He never should have married her. Look what a mess his life is turning into. Maura did try to kill Guy. And now his wife kills Crystal. She could have just told Crystal to go home."

"According to the paper and what Gene told the press, Crystal was out of her mind, intent on killing Maura."

Burke wanted to say, I wish she had, but didn't.

"Well lovey," Jackie said, "he's bound to get tired of this somehow. Although she does provide a lot of legal work for him."

Burke laughed.

"I don't understand," Jackie said, "why men always go for these vamps. It's in all the movies. The men always go for the sultry bad girls who are of course great looking. They never go for the nice plain ones."

"Well," Burke said, "maybe Maura will be convicted in some way."

"You do like to look on the bright side don't you," Jackie laughed.

* * * * *

Belinda could not believe it when she saw it on the 6 o'clock news. She had switched the television on to see what the weather was tomorrow. "Oh Paul," she said, since he was studying at her apartment. "What a horrible thing to happen. It's the same night we celebrated with them. It's so... tragic."

He too watched the screen, transfixed. Maura Howard Craig in a holding cell for murder of her step daughter, Crystal Craig. Lawyers and police saying it was in self-defense when Crystal Craig broke into their apartment with an assault rifle with intent to kill Mrs. Craig, now Mrs. McGuinness.

"But is it true?" the anchor asked a bevy of lawyers brought in to pontificate on the case.

"Belinda," he said, "during the case we sat on, did you think she was guilty?"

"No, she was way too refined to commit a murder. And she dressed so well."

He didn't reply.

"Did you?" she asked.

"Of course, I didn't murder him," he said.

"No, think she did it?"

"Well, a woman who has two murders associated with her is pretty suspicious. I mean neither of us are facing anything like that. I felt that the mistrial was kind of fortunate for her. Especially since it was orchestrated by her knight in shining armor. And now she shot the head off her step daughter?"

"Yes, it's sad. But it was in self-defense, Paul. I would shoot someone trying to kill you, honey."

He wasn't sure whether to be happy about that statement or not.

"There really needs to be gun reform," he said. "Crazy people should not get guns."

Belinda was staring out the window.

"What are you thinking?" he asked.

"I wonder if I should tell him, you know, if Maura Craig goes to jail, that my mother is single."

Too Tall Paul looked down at his study books. He knew better than to make any comment.

* * * * *

Ms. Edwards was on her way to the knitting store to find a particular skein that would suit her granddaughter. She wanted to make a chic over-sweater for her. These young people like clothes that are a bit exciting but also, they like the materials to be sustainable. Her granddaughter is always asking.

"Is it sustainable? Is it sustainable?"

It took Lilian Edwards a bit of time to figure out what she was talking about.

As she turned the corner to the wool store, she passed a newsstand. There was Maura's face on the front page of all the newspapers, once again. My God that woman is like Jackie Kennedy used to be. Always in the news. It's funny how the magazines boycotted Melania who was almost never on the cover.

Lillian came closer to the papers and then searched her handbag for her eyeglasses.

Oh my God. The headline read, OOPS. SHE'S DONE IT AGAIN. Done what? she wondered. Oh, her stepdaughter has been murdered. Oh, by Maura, allegedly. In self-defense. Oh, poor Maura or poor stepdaughter. Definitely poor stepdaughter. And Maura, just married to that nice lawyer. Some people have all the luck. Marrying that nice man. And now this.

The Pakistani owner of the newsstand was watching her.

Lillian looked up at him, "Can't say her husband is ever going to say life is boring with her."

The Pakistani owner smiled.

Lillian asked, "What do you make of it?"

He said, "It seems Mrs. Craig knows how to win an argument."

Ms. Edwards smiled and nodded, then went on walking. What a strange world, she thought. Terrible things always happening. Thank God one can always put one's faith in knitting.

CHAPTER
Eighteen

Burke couldn't wait to leave school to check up on the latest news regarding the new Maura Howard Craig case (Burke refused to refer to Maura's new husband's last name). The press tended to refer to her as Maura Howard Craig, too. Maybe because her books were written under that name.

She and Jackie had been right. Gene was representing Maura. When Burke sat down in front of the news sites on her laptop when she got home, her eye caught an op-ed piece thanking Maura Howard Craig for giving the headlines a break from Look What Trump Has Done Wrong Now. Instead, the news had taken a break to focus on the pretty face of Maura Howard Craig and what She Has Done Wrong Now.

Everyone knows the press loves skullduggery and conspiracy theories since these sell papers better than anything else, so the myriad of articles that Burke was busily viewing supported their theories that this murder was not in self-defense because, look, a third time? Something has to be amiss. Feminist presses, conversely, were supporting Maura as a victim, that she was just another woman being typecast as bad just because she is pretty and successful and lives on her own terms.

Then Burke turned to the Post, and read Maura was getting a plethora of marriage proposals from men in prison.

Burke dialed Jackie whom she knew was home practicing her lines, and would be glad for a break. Burke wanted to recount some of the headlines.

"Those men in prison must think Maura is like them or something," Jackie said.

"You mean guilty?"

"I suppose so, dearie."

"The police *are* saying it was clear cut self-defense. Crystal didn't go up there with a rifle that she bought on the black market for an arm and leg from some corrupt army and navy store to have a cup of tea with Maura. Gene will get her off."

"I suppose so," Jackie said.

"I don't think it will even go to trial. He'll prove it to the DA or something."

"We'll see," Jackie said. "What else are they saying? I don't have as much time as you to read all the news. What with rehearsals."

"When do you open again?"

"In a week."

"Oh, what shall I wear?" Burke said, joking.

"Something good because I sat you in the front row."

"Thank you."

"You know my role has changed a bit, right?" Jackie said.

"No, but it doesn't matter, Jackie. I'm happy to see you in anything. Even if it's a walk on. I'm proud of you."

"That's so sweet of you to say."

"Well, I mean it."

* * * * *

One afternoon a week later, on the same day of Jackie's opening, Burke was once again at her obsession, sitting in her living room looking at pictures on the front page of the Times and the Post, of Gene and Maura leaving the courthouse. There had been a private court session with Maura, the DA and his people, and Gene and his people. They made their case to Judge Stolzberg and there was enough evidence to not have to go to trial. The DA and the Judge both agreed it was clear self-defense. Crystal was not making a social call, with a bootlegged assault rifle.

Burke read she'd got past the doorman with the gun hidden in a musical instrument case.

Maura, naturally in Chanel, this time a mauve color, smiled and looked her usual starlet self in the photographs of them leaving the courthouse but, as Burke studied the photograph with the acuity of a radiologist looking at an x ray, it seemed to her that Gene looked tired.

"I hope he's not ill," Burke said to herself.

She dialed Jackie.

"I know you're busy."

"Yes, I'm a nervous wreck," Jackie said, studying herself in her costume and wondering how to wear it to the best effect.

"Well, here's something to take your mind off it. Maura got off on self-defense. No trial."

"Not surprising, love."

"But it's Gene."

"What? Has he murdered someone too?" Jackie asked.

"No. He just looks so down in these photos."

"He's probably just tired. Tired of defending her. Maybe he's frightened when he gets home, she'll kill the car wash man or something. He probably would like a new client, for a change," Jackie said.

"God, I love British humor," Burke said. "Drinks after your opening?"

"Of course, all great actresses have drinks after their opening."

"Some have them before," Burke said.

"Not quite ready for that. See you later."

"Break a leg."

"Thanks," and they hung up.

* * * * *

Burke had indeed been saved a front row seat and she'd made a point to wear a shiny necklace Jackie had given her on her birthday. She thought, if Jackie saw her, it would make Jackie know someone was here on her side. Burke looked at the program. Jackie had already told her that this new play is British. A modern-day Feminist Midsummers Night's Dream. Maybe I should bring my kids from the school, Burke thought.

The curtain rose and some fairies a la Shakespeare come onto the stage, and soon Burke heard the distinctive sound of her friend's voice, with a cockney accent, from upstage so Burke couldn't quite see her and then the voice came to the front of the stage, in all its glory, wearing a Geiko lizard outfit.

The play continued with its plot twists of love found, love lost, and love re-found and everyone, including Burke, roared at some of Jackie's lizard-ess activities in both getting the lovers together and erroneously driving them apart, only to have a happy ending when the lovers return. Obviously, the happy couple would have low-cost car insurance. Even a lizard girl has to make a living.

When the curtain went down and then up for the bows, Jackie got the most applause. She had wonderful comic timing.

They were to meet at a local bar, Otto's, after Jackie had got her make up off and attended to all the men waiting at her stage door, as she had explained it to Burke. It would take about a half hour.

Burke, as she walked to the bar, as usual, picked up the latest newspaper. Let's see what else has happened.

She sat down at a table, ordered an old fashioned, and waited. She really had to thank Maura for this gift of friendship with Jackie. No matter how many men come into your life or leave your life, a good friend is constant. Not to be taken lightly, Burke thought.

Not too much on Maura tonight, she thought, as she scanned the paper. Oh my God, look at this. The Mayor and the State Attorney General are asking for Gene to run for Congress. He does look like Jimmy Stewart, a tall one, with the way he never loses a case and so handsome...and good... Can he run with a wife who has been accused of multiple murders? But she is a celebrity and people are partial to that. But he is such a good person, she thought. Yes, he should run. She would have made a much better Congressman's wife than Maura, but she has to let that go. Burke, you have to let that go, she told herself.

Jackie came in all cheerful and laughing. "What a night."

"Oh, hello Lizard," Burke said. "Have a drink. What do lizards drink?"

"We lizards are partial to martinis."

"Garcon," Burke said laughing, calling over the waiter. "You were terrific, Jackie. You're a real comedienne, not that I didn't realize that at the court house."

"But I have news, Burke. I have news. I really should have ordered champagne. Oh well."

The martini arrived.

"This will just have to do," Jackie said, taking a long sip and putting the glass down. "My news is, Ms. Burke, I just got rich."

"Oh really? That mid summer's night dream sprinkled money around?"

"Almost. What happened is that it turns out that a representative from Geiko, the insurance agency, was there. They had heard about the performance somehow, God knows how, it could have been my five mailings about my role to the company, anyway the insurance agents came backstage and said they were going to talk with their people but they had been looking for a new voice for Geiko. A female lizard, they explained, since it is more politically correct. We may not be ready for a female President but we ARE ready for a female lizard. And I, for one, am delighted because I won't say in polite company how much that comes to in dollars if I get that contract but I will say, Burke, if I get it, our troubles are over."

"Oh, that is so wonderful. You WILL get it once the other big wigs see your act."

They clinked drinks to ensure the contract's success.

"I have some good news too," Burke said.

"Really? Maura was indicted for a new murder?"

"Unfortunately, no but Gene, Gene is being asked by members of the elite to run for Congress. Don't you think he would look great at that and be great?"

"I do," Jackie said. "I really do. Mr. McGuinness goes to Washington."

"Exactly."

"May I ask," Jackie said, "why that would be good news for you?"

"It's not particularly. But since he's married to her, what difference does it make anymore? I'm just glad he's getting recognition for being who he is."

"Dumb at choosing women?"

"I regret to say," Burke said, "we're all like that in love."

"Well," Jackie replied, "you're quite generous tonight in your wishes for him. I commend you Burke. You should really try and meet a new man. I'm sure Dangerous Dan would like to see you again..."

"Enough, lizard. Let's talk about how to spend your future ill-gotten gains."

* * * * *

Jackie did indeed become Ms. Geiko and, even before receiving her first paycheck, she and Burke were looking at condos on the Hudson for her. They were both partial to Nyack. "There's a good theatre there," Jackie said, "and some wonderful watering holes."

Burke did well at her school, but was not ready to look for a new man. She really did love Gene. How odd to have made a life for herself of unrequited love.

"Very Joycean of you, like in Joyce's *The Dead*," Jackie said, as they met for lunch at that place Jackie had dressed as a rabbi.

"I don't know why I can't move on. What is wrong with me?" she said, picking at her salade niçoise.

"I have no idea. You seem perfectly normal to me," Jackie said picking at her corned beef hash which Burke usually could not even look at.

"Why do you say that?" Burke asked.

"You're a good teacher, you've been very good at thinking up ways to spend my money which shows a good healthy love of life...you just chose the wrong man. I mean...Gene's the right type...but wrong in the availability department. Haven't you heard the song, "If you can't be with the one you love, love the one you're with?"

"I never liked that song," Burke said.

* * * * *

Even while recording the new Geiko ads, Jackie kept on with her success at playing her comedic role in the theatre which was a roaring success since the Geiko ads made the play the talk of the town. She even continued nursing, having moved to the day shift. But now she was seriously considering whether she should quit nursing and take her theatrical career further.

Burke would listen to this debate of Jackie's over numerous cocktails.

"I mean what is the next step up in a lizard's career?" Burke asked. "The voice of an alligator?"

"My voice is getting very well known," Jackie said. "I may not need a next step. I am making enough money. I don't need the nursing job. I am tired of bed pans and the like. Wouldn't you be?"

"I would."

The ads were currently all over the television and, now, when they had drinks, they were invariably stopped by someone asking, "You know you sound just like the new female Geiko lizard."

"Do I?" Jackie would say smiling, and then give the person a wink.

Burke would smile too. It was fun to see Jackie so happy.

Burke sipped her drink and sat back, "I mean what if they want a new lizard after you, let's say it is a baby lizard, like they just did with Baby Yoda, what will you do if you don't have nursing to fall back on?"

"I know. But I could audition for those animated movies where they need a voice over."

"Then you need to get yourself an agent. Go to Creative Artists or something and then, if they can guarantee you work, then quit your day job."

"Very good thinking Burke. Maybe you should be my agent."

"No thanks. I have my own plans."

"I hope it is not to become a lawyer so you can work with unowho."

"No. But I have my plans."

"No interest in sharing?" Jackie asked.

"After all I've been through, I think I should do something to help the world become a better place."

"Sound dreadfully boring, lovey. You're not planning on becoming a missionary or something?"

"No, I am not."

Jackie laughed, "I know you're not. You would never leave that tall lawyer that long."

CHAPTER Nineteen

Over the next few months, Gene found himself experiencing a myriad of cross-current feelings as he drove to and from work. Congressman. That had never been on his list of what he wanted to accomplish, but he had already accomplished everything else he'd written down except for trying a case before the Supreme Court. Look, he said to himself, I can exchange that for Congressman.

His fellow lawyers were encouraging him (what a boom for the firm, they said) and the more Gene thought about the prospect of running for the House, the more he wanted to do it. That would be quite the punch in the nose to his father if he was alive. His no-good son, Eugene, becoming a Congressman of the United States. He was so sure I was never going to amount to anything, Gene thought. He remembered studying in university, he thinks it was the classics, maybe Aristotle, who said the most admirable career in the world was to be in service to the people through government. It made Gene proud just to think of it.

And Washington. It would be a beautiful place to live. Maybe he'd take up horseback riding in nearby Virginia.

He sat around near the end of one of their work days with a fellow law partner, Dennis O'Connor, sharing a whiskey that Dennis kept in his desk to celebrate what he called, "Victories at Sea." He meant trials, but Dennis was a sailor.

"I think you should do it. People admire you, Gene, and it would be a blast. And you have a famous wife – that will add to the attention you get. You know how so much is about how much you are in the news."

Gene was quiet and then said, "She's famous, I know. Not only for her books nowadays, Dennis, for all those damn murder accusations."

"I know," Dennis said, taking his legs off his desk, and sitting forward. "But some believe even bad publicity is good."

"I don't know," Gene said, looking out the window at the buildings surrounding them. The grey winter sky seemed to mirror how he felt about the whole conundrum of Maura's rather checkered resume as of late.

Dennis said, "Am I hearing trouble in paradise?"

Gene kept looking out the window. Finally, he said, "I don't know."

"You just said that."

"I know," he said, standing up and swallowing his drink. "I am, as some women like to say, confused."

"Tough place to be in," Dennis said.

"Don't I know it," Gene said. "I better get back home."

* * * * *

As he drove to Tuxedo Park, the beautiful roads with their tall trees and some open farmland along the way, soothed him. The fact is it wasn't the thought of a political career that was making him confused about Maura. It was her. He had loved this woman all his life, never even looked at another woman, yet he had to face that he fell for her when he was a boy. What could he possibly have known in elementary school? After that, they'd seen each other now and then, they were always friendly, he had followed her marriages, her career, gone to some of her book parties, been really, when he thinks about it, he'd been obsessed with her memory. He had been loyal to and never changing in his admiration for her, which was really formed around age eight. True, she is a remarkably beautiful and intelligent woman. Even warm. She had lived up to his fantasy. She was easy to live with, a diligent hard worker, good tempered, and not unreasonable, unlike what he heard some of his friends had to deal with in the marriage department.

But he had to admit, as of late, he was beginning to feel she was also a woman that you fundamentally never really knew. She lived in her stories and her stories were doing the bizarre thing of spilling into their lives. She wrote about murder and murder seemed to be all around them.

And there was the Guy St. Claire issue. He had proof, thanks to that strange Burke, that Maura did want, at least for a bit, murderous revenge. No one in his circle of friends wanted murderous revenge. And Crystal, poor Crystal, with her doomed assault rifle, maybe when he is Congressman, he has to get rid of those damn things, Crystal claimed to have proof that her father had been murdered by, he hated to think of it, his wife.

Maura thought he couldn't hear on that fateful night when she and Crystal had been verbally attacking each other, back and forth. He did take too long to get out of the shower but that was because he was listening. If he'd known Crystal had a gun, he would have high tailed it to the living room. But all he heard were the accusations. It was a tragedy. He still felt guilty he hadn't run out there. But he did get to hear that Crystal said she had proof. But Crystal was crazy. Crazy people say anything, he reminded himself.

Hard to believe that sweet Maura, who has the mind of a steel trap, would murder husbands. It was something that would only happen in a book. Which is what worried him.

It wasn't for his own life that he worried. He was more concerned about what kind of woman he is married to. And also, he thought, as he swerved onto another road, the sun setting over the fields with their mansions hidden behind dappled trees, let's face it, she doesn't need him. She has enough money. She has Patricia to talk to. She doesn't need that much more.

She loves him, he surmises. But he was beginning to come to the conclusion that Maura loved one person first, herself. Maybe that is human, he thought. But when you love someone...oh this is all too much for him. He can handle legal tortes, he can handle dismaying court stenographers, he can handle obstinate judges, he can handle long weeks, but he just doesn't know what to make of love.

Who does? he thought as he parked his Mercedes. That's for artist types to figure out. From what he's read, they're not that good at it either.

* * * * *

Maura was, as always, in her office when he got home. Patricia took his coat and brought him his Jameson's which he had begun to look forward to each evening. How could he have not drunk for so long? Lord knows it's relaxing.

Those Indians were onto something.

"I'll bring up her martini," Patricia said.

"Thanks," and he and his drink began walking up the stairs.

Maura turned toward him as he came in. She was wearing a suede dress with an open neck, and high heeled sandals even though it was winter. She kept the house warm. She often wore her coat when they were chatting indoors. Maybe slender people do not have enough blood, he thought.

"How was your day, honey?" she smiled. "Thanks Patricia," as she handed Maura her martini. Patricia nodded and then retreated downstairs.

"Okay." He sat down in the brocade high back chair across from her.

"Anything interesting?" she asked.

"Dennis and I talked about this Congressman thing."

"It's amazing," she said, smiling.

"How would you feel about moving to Washington?" he asked.

"Well," she said, "I would certainly go down there a lot. But would I really have to move? I have the publishing firm here to manage and you'll be so busy anyway. You see how so many of them work nights. And even when you're campaigning, you're going to be out all the time."

It is nice to have someone to come home to, he thought, but didn't say it.

"I could come down on weekends," she said, "if you are elected. I could write on the trains."

"What about campaigning for me?" he asked, looking at her.

"Well, I'll do.... some," she said. "You know, but it's really your bailiwick dear. They're voting for you, not me."

"But your name could help, Maura."

"Yes, maybe. Although you do realize reporters will harangue me about the three cases I've been in."

"I do," he said. They'll harangue me too, he thought.

"I don't know, Gene. What about all the money you have to raise to run for Congress? Are you worried about that?"

"Not really. I already have a lot of endorsements. The AG, all of them, will fundraise for me. "

"Yes, I have put your name in the news a lot lately."

"People knew of my legal successes before that, Maura."

"But I made you a household name," she said authoritatively.

"In not the most flattering circumstances."

"We married after you won Guy's case," she said.

"I won on luck, Maura. I didn't know the Police Chief played that trick till Williams told me."

"Well, you won," she said. "That's what people remember and that's probably going to get you voted Congressman."

He took a sip of his Jameson. God, I can see why my father needed this stuff.

"And," she continued," being married to a very successful writer is going to help too. I'm telegenic and, let's face it, a household name. Our marriage after the trial, and knowing each other all our lives, will make romantic hard copy. Between that and your height, you'll get the entire female vote."

"Is that what I want, Maura? To become a Congressman because of my height? And let me say, listening to you right now, is not giving me much sense of your respect for me. “

“Oh Gene – don’t be so microscopic –”

He stood up. Yes, he thought, I am not liking this at all.

She stood up. “Let’s go out to dinner,” she said. “It’s more fun.”

“Where?” he asked.

He didn’t know why but something made him nervous.

* * * * *

They had dinner in a modern Greek restaurant close by with white walls and white tables, and big windows, and where the maître d and the waiters knew them. They didn’t have to order since they always had the same lamb dishes, the same salads and the same drinks. The food and cocktails came quickly but his mind roamed as Maura talked about her struggles with the rewrite of the book she had been writing about the jurors, and how annoying it was to her that John Grisham got movie deals but she did not.

“Why do you think that is?” she asked Gene.

“I have no idea,” he said. He was noticing that people seemed to recognize her and sometimes she would turn and deliver a movie star smile to some of the diners.

Then she’d turn back to him and continue chatting on and he found himself not listening. Now he knew what had made him nervous before. It was the possibility that he no longer loved her.

He remembered the priest in his parish saying that Love is Trust and Respect and, as he sat looking at her, pretending to listen, he thought, I just may not feel that anymore.

"Gene," she said. "*Gene!*"

"Yes?"

"You're not listening to me."

"I am. "

"Is something bothering you?" she asked.

He could not believe it but he felt tears at the back of his eyes. What's bothering me, Maura, he thought, is this may be over.

How he had loved her. With every fiber of his being. He would protect her always. She sat here now, sophisticated in her suede dress, no longer that little girl, but now, she almost felt like a stranger to him.

"Gene, what is wrong with you?" she said. "Waiter, I'll have another drink."

She did not ask him if he wanted one and he noticed that.

I am a Catholic, he told himself, we don't divorce. Till death do us part. He believed in that. Even his mother living with that horrible man, his father, never walked. You don't leave a marriage. You get through things. But can he make a life that is a lie? Pretending he loves her? Always wondering just how skilled a storyteller she really is. Is that what he, a man who upholds the law, is looking for?

The waiter brought her drink.

He still hadn't spoken.

"Cat got your tongue?" she said.

"I wonder where that expression comes from," she continued after her sip. "How can a cat get your tongue?"

He sat in silence.

"Gene, have you had a stroke or something?"

That would be convenient, he thought. She won't have to kill me.

"No, I'm alive."

"I have never heard a lawyer this quiet in my life," she said.

"It can happen," he said.

They ate dinner and then they drove home. "I'm going to work in the study," he said, "before bed."

"Alright."

She didn't even seem upset about it. But then writers are always busy in their heads. As are lawyers, he thought. That is why I thought we were perfect for each other.

She was asleep by the time he went upstairs.

* * * * *

In the morning at breakfast, he opened the papers. Maura came down in a flowered dressing gown, looking cheerful, and ready for the day.

"I am going to write first, then go to the office," she said.

"Sounds good."

"Look at these ridiculous slippers someone gave me." She pointed to sort of furry animal shaped slippers that looked like boats on her feet.

"Not quite your style," he said. "Maybe you should add heels."

"Won't go with the plushy moose ears."

He nodded and continued looking at the paper.

"Are you still feeling morose?" she asked, buttering her toast. "Where is Patricia?"

"In the kitchen."

"Oh good. I want to run a few ideas by her."

"Great," he said.

"Are we becoming one of those couples who speak in monosyllables?" she asked.

"Yes," he answered, slightly amused.

"What a relief," she joked.

He stood up, "Alright. See you later."

He didn't kiss her good bye and, as he left, he wondered if she noticed this was the first time he had ever done that.

* * * * *

He had a busy day at work, in and out of meetings, even though he wasn't on a new criminal case yet. It was as if the powers that be, he being one of them, were giving him time to decide on the Congressman bid.

He had a scheduled lunch today with the New Jersey Congressman, John Godfrey, to get some ideas.

They met at the Palm Steak House to discuss it. This steakhouse, famous for its drawings of celebrities and regulars on the wall, as well as the quality of their steaks and lobster, not to mention rob roys and old fashioneds, was a place where power meetings took place. Gene slid into a leather booth.

"Great of you to come over here, John," Gene said. "Thank you."

Gene took in the Congressman's perhaps dyed blonde hair, his ample stomach, his very bespoke suit. He seemed like a man who was comfortable with his life.

"It's a big move, Gene, and we would love you in the Congress. It's a helluva place to be. The Speaker is strong, we're getting bills drafted that are even getting through the Senate. I think you would excite the public coming in and really raise the profile of our party. I mean it could mean big things for you, Gene. And when your term is over you can certainly go back to law and you'll have even more of a name for yourself."

"Thanks, John."

"Do you have any questions about running? You need a great campaign office and you're going to have to have fund raiser experts, not to mention campaign strategists, all of that – but I can get you all those names. They do the heavy lifting. Your job, at first, is to do the glad handing and a lot of talking. Your voice is going to get hoarse.

Gene smiled. "I'm used to that kind of talking in court."

"What kind of things do you want to stand up for?" Godfrey asked.

"No assault weapons, for one."

"We're in a liberal state, of course you're going to stand up for that."

"I want to change some –"

"But you know," John said, "you could be called to be vetted for the Supreme Court. Have you thought about that?"

"I always wanted to try a case there," Gene said, "but I don't think I am fingered to be on the court. I don't write opinions that get talked about. I am not sure I would want to. But I have this sense I would enjoy being a Congressman. I would like to represent my constituents and bring about some social improvement. And I think being a lawyer is helpful to the whole process."

"Indeed. The founding fathers were, as you know."

Godfrey continued, "You just need to work out what issues you are running on and refine how you present them. Knowing you, I would guess they'll have a lot to do with the integrity of the laws, the corporations, and the system."

"Doesn't everyone want that?" Gene asked.

"Nothing is simple. You already know that. I think a politician has to make decisions for himself. Where his line of compromise is. Of course, you have to listen to your constituents and their needs and concerns but I think a politician has to have a very strong core of what he believes is right and wrong."

Gene nodded.

From there, they went on to chatting about other technicalities of the job and of running and soon Godfrey said he had a car outside to take him back to New Jersey.

"Thank you so much, John," Gene said and picked up the tab. "I know you don't have much time."

John said, "Sorry I have to run out like this but that will be your new life," and Godfrey sprung up and turned around as he left and laughed, raising his hand, "See you in Washington!"

Gene smiled.

*   *   *   *   *

When he got back to the office, Gene dug through his desk looking for a particular phone number. He had made his mind up on the drive to work. He held the card and dialed.

"Father? It's McGuinness. Yes, great to talk to you, too.... um, I have an unusual request."

"Whatever you need, Gene. Whatever you need."

Gene smiled and thought, I bet he's not expecting this. "What I need, Father, is an annulment from the Bishop."

"What did you say, Gene?"

Gene shifted his papers around on his desk. "Maura and I need you to file for an annulment of our marriage. I can afford whatever fees are necessary, you know that."

"Have you thought this through, Gene?"

"Of course, I have."

"You're both Catholics, it's true. Her other marriages, if I recall, were not in the church."

"She became a widow in both cases."

"I am aware," the priest said. "Everyone is."

"Can you do it?" Gene was now flicking the top of his pen up and down. Up and down.

"Of course, I can do it for a future Congressman, Gene."

"I beg your pardon?"

"There are no secrets in this parish, my boy! I will be rooting for your success."

"Thank you, Father. I still haven't made up my mind. But about the other issue –"

Gene's secretary walked in, dropping off some files. He looked up at her and kept silent till she had left the room.

"The other issue—" he repeated.

"I have to go, Gene, but I'll speak to the Bishop and get the paper work going."

"Thank you, Father."

Gene looked out the window and did he see a sliver of blue?

"God bless you, son," he heard. "You're a good man."

* * * * *

The part time Thai cook they had hired had already left dinner on the table. The candles were lit. The wine glasses filled. The salmon in some kind of thin parchment type roll had been placed on the plates, along with carrots (Maura had read they are good for you.)

He and Maura were sitting at the table and, beforehand, at their cocktail hour they had gone over their day. Almost.

Gene said, as they began eating, "Maura, I've been thinking."

She laughed, "With your job, I should hope so."

"Yes, well, Maura, I made a mistake."

"Oh?"

"Yes." Here goes, he thought. "I think, much as I love you, we should not continue being married."

She looked up shocked. "What do you mean?"

The Thai cook came in, "Leady for dessert?"

Maura said, "Not now, Sureelak," and waved her away. The cook could see something was going on.

Gene tried again. "I just think that ... I was in love with you as a kid, but now... I just don't feel suited to this marriage. I don't have the right temperament."

She squinted her eyes. "You mean I don't suit your political plans."

"No, I don't mean that at all. I have no idea if I will even run. I mean that I don't feel suited to this marriage."

She got up, grabbed some nuts on the sideboard, and began eating them rapidly. She always did that when she was nervous. She said eating nuts kept her company. "What exactly does that mean, Gene?"

"Exactly what I am saying."

She was silent, thinking, you can survive this, Maura. There are other men. I can survive this. And do I even need a man at this point? Of course, I do but I am a catch. There won't be a problem.

"Go on," she said.

"I feel that I am not suited to our life. It is not the kind of marriage I want."

"What kind of marriage do you want?" she asked.

"I don't know," he said.

"Is there someone else?" she asked, her voice emphasizing "else."

"Of course not."

"Well, what do you want to happen now?"

He actually hadn't thought much about that but it turned out a plan came easily to him. "I will move back into my apartment in New York. The split will all be quiet. We will just get an annulment."

"An annulment?"

"It is important to me, Maura."

"That's fine," she said.

They were silent.

"Quite a dinner," she said. "So, you want to end this happy marriage because you are not suited to it? It doesn't fit your 'temperament?'" she asked somewhat sarcastically.

"Yes," he said. "I am sorry."

"I don't understand," she said. "Gene, we were so in love. Are you sure you are doing the right thing? Maybe you are ill. You have been acting strange. Maybe you are getting dementia or something."

"Possibly, but I doubt it," he said. "You are right we were so in love but I have tried, really tried, to live with someone who has deaths happening around her like I have depositions, but I just can't, Maura. I know the last death was in self-defense, but the one before that was not and you held that from me. What else will you hold from me?"

"All couples have secrets, Gene. I am sure you do."

"I don't have secrets and I don't want to."

"If you are going to Washington, believe me you will have secrets."

"I don't follow that at all, but it can be your opinion," he said.

How different we are, he thought. She anticipates moral deterioration as inevitable. Perhaps he should also as a criminal lawyer. God knows awful things go on. But one can believe, perhaps naively, in upholding one's own principles, can't one?

"I'll miss you," she said. "Maybe you'll come back to your senses."

"I probably won't stop loving you Maura. I am going back to loving you from a distance, as I did before. Maybe I will love you forever. But it seems distance might be the best way for this love to survive."

She looked at him seriously. Had he gone crazy?

"That damn Ernie Burleigh or whatever his name was," she said. "He should never have contacted me. If he hadn't, we would stay together."

"It hasn't got to do with him."

"Oh yes it does. You blame me for Guy's murder."

"Well shouldn't I?"

"It was an accident."

The Thai cook's eyes widened as she listened from the kitchen. She couldn't speak English well but she could understand it. Is this a good place to be working?

"A helluva lot of accidents happen around you," he said.

Maura sat up rather regally. "I resent that you are blaming me for all these deaths."

"I am not. I just can't live with them all my life. You can but I can't."

He stood up. "Maura, this whole thing is too depressing. I am going to get a few things upstairs and go back into the city. We can figure all the rest out at another time. I am exhausted. This is not easy."

He walked round to the table and kissed her on the cheek. She had tears in her eyes. "Oh, Gene, this is so silly—it was all a mistake – people make mistakes –"

"Maybe I am making one now too," he said, as he began walking out, "but I just think this is the way it should be. For now, anyway."

CHAPTER

Twenty

Once Gene left Maura sitting there alone at the dining room table, the candles nearly burned out, the Thai cook came in. "You like dessert?"

"No, no thanks," Maura said, distracted. At first, she'd felt stunned, but that began to morph into an unbearably heavy mantle of loneliness, that she feared would last forever. She thought about saying something to the cook as she silently pattered in to remove some dishes, but that seemed crazy. The cook could barely speak English. "Sureelak, can you call Patricia and ask her to come over? Tell her it is important."

Forty-five minutes later, the ever sturdy, ever loyal Patricia entered the house using her own key. Maura had by now dragged herself upstairs to the bedroom and was lying down on the bed, unable to move. It as was if her whole body hurt, as if she had been physically punched.

An annulment? Why would he want an annulment?

Patricia walked up the stairs, knocked and Maura said, "Come in."

"I brought you martini."

"Whoa," Maura said. "I might pass out if I drink this but...yes, good idea. Passing out might be just the thing. I'm almost there. Thank you."

Patricia could see that Maura was practically in a ball in grief. What could have happened?

"Why chef call? Something go wrong?"

"Gene has left me."

"He what?" Patricia sat down on the bed. "He go work?"

"No, no, no. He says, inexplicably, he does not want to be married anymore. He doesn't feel we 'match,'" Maura said, raising her eyebrows.

Patricia studied Maura, and then said, "Who matches?"

"Some do, I guess," Maura said. "I thought we did. Didn't you?"

"He is not serious man to think this, to leave marriage for this."

"What? Gene is the height of seriousness. He's *too* serious. All we did was work together. No traveling as I did with Guy or skiing or sailing or, for that matter ...sex."

Patricia looked a bit surprised. "No?"

"Frankly," Maura had no idea where this was all coming from but she was beginning to feel angry, "being with him was, not to put a spin on it, boring. "

"You mean bed?"

"I mean everywhere. When I really think about it, Gene was dull. Tall but dull." Maura sighed. "But I don't want to start all over again. Who does?" Maura said. "And he is smart."

"You more friends," Patricia said. "Everyone like him but artists need passion, Maura. Maybe that is why you don't so-called match. Lawyers like everything in box. Artists do not."

Maura was quiet, realizing, as usual, Patricia was making sense. It was true. She and Gene were more like friends. Childhood friends, for God's sake. So what if he kissed me in a cupboard or wherever it was?

I had thought he would be a knight in shining armor. And he is, sort of, but really, do I need someone who idolizes me, rather than someone who brings some powerful heterosexual male energy to the table? Do I need someone who THINKS all the time? I do enough of it myself.

"He admire you," Patricia said, interrupting Maura's thoughts.

"Yes, maybe I was just grateful he took care of me at that trial. Or maybe I was just exhausted and would have married anyone. All the terrible things being said about me. Remember that? It was horrible."

Patricia wisely listened.

"He made me feel old now that I think about it. I couldn't let my hair down. He is so ...righteous. It' s like being with Abe Lincoln or something. I had to be so damn...well behaved. It was a strain." Maura took another sip of her drink, an unconscious sign to herself that her well-behaved days might now be coming to an end.

"So, you not hurt?" Patricia asked.

"Maybe I wanted out as much as him but I didn't know it. He never listened to me when we were having dinner. Always thinking about his cases. "

That was not quite how Patricia remembered it but she thought it best to say nothing.

"Patricia," Maura asked, "why do YOU stay alone?"

"When I marry, I wish I'm alone. When alone, I wish marry."

"Yes, it's the conundrum, isn't it?" Maura said.

"Maybe though," Patricia said, patting Maura's hand, "easier be alone. Live life you want."

"True, true. What's so wrong about being alone? I can find someone to sleep with. And have dinner with without putting up with someone's morose and banal moods. Now that I think about it, I should have been the one to ask for an annulment, not him."

"Everyone need love," Patricia said. "You beautiful, smart woman. Easy for you to find when ready. Don't marry friend. Marry someone cannot live without."

"I thought you said being alone is better," Maura said.

"Both are good," Patricia said, plumping up the pillows. "If be with man, find someone who is everything. He still drive you crazy but you stay interested. Otherwise waste of time."

"Patricia, you missed your calling. *You* should have been Dr. Ruth."

Patricia had no idea who Dr. Ruth was, she had no interest in medicine, maybe the martini was working. "Okay, Maura, sleep well. We discuss everything tomorrow."

With those words, Maura, fully dressed, closed her eyes, like a child, and Patricia went downstairs. Sureelak came out and said, "Need help?"

"No, you take day off tomorrow," Patricia said. "I cook for her."

Sureelak had just been furiously texting a man looking for a date so this plan seemed like a positive portent. "Thank you," and then she quietly left the room.

* * * * *

Over the next few months, Maura took solace in focusing on her work and found, when she was writing, or paying attention to the publishing company, she didn't really miss Gene. It was odd.

Maybe the lives she lived in books were just easier for her than real life. She preferred being there.

And Patricia had done the oddest thing that made getting home from the office rather fun. Patricia had arrived with a rather large hound dog, saying "We need love in house." This dog seemed to consider himself a comedian, jumping up on couches and beds to get into a fun bidding war on who was boss in the mansion. Not to mention this new male in the house was consistently affectionate and generous.

As an example, Maura had some kind of infected toe and she noticed that the dog would lick her ailing toe whenever she sat barefoot.

Patricia noticed, too.

"You know what he doing?" Patricia said. "He have antibiotic in tongue. He being doctor," and Patricia watched him with a softness that Maura rarely saw on Patricia's face.

"Really?" Maura asked. "How interesting," and she found her heart smiling at the big dog too.

He liked to hide and then show up as if he had played a trick on her. She loved seeing his loping figure run to her, victorious at his disappearance and reappearance game.

Sureelak, the cook, asked, "What his name?"

"Sherlock," Maura said.

Surreelak nodded and left the room quickly. She never heard of the name Sherlock, confirming for her, once again, that these people are strange.

It wasn't long before Sherlock had totally charmed them all and so it was only natural that Sherlock started making appearances in Maura's books. Everyone knows people like to write about what they love.

Maura would read some of the sections to Patricia who took to the stories enthusiastically, since if Maura liked writing about Sherlock, Patricia liked hearing about him.

Patricia said, "I have new suggestion. We get artist to make funny pictures."

Maura who now wore glasses when working since no man-made interruptive appearances, looked over her frames at Patricia. "You know I don't think books need illustrating. The words should do the work."

"People on their phone looking pictures all the time," Patricia said.

"True. True. Okay invite my old friend Sandy. She is a good illustrator." By now, she had learned to heed Patricia's "intuitions."

* * * * *

When Sandra Frost-Piatti (Sandy had just married) showed up, the first being to be smitten with her sunny and warm presence was Sherlock himself. The romance turned out to be mutual. It seems he had chosen his own portrait artist. Maura was glad to see her old friend, but also found Sandy's work very attractive, with its almost Japanese brush work. Maura had been against the idea of illustrations all her life, yet she found some of the ideas Sandy came up with for the book to be exciting, even if they did take some getting used to.

She also was surprised by how much she enjoyed the three women, Patricia, Sandy and herself, ending their sessions, feet up on ottomans, each with a martini, trying to come up with more and more storylines.

If James Patterson can have an entire writing staff, why can't I? thought Maura.

Sherlock would attend these meetings, his long body prone on the floor, and his long face following the conversation as if he understood every word. Of course, eventually he fell asleep, the women positing their storylines not up to his standards.

Sandy said, "If you two treated a man with the same love you give Sherlock, you'd both have huge diamonds on your hands."

Patricia replied, "Men not so loving as Sherlock."

"Or as funny," Maura added.

And then the three women looked over at him, dotingly.

* * * * *

That night, Maura was finishing up and Patricia was still there. "You know Patricia this is not a bad life. We are being very productive at the company and even here with these new stories. I finally have a leading male in my life who doesn't aggravate me, and..."

"Yes?" said Patricia turning down the bed.

"I have friends like you two and, Patricia..." she said, just like Scarlett making a pronouncement, "I can feel it."

"What?"

"I can feel we're going to make a helluva lot of money."

Patricia smiled. These Americans. Money. Money. Money. But it good, she thought, Maura always take care of her. Of that she was sure.

Maura looked round the room with satisfaction. Like Scarlett, she had rebuilt her plantation.

CHAPTER

Twenty-one

Burke's cell phone rang as she was on her way to her volunteer work. She had decided to do something worthwhile for the world, besides her teaching. It was much better than staying at home and following the news. She had just parked her car and was turning the block, when her phone rang. She fished it out of her pocket and answered.

"Oh Jackie, where are you? At Nyack Hospital? Good, good. Do you like it there?"

Burke listened as she looked in the shop windows. The store windows had become like friends as she passed them the three late afternoons she went into the office.

"How do the patients feel about a lizard giving them needles?" Burke asked and laughed.

"Oh my God," Burke said. She had just passed the usual bookstore she passed when she went to volunteer. Initially, that there was a bookstore at all was a shock since so many of them had closed. "I'm just passing Barnes and Noble and there is a pyramid of books being displayed in the window. All the same book. Guess whose it is? No... it's not Dangerous Dan's memoir. It's called *Sherlock Solves It* written by our dear friends Maura Howard Craig and Patricia Lawzarkewica. Can you believe it?"

Burke now put Jackie on speaker phone.

"*Sherlock Solves It*?" Burke and anyone passing heard from the infamous female lizard. "Is there a man with a magnifying glass on the cover wearing a hat smoking a pipe? Doesn't she know it's someone's else idea?"

"No, there's a hound dog on the cover."

"God, how ridiculous," Jackie said.

Burke was looking at the cover. "I think it's kind of cute. The dog must be Sherlock."

Now she began walking again. "I'm almost at my post," Burke said. "I'll talk to you later. Don't let anyone step on your tail at the hospital."

"I am wearing a uniform, darling. Actually, it feels good to do something normal for a change. Doesn't pay as well, but feels good, frankly," Jackie said.

"Gotta go. Talk later."

* * * * *

Just then Burke turned into the McGuinness for Congressman Campaign Headquarters. It was a big office with a view of Columbus Circle and lots of desks and mostly young people, younger than her, rushing about with cell phones studying their to-do lists. Still, it was energizing and people were friendly. Gene has a lot of support, she thought, as she entered the fray.

Burke went to her desk, her job currently to make calls to people on lists she was given by one of the twelve-year-old managers. She didn't mind. She sat down and took off her coat. She had a cheat sheet of what to say about Gene but, in truth, she had it memorized. She actually enjoyed these calls because strangely she was never treated rudely.

The staff had warned her she would be. But it seemed that people were eager to hear about the new Congressman, the press so far had been kind to him, and they liked to ask her questions about him.

She always answered so freely and enthusiastically that one older woman asked, "You're not his wife, are you, dearie?"

Burke thought about lying but the thing is it was all over the papers that his marriage had recently been annulled. Just like she had asked that priest at St Francis about. She must tell Jackie that, in her opinion, she had foreseen the future. Obviously, this older woman on the phone doesn't read the papers, though.

Suddenly she heard clapping in the big room. She turned around.

There was the big man himself. In a blue suit, excellent slightly lighter blue tie, she thought, unbelievably handsome.

He was shaking hands with people and soon he, along with the campaign managers, went into his office. They closed the door but she could see them talking through the glass window.

She went back to her phone calls.

Two hours later he came out to get himself a coffee.

He went down her aisle and then, she imagined, he must have espied her red hair.

He stopped, looked down at her. "Ms. Burke? Is that you?"

She turned around smiling. "The one and only."

"You're working here?"

"Yes. I support Gene McGuinness for Congressman. How do you feel about him? Do you support him?" she asked flirtatiously.

"I do," he laughed.

Oh, how she longed to hear him say those words in different circumstances.

"Although I think he has a lot to do," he said, smiling. "Have you been working on the campaign long?"

"Last two months. I am sure you're going to win," she said smiling.

He laughed, "I hope so. It's very kind of you to be doing this, Ms. Burke."

"I enjoy it. Oh, and I was sorry to hear about you and Mrs. Craig," she lied.

"Yes," he said. "These things happen."

No, they don't, she wanted to say but was uncharacteristically polite right now.

"So odd how I keep running into you," he said.

"I wouldn't say it's odd."

"Well," he said, and now he seemed a bit uncomfortable.

Is he going to ask me out? she thought. Her face flushed. She tried to keep the smile on her face under control. Alluring but not pushy.

"Well, Ms. Burke. It's good to see —"

"You know I can imagine having to campaign all the time as well as doing your job never probably leaves you time to eat. I could bring over a pot roast dinner, if you like," she said.

He smiled. "That is very kind of you Burke. But I like what you're doing here better. I'll pass on the pot roast and look forward to running into you here again. I appreciate all your efforts for us."

And then it seemed, although she would never admit it out loud, he ran off to the coffee machine.

A young campaign worker, a young man with floppy brown hair and Harry Potter glasses turned to her from his section. "I didn't know you know him personally."

"Oh yes," she said. "I've known Gene for...some time."

"Interesting," the young man said. "Lucky you."

"Yes."

"Well back to work," the young man said.

"Yes," she said, picking up the phone and having a bit of trouble finding her place on her call list. Gene had already rushed back to his glass office. She dialed another number and began her spiel. Another older woman.

"Oh dear," the older woman said, "don't be so down. Whatever it is will pass."

Burke looked at the phone, incredulously.

"Uh...thank you. So, about Mr. McGuinness..."

"Dear," the woman said, ignoring Burke, "you never know how things will work out. Just be cheerful and carry on. Things always do. Just like in novels."

"Well thank you," Burke said, strangely reassured, although the novel reference didn't make much sense but the thought that one never knows how things will work out did help.

"So," Burke said, "may we talk about Mr. McGuinness and what he can do for you."

"Oh yes, dear, and what about his having to get away from that awful writer woman. Now she's writing about dogs, I hear. She's probably killed off all her other detectives."

Burke thought this woman might be a bit demented, but Burke put a star by her name, to call her again. She liked this woman's attitude.

Burke swung her chair closer to the desk and said into the phone, "I couldn't agree more. I am sure he will find someone more deserving of him one day."

"Oh," the woman said, "of course, dear. Life always works out in our best interest."

Burke debated arguing with her about that but she kind of preferred listening to this reassuring fairy godmother on her call list.

"So, you know that Mr. McGuinness is dedicated to hearing all your issues and will fight for you. He is particularly devoted to the elderly and..."

"Yes, I do, dear. I must go. Of course, I will vote for him and it was so thoughtful of you to call me. Please remember that even though you don't know it, things are always working out in your favor. So hang on dear. Your wildest dreams will come true."

"Well, I certainly hope you're right, Mrs...." she looked down to the call list, but the woman had already hung up.

The Harry Potter guy was staring at her.

"What?" Burke asked.

"Nothing. I just wondered if...you are free for dinner one night, after working here."

He seemed a bit young for her. "No," she said, "I am not really available, but thank you for asking," but she did think it was kind of nice that someone felt her to be attractive.

She went to the next number and picked up the phone. She saw Maura's name. Unbelievable. She immediately crossed that out with a profound fury. Onto the next, she dialed, and a person answered, "Hi, I am Ms. Burke from the McGuinness for Congress Campaign Headquarters and..."

She began her spiel about all Gene's qualities. As she did so, she thought that loving and respecting someone can sometimes be enough. It makes for a full life no matter how you slice it. She must remember to tell Jackie about it.

.

Epilogue

On an uninhabited island in the Caribbean, a developer uncovered the skeletal remains of a man. He was identified by his dental records and an inscription on his Rolex watch. The remains were that of John Thomas Craig who was reported lost at sea twenty years ago. The skull had a bullet hole through it.

Maura was informed the same day the tabloids announced the end of the mysterious death of the billionaire: MURDER.

She made two phone calls. One to her psychiatrist who was the only other person who knew the truth, and the other to her ex-husband, Congressman Eugene McGuinness.

You be the Judge.

About the Author

Kathie Keppler taught Special Education in Rockland's Psychiatric Center, NY and has a post graduate degree in Psychology from Fordham University. She raised three children before retiring and relocating to Florida. This is her first novel.

Acknowledgements

A special thanks to the friends and family whose names I borrowed and may have unwittingly disparaged. I hope I have given you seven minutes of fame.

Kudos to Gay Walley, my scribe and friend for her advice and patience and publisher Linda Langton, for her faith and fortitude.

www.ingramcontent.com/pod-product-compliance
Lightning Source LLC
Chambersburg PA
CBHW060602310726
48982CB00008B/1209/J

* 9 7 8 1 7 3 5 2 9 6 4 5 6 *